Between the mansion and the dress, she was beginning to feel like Cinderella. Honor grinned and tugged the princess-seamed bodice up over her bra. When the door swung open, she clutched the top of the dress to her chest as she jerked her head up with a gasp.

The sight of her equally shocked neighbor filling the doorway lodged her pounding heart in her throat.

"Whoa…hello."

She darted a hasty glance down to make sure her bra was covered. "What the hell are you doing here?" she demanded, making necessary adjustments while heat seared her cheeks.

"*I* am here for my parents' anniversary party. What are *you* doing here?"

Her jaw went slack for a second even as her stunned subconscious registered his tux and how devastatingly gorgeous he looked in the black and white. "Your *parents?*"

"Yeah." A brief smile ghosted over his lips. "I guess we haven't been formally introduced yet, have we?"

"No. You haven't taken the time to bother with that."

His head dipped with the slightest bit of acknowledgment of her pointed barb. "Asher Diamond."

Trying to salvage some of her dignity, she asked, "And do you always walk into your sister's room without knocking, Asher Diamond?"

"Never," he replied gravely. "My room, however, always."

"Your room?" Her stomach dropped as she darted her gaze toward the bare dresser top. "But…you don't live here."

"Not now, but I grew up here. It'll always be my room."

"Oh." The darker masculine colors and lack of anything girly made perfect sense now. Her embarrassment jumped another notch when he reached to set an overnight bag inside the door. "Right. Well…Celia said her room was the third door on the right, and this *is* the third door on the right."

PRAISE FOR STACEY JOY NETZEL

"Stacey Joy Netzel meets Indiana Jones. **CONNED** has it all, intrigue, suspense, danger and a incredible ending. Awesome writing, Awesome book." ~ Bev, Amazon Reviewer

"**SPRING SERENDIPITY** is a sweet romantic book, that had me crying, smiling, mad and happy which is my kind of romance story." ~ Rhonda, Amazon Reviewer

"As usual Stacey has an exceptional way of making her characters come alive both on the page and in the reader's heart that never misses leaving the reader satisfied and believing they are real."~ LovesToRead, Amazon Reviewer for **SUMMER SCANDAL**

"Summer Bride has become my new favorite by this author. This book just seemed to hit it out of the park with its genuineness and real life situations and problems encountered by the couple." ~ Jan, Amazon Reviewer for **SUMMER BRIDE**

"This one had me biting my nails and the tension and anxiety were palpable. Stacey's characters are real, hot, sexy, and determined." ~ Bev, Amazon Reviewer for **SUMMER SECRETS**

"[**EVIDENCE OF TRUST**, Colorado Trust Series] grabbed me from the beginning and I couldn't put it down. I loved Britt and Joel! I loved the action and the suspense and of course the romance!!" ~ Angie, Amazon reviewer

OTHER TITLES BY STACEY JOY NETZEL

Say You'll Marry Me, Book 10

(books 1,3,5,7,9 written by Donna Marie Rogers)

ROMANCING WISCONSIN SERIES

Mistletoe Mischief

Mistletoe Magic

Mistletoe Match-up

**Mistletoe Rules – short bonus story

Autumn Wish

Autumn Bliss

Autumn Kiss

**Autumn Glimmer – short bonus story

Spring Fling

Spring Serendipity

Spring Dreams

**Spring Spark – short bonus story

Summer Scandal

Summer Bride

Summer Secrets

**Summer Wager – short bonus story

STAND ALONE ROMANCE TITLES

More Than a Kiss, contemporary romance

Chasin' Mason, contemporary western romance

Ditched Again, high school reunion novella

Dragonfly Dreams, Christmas novella

Nina, Beach Brides sweet contemporary novella

PARANORMAL ROMANCE TITLES

If Tombstones Could Talk, paranormal novella

Beneath Still Waters (Part One), paranormal novella

Rising Above (Still Waters Part Two), paranormal novella

FREE READ

Holding Out For a Hero

PUZZLE BOOK

Passion & Puzzles

a Word Search and Crossword Puzzle Book of Stacey Joy Netzel
Romance books

Must love Frosting

BOOK 1

MUST
LOVE
DIAMONDS

BY
STACEY JOY NETZEL

DEDICATION

To Patti
Friend, fellow author, and Authors4Veterans co-founder...
Here's to doing this job we love for many years to come!

*A*sher Diamond glanced through the front screen door on his way to the kitchen, but caught the doorjamb and leaned back for a double-take when he saw a man down on one knee in the yard across the street. Ah...the mysterious new owner to go with the SOLD sign. Just in time for summer. The house had been on the market for six months with no more than an occasional looker.

Truth be told, it had been nice and quiet since the Zimmermans moved to California in December with their three boys, twin toddler girls, and two dogs—all of them Tasmanian Devils in disguise.

He squinted through the screen. What the heck was the guy doing, testing the texture of the grass? He rolled his eyes and resumed his mission for a second cup of coffee—until *she* strolled into view.

Whoa—hold the hell up.

He halted and leaned back. Hmm. Caffeine could wait.

Moving to the screen door to lean against the frame, he took his time scanning tanned legs topped by jean cut-offs and a white baby doll tee working overtime. God bless the warm May sunshine. This new scenery would be a helluva nice addition to the neighborhood, and that was going off only a long-distance-through-the-screen appraisal that hadn't reached her face yet.

He lifted his gaze when she halted in front of the kneeling man. And suddenly the man's position made perfect sense. Well, that, and the box he'd extended to the red-haired beauty before him.

Asher almost retreated from spying, but decided if the guy didn't want the whole world to know his business—well, this one street in Lakewood, Colorado, anyway—then he shouldn't propose to his girlfriend on the front lawn while the neighbors salivated for a glimpse of the new residents of 129 Hopewell Lane.

And, what if she said no out there? How humiliating.

As if on cue, the woman's smile dimmed and disappeared, leaving her looking altogether too serious. Very beautiful in an intense sort of way, but not a good sign for her would-be fiancé.

Duncan Collins from down the street drove by in his restored '57 Chevy, drawing the redhead's gaze for a long, covetous look before she refocused on the man kneeling at her feet.

Ooh, ouch. A woman madly in love shouldn't look away from her lover's eyes—or the ring—when he was on one knee offering her the rest of his life.

It was like seeing a car wreck; he didn't want to stare, but couldn't help himself. Pity rose for the poor man at her feet who was about to be rejected. The guy's heart would be ripped from his chest and stomped into the lush grass the real estate company had cultivated after the Zimmerman wrecking crew departed.

Yeah, he was jaded. That tended to happen when a guy had been cheated on by a superb actress who was less interested in his heart and more interested in the social and political standing that came with his last name. And while his parents were going to celebrate their thirty-fifth anniversary next weekend, and his grandparents had celebrated their fifty-fifth back in January, he and his oldest brother combined for a complete strike-out.

Loyal had fallen head-over-heels in love twice. He'd proposed twice, too.

The family had yet to hear him say, *"I do."*

Asher hadn't proposed to Brianna, but he'd been about to. And while his brother swore off marriage and moved eight hundred miles away to Dallas six years ago, Asher's method of purging the past was to throw himself into his photography career. He still wanted to get married and have a family, but with Grandpa Ira's *"Dodged a bullet on that one, son. Diamonds don't do divorce,"* echoing in his head, he'd make sure he found the absolute right woman the next time.

He was only twenty-nine, after all. He had more than enough time.

Across the street, the redhead out on the lawn extended her left hand while she beamed down at the man still kneeling before her.

Huh.

He hadn't seen that coming.

Asher shoved his shoulder off the doorjamb and straightened. His gaze lingered on her face. Man, she was something with a smile brightening her features. The guy's hand shook so hard, he dropped the ring. He stared down for a moment, then frantically pawed through the trimmed blades in search of the rock that'd flashed in the mid-morning sunlight on its decent to doom.

Legs—it was as good a name as any—dropped to the ground beside him and helped search. When she held it aloft and stood with a victorious smile, Asher experienced a tiny twinge of jealousy. His gaze travelled over her curves once more. The dude kneeling at her feet was one lucky man.

However—thou shalt not covet thy neighbor's fiancé, so he mentally knuckled the green-eyed monster aside and waited for the happy ending so he could go get his coffee. Time for the passionate kiss to put the cherry on top of the romantic scene. Too bad he didn't have his camera in hand to capture the moment for them. He could frame it as a *welcome to the neighborhood* present.

The redhead nodded and extended her left hand again. After the ring was successfully placed on her finger, the man stood, they shared a smile, and then they—

Hugged?

Asher snorted as he swung back to the kitchen. Camera definitely not needed, and a hug didn't bode well for the future of that marriage.

He couldn't speak for Loyal, but looking back, he should've realized that in his own relationship. Even though Brianna had been one hell of an actress, he should've recognized the lack of true, unadulterated, lasting passion.

Like his parents, who still shared R-rated kisses when they thought they wouldn't get caught. And his sister Celia, and her fiancé, Robert, who were always sharing glances, smiling, and touching even after six years. Not to mention, the night of their engagement party, he'd walked in on them in the wine cellar.

The image seared into his brain still made him cringe as he refilled his coffee cup. Robert had an obscenely white ass.

CHAPTER 2

"Got a big enough slab there, Ace?"

In the middle of lifting his fork to his mouth, Asher shifted his gaze from the dance floor to his best friend, Roxanna Kent. The tall, feisty brunette sauntered up to his corner table, still flushed and disheveled a half-hour after the Grand March and the recent departure of their newlywed friends, Shawn and Miesha.

"I've been working, remember? Other than a few appetizers earlier, this is the first thing I've had all night." He shoveled the chunk of marble wedding cake into his mouth before slouching down into his chair with a guttural groan of ecstasy.

Marble wasn't fancy or gourmet, but the cake went light-years beyond basic. Exquisitely moist, it had the perfect hint of butter and almond flavoring in the yellow cake to combine with the rich swirls of chocolate.

After a second bite topped with a delicate green frosting rose, he held up his fork and spoke around the sensory orgasm seducing his taste buds. "This is the only reason I still do weddings."

Roxanna dropped down onto the chair beside him and brushed her long hair back over her shoulder with a tired smile. Kicking off her shoes to prop her feet on a neighboring chair, she grabbed his Nikon and started flipping through the images.

"Right. It has absolutely nothing to do with the hopeless romantic you keep locked behind that sexy, rugged exterior."

"You think I'm sexy?" he inquired with a grin.

"All you Diamonds are—though not quite as sexy as Merit," she teased as his younger brother danced past with a blond guest from the bride's side. Miesha's cousin or something. Roxanna gave Asher a quick sideways grin, then rolled her eyes. "Except I can't even give you credit for shaving when you have green frosting in your teeth."

"Want some?"

"I'm gonna pass. There's something off about that cake."

"Such blasphemy. There's something off about *you.*"

She scrunched up her nose and kept scrolling through his pictures.

Asher didn't care what Roxanna said, the cake was pure heaven. Any masterpiece by Honor Hartman was nothing short of amazing. Didn't matter if it was marble, lemon, red velvet, carrot, chocolate rum, or any of the other flavors he'd been lucky enough to taste the past couple years. His mouth watered whenever he saw the signature double H's creatively swirled into the design on the back side of her cakes.

Since he was usually photographing the ceremony while she was delivering to the reception, he'd never met the baker, and frankly, he didn't want to. In his mind, Mrs. Hartman was a sweet grandmother wearing a matronly apron as she baked wedding cakes filled with love for young couples starting their lives together. When he did find the right woman, they'd have an Honor Hartman cake at the wedding.

Oh, crap.

There was that hopeless, romantic sap Rox had accused him of harboring behind his rugged exterior. But in his defense—and the romantic sap's—eating the woman's cake was an erotic enough experience by itself. No way he wanted to picture some sexy young baker in a skimpy apron unless he had the flesh and blood woman at hand to complete the fantasy.

Speaking of sexy…he turned to scan the wedding guests until he located the slim redhead in emerald green he'd been watching on the dance floor—and pretty much most of the night. Disappointment drew his brows together as he watched the woman with her partner. Too bad she didn't match that beautiful dress.

Well, her body *was* equally breathtaking, but—

"In-ter-rest-ing," Roxanna murmured beside him.

Asher nonchalantly returned his attention back to his plate, hoping his friend hadn't noticed the direction of his frown. He relaxed when he saw she was still looking at his camera screen.

"What?"

"Some-one's got a girl-friend."

Her teasing, sing-song tone made him snort. "What are you, seven?"

"Hey, at least I didn't take more pictures of a certain female guest than the blushing bride at our friend's wedding."

Asher's stomach lurched as he set his cake aside with one hand and snatched his Nikon from her with the other. It didn't take long to see what she meant. *Shit.* So much for *thou shall not covet.* He angled the screen toward his friend. "Miesha's in this one."

Roxanna chuckled. "Yeah. Great picture of the back of her head."

"I was capturing the design on her veil," he muttered.

She laughed at the weak excuse. "Who is she?"

She meaning the woman in the green dress—Legs.

Asher set the camera aside and picked up his dessert again. "I think she's my new neighbor across the street."

"Oh, wow. The house finally sold?"

"Yes. In fact"—he scooped up some of the butter cream frosting—"her boyfriend proposed on the front lawn this morning."

Roxanna sat up and craned her neck to get a glimpse of the redhead snuggled up close and personal to her curly-haired blond partner. "Mm. He's cute."

His fingers tightened around his fork. "That is *not* the same guy who proposed."

Her brown gaze met his, her eyebrows arched high. "Reeeally?"

Turning his gaze back to the dance floor, Asher nodded before stuffing another bite of heaven into his mouth. He had his cake, damn straight he was going to eat it, too. And why *he* was angry that some woman he didn't know appeared to be cheating on her brand new fiancé, he had no clue. It certainly wasn't any of his business.

Rubbing her hands together in gleeful anticipation, Roxanna slipped her shoes back on and moved to stand. "I'm gonna check this out."

Asher caught her arm to keep her in the chair. "Don't you dare."

"Why not? I'll get your brother to provide cover, and she'll never even know."

"Leave Merit out of it." Last thing he wanted was his horn-dog little brother noticing Legs. Except he really shouldn't care, damn it.

"Fine." Roxanna sat back with a sigh. After a long moment, she lolled her head in his direction while keeping her gaze trained on the dance floor. "Think we'll ever have this? Weddings, I mean."

"Sure we will."

"Once we find the right person." She sounded almost sad as she said it. Like she didn't hold out much hope. He cast her a quizzical look, but she was still staring straight ahead. Another beat of silence passed before she asked, "Did you hear Adam and Amy separated?"

"No way." She nodded, and he frowned. "What happened?"

"I don't know. No one's talking other than I heard he moved out last week."

"Wow. That sucks. Their first anniversary was only a couple of months ago." The news set off a ripple of discontent. He'd photographed their wedding, too, with their white velvet Honor Hartman cake.

Roxanna sat up and craned her neck, still surveying his faithless neighbor. "If anyone was rock solid, I'd have thought it was those two."

"I know what you mean." Realizing she'd shifted forward in her seat, Asher gave her a warning look. "Don't do it."

"What?"

He didn't buy the innocent expression for one second. "Shawn and Miesha said no readings at the wedding. You had direct orders to relax and enjoy yourself."

"I just want to examine her aura up close."

"I'm not psychic, and *I* can see her aura from here," he muttered as she ignored his advice and rose to her feet. He couldn't really, but still. "It's bad news no matter where you view it from."

"I don't know. I see a subtle variance around the edges that—"

"Let it go, Rox."

She spun around to face him and stuck her hands on her slim hips. "You like her."

He set his empty plate aside and stood. "Pretty wrapping doesn't change what's inside. After Brie, you know I wouldn't touch another cheater with a ten foot pole."

"Brianna was more than just a cheater, Asher."

"Yeah, but it doesn't change that she *was* a cheater."

"Fine." She glanced over her shoulder. "I'm curious, that's all. Call it job research. And technically, I'm not ignoring Shawn and Miesha's orders because I love what I do."

Knowing she'd set her mind, he swiped up his camera. "Do what you want. I'm pretty much done here now that the bride and groom have left, so I'm calling it a night." He leaned in for a quick hug goodbye. "Behave."

"I'll talk to you tomorrow." She fluttered her fingers as she spun away.

Asher went the opposite direction to gather the rest of his equipment. On his way out with his bag slung over his shoulder, the cake table distracted him long enough for him to wrap two thick slices in Hulk-green napkins. Shawn had hissed at him to shut-up when he wise-cracked about the color, because Miesha loved the sage and cream color combo, but then they'd shared a chuckle the moment the bride stepped out of ear-shot.

Before he left, a cream-colored clump of frosting on the cake knife hailed his addiction. The silky-smooth, sugary indulgence melted on his tongue, triggering another involuntary throaty groan.

"You like the cake?"

The husky-soft female voice sent a jolt of physical reaction through his body. He sucked the remaining frosting from his thumb as he spun around. "I love the—"

His voice froze when he saw the woman he'd been avoiding all evening. Gleaming red curls in a sexy, messy pile on top her head, sparkling green eyes brightened by the luxuriant emerald of her dress, and the sensual curve of glossed lips all combined for a triple threat without the safety filter of his camera lens.

"Cake," he finished as he lowered his hand. "Have you had a piece?"

Humor warmed her smile, as if his answer pleased her. "I've tasted it."

To combat the flustering effect of that smile on his racing pulse, he dropped his gaze. Her dress revealed an alluring hint of cleavage before skimming along the rest of her curves. The high, strategic slit along her right thigh gave him a glimpse of one of the shapely legs he'd appreciated from across the street earlier that day.

The top of her head barely reached his chin, and without heels, her petite height would no doubt stimulate a man's protective instincts. His were fired up and ready to go right now—until he realized he'd given her a thorough once-over as if he were a man who hadn't eaten in weeks and she was a freshly grilled steak.

Or a slice of Honor Hartman wedding cake.

Asher cast a casual glance around for the boyfriend. Nothing like another guy—or two if he counted the proposer on the lawn—to put his mind back where it belonged.

Instead of the blond boyfriend, he caught sight of Roxanna, shaking her head while waving her hands in a strange circular motion in front of her. She started making some other gestures, none of which made any sense. He shifted his gaze to his brother standing next to her, but Merit just shrugged with his palms up.

What the hell? *You'd think a psychic could communicate better.*

"You're the photographer, right?"

The question brought his gaze back to the woman in

front of him. Her green eyes had flecks of gold around the irises. The right one had an intriguing freckle next to the pupil that made him want to lean in for a closer look.

He managed to stay right where he was as he replied, "Guilty. Actually, I was pulling double-duty today; Shawn and I have been friends since the second grade."

"Ah, got it."

When her gaze dropped slightly, his pulse leapt with the realization she was staring at his lips. He quelled the urge to lick them even as her eyes darkened the slightest bit. A heady thrill of anticipation shortened his breath, and then she lifted her hand to swipe her thumb against the corner of his mouth.

A spark of electricity transferred from her skin to his. Asher automatically lifted his left hand to cover hers, but she'd already pulled back. He had a split-second glimpse of cream-colored frosting before her lips parted and her tongue darted out to lick the sweet confection from her thumb.

A molten tsunami of heat shot straight to his groin as their gazes locked once again.

Her eyes widened. A fierce blush camouflaged the freckles on her cheeks and she slapped a hand over her mouth. "Oh, God, I'm sorry. I can't believe I just did that."

Smiling to put her at ease even as his body tightened with primal hunger, he swiped the back of his hand across his tingling lips to remove any remaining frosting. "No problem."

"Occupational hazard, I guess."

He cocked an eyebrow at the odd comment, trying to muddle through the lust fogging his brain.

"I can't help but taste," she explained with a cute, sheepish grin. "Um, when I'm baking, I mean." She gave a roll of her eyes and another smile. "Not that I'm baking now, *obviously*, but when I am, I can tell by the taste of the batter if it's missing something. Everything has to be just right."

Batter?

Asher turned to eye the cake.

No.

"Oh, no—don't worry, the cake is safe," she quickly assured him. "I don't lick my fingers and put them back in the bowl. I always wash my hands. Well…almost always."

The admission brought his gaze back to her as the dread in his gut mushroomed.

She laughed and cringed at the same time, her hands rising to press against her red cheeks. "I'm going to shut up now. Please don't tell anyone I said that."

"How is it you know Shawn and Miesha?" It was a dumb question. He already knew the answer. He didn't want her to confirm it, and yet he hadn't been able to keep from asking on the off chance he was wrong.

Please be wrong.

She lowered her hands to her sides as she said, "I designed the cake."

Shit. "You're Honor Hartman."

Her smile faltered at his flat statement. "Guilty."

His lewd libido jumped up and kicked the romantic sap's ass while he imagined this real life version of Honor Hartman across the street from his house, in the kitchen wearing a skimpy apron—and nothing else.

"Son-of-a-*bitch*."

CHAPTER 3

"*E*xcuse me?"

Honor's shocked, offended question was spoken to the man's back as he strode for the exit. She blinked when Mr. Tall, Dark, and Rude disappeared out the door, realized her jaw hung ajar, and snapped it shut on a disbelieving laugh.

The outright rejection stung after he'd seemed interested. Hell, at one point he'd seemed more than interested—right after she wiped the frosting off his lip and his amber eyes darkened beneath the wavy locks of near-black hair falling over his forehead. Everything inside her had gone on alert, her breath seized in her throat, and her already racing heart stumbled in her chest. With the way she'd been single-mindedly focusing on her business the past year, the visceral reaction had knocked her totally off-balance.

Speaking of which, she still couldn't believe she'd touched his mouth and then licked the frosting off her thumb!

Belatedly, she turned and swept her gaze around the room. Hopefully, no one else had noticed the intimate gesture. Sam wouldn't be happy if she goofed everything up after they'd carried their charade through the entire evening.

She did some unnecessary arranging of the sage green napkins while thoughts of the photographer crowded back in, along with a twinge of disappointment. Obviously, he'd heard of her, but *what* had he heard about her that sent him running for the foothills? He'd looked distressed when she confirmed she'd baked the cake.

Maybe it was the finger-licking?

No. She hadn't mistaken the smoky flare of desire in his gorgeous eyes. And she'd never met a guy who didn't find that somewhat of a turn on—even if she hadn't done it intentionally.

Still, she wondered at his abrupt departure. She didn't think it was the tall brunette she'd seen him with—they acted more like friends, or siblings. They hadn't even danced once.

Hmm. The rare man she dated more than once or twice didn't usually run away until *after* they met her mom. Much as she loved her mother, Honor silently agreed with anyone who had the nerve to declare her certifiable. As for her dad, well, no one had ever stuck long enough to meet him.

You've never kept them around long enough.

True. But better to leave than be left. A fact she witnessed up close and personal with her mother four times now. And each time, her mother fell apart until she found the next man to take care of her. Until he didn't. Made it a little hard to buy into the whole *I love you 'til death do us part* thing when exposed to that kind of carnage over and over.

Honor sighed and scooped up a finger-full of frosting like she'd seen the sexy photographer do. No matter how many cakes she made, she still loved the decadent butter cream.

Too bad sugar doesn't solve man problems.

Problems? She stiffened her spine as the thought triggered a spike of annoyance. The man's snub wasn't a problem—it was a blessing. Right?

Right.

Well...maybe.

Honor sighed. Okay, fine. She didn't have time to date at the moment, but some fun with the hot photographer would've been a nice change from twenty-four-seven work. She wasn't a one night stand kind of girl, but man, it had been a while, and with a guy like that, rules were meant to be broken.

"Hey, Sweetie Pie."

She jumped at the male voice directly behind her.

Nope, she was going back to the snub definitely being a blessing. She had enough man problems. Make that *friend* problems. More like issues—or situations, or...whatever.

Sam's arms slid around her waist to pull her back against his broad chest. As she considered who might be watching, suddenly the past few minutes made sense. He—the photographer—had seen her with *Sam* all night.

A new wave of disappointment rushed forward. Wasn't that just her luck? Now she wanted to run after the guy and explain, but of course, she couldn't do that.

Why did I let Sam talk me into this?

She turned around in her friend's arms and leaned back a few inches. "We both know Penny's gone already so ease up, Romeo."

He dipped down to kiss her nose with a grin. "Her mom is still at the bar, and I can feel her sister's glare stabbing between my shoulder blades as we snuggle."

"What about the bride and groom?" she asked with a discrete glance past his shoulder. "I know they're your friends, but I can't afford to jeopardize my business with this little break-up scene."

"They left after the Grand March so it's not going to ruin anything for them. It's the perfect time."

Too bad they couldn't have done it half an hour ago. Before she met the hot photographer. Maybe he would've offered her a shoulder to cry on.

No. *Forget him.*

"All right, then," she said. "Let's get this over with."

"Let's do it."

Honor took a deep breath and pushed against his chest. Sam tried to grasp her arms, but she twisted free and strode toward the main entrance. His footsteps shadowed hers, and she threw a disgusted look at him over her shoulder. He gave her an awkward smile and reached to take her hand in his. She yanked her fingers away and kept walking.

"Honey—"

She whirled around to glare at him and felt a couple of her curls tumble loose. "Don't try to make up for it now."

With a self-conscious look toward the bar, Sam took her arm and attempted to usher her toward the door while speaking in a low voice. "Let's go outside."

"No. Right here's fine." She forced her voice louder. "Everyone saw what you did."

"What did I do?" Sam asked, looking genuinely confused. *Good.*

"You couldn't take your eyes off Penny all night."

"And I suppose you hitting on that guy over by the cake was okay?"

Honor lifted her eyebrows.

"Yeah, that's right, I saw you." Sam winked to soften his accusatory tone.

Her face warmed. "He had frosting on his chin—big deal. At least I wasn't staring at my ex all evening." She shoved a curl behind her ear and crossed her arms. "It's obvious you still have feelings for her."

"She was in the bridal party—"

"Are you still in love with her?" Honor made sure her voice trembled with just the right amount of heartbreak. It wasn't hard. She'd heard the emotion in her mother's voice many times.

Sam's cheeks flushed, and he shoved his hands in his pockets as his injured gaze locked with hers. *Oops...too much?* They hadn't scripted this part, and he obviously hadn't expected her to go that far. But the whole public breakup had been his idea, and it seemed to fit in the scene.

"Are you?" she pressed, despite a prick of guilt.

Sam's Adam's apple bobbed, his expression rigid as his jaw clenched. "I refuse to have this conversation here."

He brushed past her, and for the second time in ten minutes, a man walked away from her.

CHAPTER 4

*H*onor donned a black tank top, zip-up sweatshirt, and cut-off jean shorts before heading straight for the coffee pot in her brand new kitchen. With a steaming cup of crème brûlée roast in hand, she wove through the pile of boxes the movers had deposited in the living room yesterday afternoon before the wedding.

Mae was coming to help unpack tomorrow after her son's tee-ball game, but as soon as Honor had her coffee, she planned to get as much done today as possible. Between being a single parent to six-year-old, Ian, and operating her own construction and remodeling business, her best friend worked even more than Honor did, and it had been ages since they'd been able to sit down and visit.

Out on the sunlit porch, she curled one bare foot underneath her on the swing, pushed with the other, and sipped her coffee pensively. Sam still refused to answer her calls or texts. Yes, it was early, but she wanted to apologize as soon as possible. They were only supposed to make his ex jealous, not shout out to everyone and her sister that he was still in love with the woman.

Honor ran a hand through her damp hair, hoping he'd forgive her. The question had slipped out because she wasn't sure Penny was worth all the heartache Sam had gone through. Then again, after watching her mother's fourth divorce and her father's third, the whole concept of soul mate love seemed absurd. But, she now realized, that was for Sam to decide, not her.

She dated for fun, occasionally enjoyed the opposite sex for obvious reasons, and then she moved on before anything got too serious. The only life-long commitment she planned to make was to her business and her mortgage.

Tracing her gaze up along one of the massive, rustic wood porch columns, she rejoiced in the fact this house was all hers. She'd fallen in love the moment she saw the internet listing a month ago. Wraparound porch—with a swing. Two stories, three bedrooms, two baths, lush, green lawn with mature trees in the backyard—all in a quiet, suburban neighborhood.

One drive down Hopewell Lane, and the place had called to her soul like a man never had. She'd felt it in her bones— for the first time in her life she could have a real *home*.

Her brother Joshua had gone over the financials, all the while pointing out the impracticality of such a large house for just her, but she'd weighed it from all sides and was confident in her plan. The gourmet kitchen with double ovens meant she would no longer have to pay a percentage of her profits to use the kitchen in the bistro across from her old city apartment. Better yet, no more third shift baking because that was the only time the ovens were available.

With more time available, she could bake more cakes, which would easily offset the couple hundred more per month between her house payment and what she'd been paying for rent. Not to mention, padding her calendar with bookings wouldn't be a problem if she landed the Diamond wedding.

No, *when* she landed Celia Diamond's wedding.

She took a sip of her cooling coffee and sent a quick prayer heavenward. Rumors were circulating that Governor Mark Diamond was planning a run for the United States Senate. Crafting the cake for his daughter's big day would showcase her work to the upper echelons of Colorado's social and political elite.

One cake could boost her up to the next level and get her another step closer to her ultimate goal of opening a shop with an actual storefront.

The bride had loved two of the three custom designs she'd emailed, but the real test would be Saturday night, when she provided four cakes for the governor's thirty-fifth wedding anniversary. It was the equivalent of a paid taste test, with the added bonus of Mrs. Diamond inviting her to attend the party as a guest.

Her stomach flipped with a combination of excitement and anxiety as she thought about the opportunity to mingle and network, even though it was a whole week away.

Taking a deep, calming breath, she leaned her head back to let the peaceful morning soothe her nerves as a cool breeze skimmed over her skin.

Hmm...heaven.

After another moment, she forced herself to move her butt. As much as she wanted to, she couldn't sit out here all morning. Not if she wanted Mae to actually relax and eat pizza with her and Ian instead of the two of them one-handing their lunch while unpacking all her stuff.

She started inside with her empty cup when her gaze caught on the *For Sale/Sold* sign still in her yard. The realty company was supposed to have come by to remove it yesterday.

Leaving her cup on the railing, she headed down the front porch steps. Cold dew slicked her bare feet, making her shiver as she skimmed across the grass to the edge of the lawn. Grasping the wood post with both hands, she tried to pull it from the ground. It didn't budge. The sign was set deep into the earth; no cheap posters and wire here.

Honor pushed one way, pulled another, and succeeded in gaining about a quarter inch wiggle room. Unfortunately, when she tried to pull the post out, it still wasn't enough.

Waggling it back and forth some more, she glanced up as a bicyclist zoomed around the corner on a black mountain bike. The guy slowed as he approached, and though she couldn't tell if he was looking at her with those mirrored sunglasses, she offered a friendly smile and half-wave. His fingers lifted slightly in response before he made a sudden turn into the driveway of the house across from her.

She watched with increased interest as the garage door rose. Looked like she'd get to meet her first neighbor.

Please let him be nice.

Her gaze traveled over his athletic build as he got off the bike and reached up to remove his helmet. Black shorts and a black sleeveless T-shirt emphasized broad shoulders, trim hips, and very nicely defined arms, ass, and thighs. He hung the helmet on a handle bar and shook his head before reaching to run his fingers through dark hair that was a little longer on top compared to the sides and back.

She smiled to herself. The view across the street was almost as impressive as the Rocky Mountains to the west.

Absently working the sign post back and forth, her focus remained on the man as he wheeled his bike into the garage. Only when he disappeared did she notice the back of what looked to be a blue Camaro SS. She would recognize that rear end anywhere, and man, would she love to get a look at that car up close. Yesterday, she'd nearly drooled when she'd watched that '57 Chevy that had driven by.

Maybe she should walk over and introduce herself. The car could be the perfect ice-breaker.

Just then, the guy came back out of his garage without his sunglasses, and Honor's stomach bottomed out as she sucked in a gasp of surprised dismay. Even with a dark shadow of scruff on his jaw, she recognized the photographer from last night—hard to forget that unsmiling face.

She quickly returned her attention to the stubborn post, shoving hard, then jerking the wood back toward her while her entire body flushed with heat.

Un-freakin'-believable.

She fought the urge to turn and go back into her house immediately. Not only would the retreat be too obvious, but she didn't run away from anything.

Then again, if she got the damn post out, she'd have a valid reason to go back inside and avoid acknowledging the jerk.

There was a good inch of wiggle room on each side by now. Bending her knees slightly, she braced her shoulder under the part that held the sign, then pulled up with her hands while pushing with her legs. The wood bit into her shoulder, but the post rose a few inches. Another forceful shove back and forth loosened it some more as she spotted Hot Photographer Neighbor Guy walking down his driveway, water bottle in hand.

Seriously? He's coming over after being a jackass last night?

Maybe he was going to apologize now that he realized they were neighbors.

He better apologize.

Resentment from last night fueled her second attempt on the post. The four-by-four burst free more suddenly than she expected, and the momentum threw her off balance. She stumbled under the weight before landing on her back in the wet grass, hugging the wood for dear life.

A few blinks to clear the stars from her vision brought a pair of amber eyes into focus overhead. The heaviness of the sign lifted from her body, and then her neighbor crouched at her side. Her fingers twitched with the desire to reach up and brush aside the damp hair tumbling over his forehead. She fisted her hands against the odd urge.

"You okay?" he asked.

She pushed up to sitting and realized too late the move put her very, very close to his face. A deep, shaky inhale to calm her nerves ended up being an even bigger mistake. Mind-muddling waves of heat radiated from his body, infused with the scent of sweat, citrus, and morning sunshine. Up close, with his shadowed jaw and sexy hair, he looked good enough to eat for breakfast.

Too bad he didn't have more frosting on his lips—this time she'd be tempted to lick it off. Her gaze dropped to his mouth. Time slowed. She swallowed hard, and could've sworn he did, too.

And did he just move closer?

Honor lifted her gaze to his and suddenly drawing a breath of air into her tight lungs was impossible.

Who needs frosting?

He shifted his attention past her, to her house. When his gaze returned, his eyes were cool and shuttered. Any awareness she may have imagined disappeared as fast as the man had last night.

She clenched her fingers in the cool grass as his stinging rejection flooded back. Sheesh. One look into his mesmerizing eyes and how quickly she forgot.

He shifted away from her, and when he held out a hand to help her up, she pretended not to see it. If looking into his eyes could so effectively mess with her common sense, touching was absolutely out of the question.

Once on her feet, she turned awkwardly for a glimpse of her wet shorts while forcing a smile into her voice. "I'm fine. The only thing hurt is my pride."

"And your leg."

Honor twisted back around as he knelt in front of her. His palm closed around her calf as he leaned in closer. The thrill of his warm touch was tempered by the sight of blood trickling down her shin and a sudden stinging sensation in her leg. She braced a hand on his shoulder for balance, then had to fight the urge to run her fingers over firm muscles and heated skin.

"It's just a small scrape," he pronounced. "But you'll want to wash it good."

His fingers flexed ever so slightly, then left a trail of tingles down her calf before he pulled away and stood in front of her again.

Surprised by his doctorly advice, she murmured a soft, "I will. Thanks."

He nodded. He looked ready to say something, but again, his gaze focused behind her.

What the heck was wrong with her house? She glanced back with a frown, but didn't see smoke or anything else to set off alarm bells. When she turned back, her neighbor was already at the curb, scooping his water bottle up off the ground to head back across the street.

"Don't forget to fill in that hole," he instructed over his shoulder, his tone brusque. "Someone could break a leg."

So much for an apology. What the hell?

She glared after his back for a frustrated moment before lifting the realty sign. After plunking it against the front of her garage, she covered the hole with a large rock from her landscaping until she could find some dirt to fill it in later, then went inside to wash the scrape on her leg.

Finally, she transferred her simmering hostility for the man across the street to the boxes in her living room. While setting up her kitchen, she went over both meetings with the testy photographer in her head. She still didn't even know his name, for heaven's sake.

He may have confused the hell out of her, but she wasn't some naïve little virgin. No way she'd only imagined the sexual chemistry zinging between them. The air practically crackled with electricity whenever their eyes met. Yet, each time she would've encouraged him, he'd stepped back and put distance between them. *Lots* of distance.

"You're Honor Hartman?"

Yes, she was, damn it, and what was wrong with that? They'd never met before last night—she damn sure would've remembered meeting him—so what was his problem? By his own admission, he loved her cakes, so that couldn't be the issue. And her apparent relationship with Sam didn't cover the surprised dismay in his voice when he confirmed her name.

Maybe he knew someone she'd gone out with? Someone who'd received the brush off? Some guys gossiped as much as women did, so it wasn't a totally crazy idea that he could've heard her name at some point. What was crazy though, was after running into him last night, she found out they were neighbors this morning.

Setting the box in her arms on the island counter, she rested her hands on the open flaps. Hmm—maybe *that* was the issue. Maybe he knew her name from the real estate agent. In that case, his brush off would be understandable. Prudent, even. Because, really, no matter how hot the attraction, a fling with the guy across the street from her brand new home would be stupid when she planned to be here much longer than any relationship would last.

Disappointment filled her sigh as she dug into the box to get back to work.

She was unpacking the last box of kitchenware when her cell phone rang shortly after one p.m. Swiping it off the counter, Honor glanced at the caller ID before answering and turning on the speaker.

"Hey, Jim...how's it going?"

"I'm freaking out."

She rolled her eyes at the phone and unwrapped a plate before reaching for another. "Try to relax. You've got a whole week yet."

"Not anymore. I've decided to do it tonight, and I need to see you right away."

She faced the phone, a plate in each hand. "Wait, slow down. Tonight?"

Geez. First Bryan yesterday, now Jim today? Had the stars somehow mystically aligned to make this the perfect weekend to propose, or were her clients trying to drive her crazy?

"Yes, tonight."

"But I've got your tickets for the Rockies next Saturday, and the jumbotron guy knows to display the question in the seventh inning stretch."

Not terribly original, but Jim's girlfriend was a baseball fanatic, and he'd insisted she'd love it. Especially when the flowers, chocolate, and champagne arrived after she said yes.

"Heidi's parents invited us to some ballet in Denver next Saturday. I couldn't say no without her suspecting something."

"Oh." Her shoulders drooped as she set the plates on the counter. "That is a monkey wrench."

"Yeah."

Bracing her palms on the kitchen island, Honor frowned out the window, her mind racing. "I'll tell you what, give me a few minutes to make some calls, and I'll see what I can do."

"You're the best."

She smiled briefly. "Don't jinx me, Jim."

"Whatever you come up with will be great. But can we meet to go over the details, please? You know I need the face to face interaction."

Her attention honed in on the house across the street where her neighbor sat on his front porch, bare feet propped on a chair, laptop across his thighs. He lifted a hand to his mouth and took a bite of food while poking at the keyboard with his other hand.

"I'm in the middle of unpacking," she told Jim. "I'm a complete mess."

"I'll come to you. Please?"

She reminded herself if Jim walked away happy, any referrals he sent her way would help pay for her new home. This particular arm of her business was all based on word of mouth. "All right. I'll text my address once I've got everything set up."

They disconnected, and she dialed Alex—the jumbotron guy, and also her ex-brother-in-law. Thank God Glory had had an amicable divorce.

She didn't even realize she was staring across the street until her neighbor tossed a crumpled green napkin on the table beside him, downed half a glass of milk in a couple swallows, and then lifted another chunk of food to his mouth.

Cake. He was eating the extra pieces of cake that he'd taken home from the wedding last night. Her cake.

Honor smiled as a light bulb flicked on in her head. *Ha!* It was so obvious. The way to this man's heart was definitely through his stomach.

Well, not that she actually wanted to get to his heart, but she did want to be friendly with all her neighbors. And if he loved the marble wedding cake with butter cream frosting, he would roll over panting for her sea salt caramel and triple chocolate pudding cake.

Oh, God, no. Get that *image right the hell out of your head.*

"Hello?"

Alex's voice on the other end of the line snapped her back to reality. She had a proposal to rescue before she could even think about making her neighbor pant.

Geezus. Rein it in, Honor!

"Hey, Alex. I need your help."

CHAPTER 5

*a*sher hadn't been able to stop thinking about Honor Hartman since he walked away from her last night. Then he did the same thing again this morning. It had been a shitty move, but he was having a hell of a time keeping himself from picturing someone else's fiancé baking cakes naked—even if she was two-timing the guy.

The redhead had haunted his dreams, trailed along on his ten mile bike ride, and was waiting for him out on the curb when he got home. One touch on her leg confirmed her skin was as soft as it looked—and he was in trouble.

Especially when the chemistry sparking between him and the sexy cake baker nearly had him leaning in to kiss her right there on the lawn—with her fiancé probably watching from inside. After Brie's betrayal, he wasn't about to knowingly be that scumbag of a guy, which meant his best bet was to avoid the attraction by staying the hell away from her.

Out on his front porch after lunch, he started preliminary work on Shawn and Miesha's wedding album, only to discover way too many shots of the woman he needed to stay the hell away from. Grimacing with annoyance, he switched over to his shoot from the nature preserve for Colorado Conservationist magazine. They'd requested proofs for a number of articles, as well as for their website.

Once he completed the magazine contract, he still had to sort the shots from his whitewater rafting trip the previous week, and plan his shot list for the Pike's Peak climbing school the week after this. He had more than enough to keep himself busy, so why was he so damn restless?

Asher glowered through his lashes at the house across the street as his cell phone vibrated on the table. He nearly dove on the distraction. "Afternoon, Rox."

"Afternoon, Ace. Did you have sweet dreams of your new neighbor?"

The too-perceptive question of the subject he was trying to ignore deepened his frown. Maybe he shouldn't have answered the phone. "I'm not talking about my neighbor with you, other than to ask what the heck were you spazzing out about last night?"

"I was letting you know to be nice to her."

He scrolled through a couple of pictures of a fox and her kits to find the right one for the magazine article. "And I was supposed to get that from your freaky psychic sign language?"

"Yeah, sorry, sometimes I forget you're normal. Turns out she's the one who bakes those cakes that give you mouth orgasms. How convenient is it to have her right across the street?"

"Not convenient at all," he grumbled.

"What'd you two talk about?"

"She told me she baked the cake. That's all."

He wished that was all. Wished he didn't have the memory of her feather-light touch on the corner of his mouth. Or the image of her licking frosting off her finger burned into his mind. It made him want to dip his finger in some batter and let her suck it off as those mesmerizing green eyes of hers widened with desire.

He bit back a groan and swiped to the next image on his laptop screen.

"Come on, it had to be more than that," Roxanna pressed. "She and the cute blond guy broke up right after you left. Made a big scene, too, so I'm thinking you should go for it. Could be a match made in heaven."

His pulse leapt at her words, but then settled right back to steady. "And screw the guy who proposed out on the front lawn?"

"Oh. Crap. I forgot about him."

"Some psychic you are."

"Hey. Anyway, forget the girl, then. I *am* psychic enough to know you already ate the cake you took last night."

He'd finished both pieces for lunch. Even a day later and dried out on the edges it was still groan-worthy. "Any one of my brothers or sisters could've told you that without being psychic."

"Well, they didn't," Roxanna retorted. "So if you want me to stop by tomorrow with the slab I wrapped up on my way out, you better be nice to me."

"I thought you didn't like the cake?"

"I didn't say I didn't like it. I said something about it felt off. But clearly that doesn't bother you, so, you gonna be nice or not?"

"Times like this, I'm glad you're *not* normal."

"Aw, you do say the nicest things." Laughter echoed in her voice. "I'll see you around ten."

After they hung up, he managed to focus his concentration long enough to cross two items off his To-Do list before his phone rang again.

"'Lo, Mom," he answered with a smile.

"Hi, hon. How was the wedding yesterday?"

"It was great. I was just about to work on the album. How was your dinner?"

"Good. Your father lined up some firm backing for the senate bid."

The news wasn't unexpected, but it produced a flicker of unease. Campaign years could get tough on the family. "He's going to announce at the party Saturday, isn't he?"

"Yes."

Asher dusted his forefinger along the row of keys at the top of his laptop. "You sure you're up for this, Mom?"

"I will never stand in the way of your father's ambitions, Asher. He can do a lot of good for our country."

"That's not what I asked. I know it was hard on you last time with all the negative campaign ads. A Senate run will garner national attention. The spotlight is going to be twice as bright and they're going to spin every little thing they can to make Dad look bad, whether it's true or not."

"I know all this, Asher. I dealt with it last time. I'll deal with it again," his mom assured him. "Your father and I made this decision together."

Like they did everything. "Okay. I just wanted to make sure."

"And I love you for that. Thanks. But I actually called to see if you heard from Merit today, and to ask if you plan on bringing a date on Saturday?"

Both questions made him cringe. "I haven't talked to Merit since last night. You know, he is twenty-five, Mom. He's a big boy."

"A big boy who doesn't have a job, dates too many women, and doesn't bother to let us know when he isn't coming home," she complained.

Dating was a generous way to describe Merit's escapades. Her frustration was understandable, but seeing as his parents were the ones financially supporting most of his youngest brother's bad habits, it was up to them to deal with the problem.

"You'll have to talk to him before the campaign kicks off."

"I will," she said with a heavy sigh. "Or your father will. Right now, I just want to know he's okay."

"You never worry if I make it home at night," he teased.

"Of course I do, but you have your own place. I don't expect to see you at the breakfast table in the morning."

"Even when Merit is home, does he make it to the breakfast table?"

"You have a point," his mother conceded. "But he still sweet talks Elena into making him a plate in the kitchen, so at least I know he's alive."

"He's alive, Mom. Probably hung over in a bed with one of the bridesmaids, but he's alive."

"Don't be so crass." Despite the admonishment, there was grudging humor in her voice.

"Just trying to make you feel better before I let you go."

"That doesn't make me feel better at all. And you didn't answer my other question. Plus one or no?"

Darn. Merit wasn't even good for an effective distraction these days. "No, I'm not bringing a date, but you know I'll be busy taking pictures at the party, so don't even think about setting me up or introducing me to anyone."

"Asher, it would be rude of me to *not* make introductions if there's someone there you don't know."

Deep breath. She means well.

"There'll be a ton of people there I don't know, Mom. You invited half the state." Not quite, but since his dad was going to announce his senate run, the guest list would be longer than usual.

"Then don't be upset with me when I make introductions," she reasoned, the happy grin back in her voice.

"Introduce Loyal. He texted and said his flight gets in Thursday night."

"I'd like him to move home for good, not drive him away."

"*I* can always move away," he threatened.

"You wouldn't."

They both knew it was true, but he still said, "You'd still have Celia, Merit, and Shelby to drive crazy."

"I want all my kids here, not spread out across the country. You're not allowed to move away, so stop teasing."

"But it's fun."

"You're sassy. Tell me, is Roxanna coming on Saturday, too?"

"She said she wouldn't miss it."

"Good, then I'll let you get back to work now."

Thank you.

"Tell Dad I said hi. Love you both." The sign-off was automatic, but no less sincere.

As he set his phone aside, a red pick-up truck pulled into the driveway across the street. He couldn't help sneaking glances as the driver spoke to his red-haired neighbor at her door, then loaded the realty sign into his truck, filled the hole with dirt, topped it with a chunk of sod, and left.

Not long after, another guy showed up in a gray Charger with a briefcase and went inside for about fifteen minutes. When Honor walked him back out to his car, she hugged him and kissed his cheek. Compared to the sign guy, this one didn't give her a second glance, and going off similar ginger hair and mannerisms, Asher guessed him to be a brother or some other relation.

At least he hoped he was.

Why? Why do you care?

About the time it dawned on him he was approaching stalker status and closed his computer to take his sorry ass inside so he could actually get some work done, a black

Porsche convertible glided into her driveway. He admired the sleek car through the living room window until a tall, dark-haired man stepped out, looking like he was right off the cover of some men's fashion magazine.

The guy swung a bouquet of red roses at his side as he hurried to the front door. A rose bearer who was neither yesterday's fiancé nor last night's date? Curious suspicion shifted into overdrive.

Honor gave the man one of her brilliant smiles when he handed over the bouquet. When she buried her nose in the flowers, Asher shook his head and decided enough was enough. He didn't want to know anything more about his neighbor across the street.

Ten minutes later, he paced restlessly to the window while fully acknowledging how ridiculous it was to be so agitated by a woman who wasn't even available. His eyebrows rose when he saw her sitting out on her front porch swing with Porsche Guy, her left hand extended.

No way.

Yet, there they sat, smiling at each other as the guy slipped a ring on her finger.

What the ever-loving-fuck was going on over there?

CHAPTER 6

*H*onor opened her front door as Mae parked in the driveway shortly after noon the next day. It always made her smile seeing her petite, blond firecracker of a friend climbing down from her heavy duty work truck. She always said she didn't want to waste money on a second, leisure vehicle, and reasoned it was great advertising.

It made sense, and Honor also knew she had a lot to be proud of with her *Lockhart Construction* prominently stenciled on each door. At only twenty-two years old, single mom to a one-year-old, she'd started her business with sheer guts and determination. Over the past five years, she'd built it into a successful company that provided a steady paycheck for eight employees.

Although they were now both twenty-eight, Honor still joked she wanted to be her when she grew up. Only her signs would someday advertize her specialty cake shop.

"Auntie H!" Ian jumped out the passenger side and ran up onto the porch. "We got pizza *and* root beer! Mom said if I help unpack, I can have soda, too!"

"Milk first," Mae reminded from the truck. She shouldered the door shut, pizza box and soda in hand.

"I've got chocolate in the fridge, Scoob," Honor told her favorite six-year-old while lifting her arm for a high five. "Just for you."

"Jinky." He slapped her hand, hugged her waist for about two seconds, then scampered inside to flop on the couch where she'd cleared off the last of the boxes an hour ago.

"How was your game?" she called as she crossed the porch to help his mom by taking the two liter bottle of soda.

"We won!"

"Awesome."

"He did great," Mae agreed as an engine fired up across the street. "Hit a double and they got two runs off it."

"Nice job." Unable to stop herself from checking out the sound of the motor, Honor's pulse skipped when she saw her neighbor outside on his front lawn with a push mower.

Look away. Now.

And yet, her gaze followed his long stride down one side of his driveway, then along the curb by the road. She would need to buy a lawnmower for her own yard now, so of course she was going to check out his equipment.

That was her story, anyway.

"*Holy moly.* I vote we set up chairs and eat out here."

She tore her gaze away to see Mae swing around to watch her neighbor, the pizza held over her shoulder on the tips of her spread fingers, like the cocktail tray she'd wielded during college for her second job. Until she'd gotten pregnant.

Despite her best efforts, Honor turned to watch again. The man's low riding jeans and faded blue T-shirt showed off all the mouth-watering aspects of his tall, athletic body. He was wearing those mirrored sunglasses, and his hair was an untidy mess that looked like he'd just rolled out of bed.

Maybe he had. It was the first she'd spotted him all day.

Not that she'd been looking.

"Mmm, *mmm*," Mae murmured.

"He's kind of a jerk." The abrupt statement was as much for herself as it was for her friend. His brush off couldn't have been clearer, so there was no reason for her to be imagining him sprawled in bed.

Shirtless.

The covers sliding down—

"Really?"

"Really," she insisted. "*Both* times I met him."

"Well, double damn, then." Her friend sighed with disappointment. "Okay, so we won't go talk to him, but we can still enjoy the scenery."

Tamping down on an irrational spurt of possessive jealousy, Honor pointed out, "You have plenty of scenery on your crew to drool over all week long."

"And a lot of weekends, too." The brag was accompanied by a cheeky grin. "But I can't *openly* drool over the guys without risking a sexual harassment suit *or* a screwdriver in the back from Jen or Becca."

Jen and Becca had been her first employees, and after each of them married, their hunky husbands had been hired at Lockhart Construction, too.

As Mae stared across the street, her expression turned wistful. "Besides, there's no such thing as too much scenery when I haven't been with anyone since Ian was born. Fantasies are all I have these days. Don't deny me this tiny bit of pleasure."

Honor's grudging laugh lodged in her throat when her neighbor swung the mower around to go back across the yard. He glanced over as the two of them stood there ogling him.

She quickly spun around, cheeks burning with mortification. "Let's eat before the pizza gets cold."

Mae sent her a narrow-eyed glance, then gave a cheery wave across the street before finally turning to precede her inside.

Ian had already found the remote and a cartoon on the TV, and two steps into the open concept foyer-slash-living room-leads-right-into-the-kitchen, his mom pulled up short to scan the furnished room.

"Wow. Did you leave anything for us to help with?"

She snagged the pizza on her way past, carrying it and the soda to her kitchen island. She hadn't had one in her small apartment and loved it already. "I've got a few boxes left in the spare bedrooms upstairs, and most of my pictures to hang, but they can wait. As much as we've both been working, it feels like we never get to visit anymore, so I made an executive decision to take the afternoon off. No arguments."

Mae braced her palms on the island, eyebrows raised in question. The glint of hope in her expression made Honor doubly glad she'd worked past one a.m., then gotten up again by six to get everything done—all the while drinking tons of caffeine. She was used to working into the night at the bistro, but not so much the getting up bright and early. Especially two mornings in a row.

"Fine, twist my arm," Mae relented with an affectionate grin as she glanced toward the roses in a vase off to the side. "But if I'd have known, I'd have brought wine, too."

"Not to worry. I've got wine. We'll have some with the pizza now so you don't have to worry when it's time to drive home later."

"This is why I love you so much."

She slid the bottle across the counter with an air kiss.

"Speaking of love…" Mae looked pointedly at the flowers.

"Oh, please. You know better than that. They're from a client, nothing more," she insisted as she grabbed paper plates and napkins before pouring a small glass of chocolate milk for Ian.

Three gulps later, he waited for his root beer refill with a milk-mustache grin while his mother poured their wine. The three of them sat at the island, eating and talking around bites of hand-tossed pepperoni pizza.

While Ian recapped his tee-ball game, Honor braced her chin on her hand as she listened to her godson. She'd known she was missing these moments together with her second family, but hadn't realized how much until now.

"Dude, I think you're ready for the pros," she teased after he told her about his second base hit.

He giggled as he chomped down on the crust of his slice of cheese and pepperoni. "I'm way too small for that yet, Auntie H."

She reached out to ruffle his hair. "You'll get there, little man. You will get there."

He ducked out from under her hand with another grin while turning to his mom. "Can I go watch Scooby and Shaggy again?"

"After you put your plate in the garbage, and rinse your cup for the dishwasher."

Once he was settled back in the living room with his favorite cartoon dog on the screen, Honor commented in an undertone, "You're wasting no time training him, are you?"

"Gotta start early." Mae tucked her blond hair behind her ear and snuck a glance at her son while lifting her wine glass. "I'm a single mom who runs a business, I don't have time to be a maid, too."

"His future wife is gonna love you."

"She better."

They shared a laugh as Honor slid her third slice onto her plate. "Considering what you said before, I think it's high time you get a man in your life again. I'll even volunteer to take Scoob since I don't have to bake at night anymore."

"You know I don't have time for a relationship."

"It's not like you have to get serious with anyone. You just need to have some fun in your life."

She shrugged, then her green gaze cut toward her son. "I do have fun."

"*Woman* fun. With an adult *man*."

"Okay, Kettle." Mae arched an eyebrow. "Or are you Pot?"

"Hey. I get out. I have fun. I even date."

"Your fake date with Sam does not count."

"Even so, it hasn't been over six years since I've had sex." It'd been about two. And she'd been fine with that until her neighbor had her thinking maybe she wasn't.

Good God, she had to stop thinking of him.

"Well, me having casual…ah…relations don't mix with being a single mother, so it is what it is and isn't going to change."

Honor held up her hands in surrender. "I can respect that."

Her friend drained her glass of wine and refilled it about half. "How did things go for Sam the other night?"

Ironically, that question gave her a heat-inducing flashback of the encounter at the cake table. Her pulse beat faster as she recalled amber eyes framed by thick lashes and full sensual lips accented by a dab of frosting.

But Mae had asked about Sam, not Tall, Dark, and Jerky.

"Not so great, but getting better." She gave her the rundown, then added, "He *finally* responded late last night. Turns out Penny called him yesterday, and they met for coffee. They're having dinner Friday."

"Well, then, all's well that ends well."

"Time will tell." And time told her to change the subject before more wayward thoughts of her wedding photographer neighbor could sneak in to mess with her mind. "Speaking of next weekend, any chance you could be my date for the Governor's anniversary party? Mrs. Diamond sent me an invite to attend this week. It's black tie and everything, so we can dress up fancy."

Mae winced in apology. "As much as I'd love to say yes, Ian has a Scouts meeting."

Nervousness pinched her stomach at the prospect of going alone. It'd been a long shot asking Mae on short notice, but she'd still held out some hope. "So much for my networking wing-woman."

"I'm sorry. What about Glory?"

Honor shook her head at the mention of her older sister. "It's her weekend with the twins."

"Your mom?"

She nearly snorted wine from her nose and reached to snatch her friend's glass. "That's it. You're cut off."

Mae's eyes sparkled with mirth as she held the last few sips of her one and a half glasses out of reach. "You certainly wouldn't have to worry about coming up with any ice-breakers if Camilla was there."

"A perfect reason to go alone." The idea of her mother in a room full of rich politicians made her shudder. With divorce number four final only three short weeks ago, she would be on the hunt for husband number five the second they entered the governor's mansion.

"What are you gonna wear?"

She'd been pondering that as she unpacked yesterday. Choices were slim, and money was tight. "Probably the same dress I wore to the wedding the other night."

"No. You just wore it."

"I'll get it cleaned, of course."

"That's not what I meant."

"It's the only thing I have that's formal enough."

Mae leaned forward. "What about that dress I got when we went to Vail last fall? The off-the-shoulder one, with the slit up to mid-thigh?"

Honor sighed with longing. "I do love that dress—but you haven't even worn it yet, have you?"

"No, but the way things are going, I never will. I'm serious, you should wear it. It'll go great with your black sandals."

Four inch heels with a simple strap across the toes and a second around the ankle. Of course Mae remembered the sandals, because Honor had bought them on clearance during the same trip. And her dear friend was kind of a shoe slut when she wasn't wearing her steel toed construction boots.

"I don't want to wear your dress before you do. Besides, burgundy doesn't go so well with my red hair and freckles."

"It'll be *gorgeous* with your red hair and freckles. Trust me."

CHAPTER 7

*H*onor carried the final cake outside to the dessert table set up on the huge, pergola-covered patio of the Diamond mansion. There were a multitude of individual treats set out by the caterers bustling about between the kitchen and the patio, but her four designs were front and center as the main attraction.

The first was triple layer red velvet with snow white butter cream frosting, a replica of the top tier of the Diamond's wedding cake from thirty-five years ago—original topper supplied by the bride-to-be daughter, Celia. The second was chocolate with chocolate ganache frosting featuring a hand scrolled family tree, with leaves for each of the couple's five children: *Celia, Loyal, Asher, Merit,* and *Shelby*.

At the request of Mrs. Diamond, the third was a southern favorite, hummingbird spice cake with cream cheese frosting, in the shape of the Colorado state capitol building to honor the governor's political career. And last but not least, lemon poppy seed with Bavarian cream filling. She'd shaped that cake into a pair of interlocking wedding bands, frosted with butter cream, airbrushed silver, and layered with delicate gold fondant lace.

Sliding the fourth cake into position, Honor stood back to survey the table. Other than the capitol building, the cakes had been fairly simple, but she'd still taken time with all the little details, plus triple taste-tested the batter to make sure each was exactly right. Everything was as perfect as she could make it. If this didn't secure her the job, nothing would.

As she started to turn back to the kitchen, she pulled up short. She'd been so focused on her work, the beauty before her hadn't even registered. Of course she'd noticed the sheer size and grandeur of the mansion when she arrived, but the grounds out here in the back were nothing short of amazing.

Her awestruck gaze swept over a massive swimming pool and sprawling flower gardens, past a combination tennis and basketball court, all the way across the lawn to a large stable with pristine white fences. At least a dozen horses grazed in the spring green pastures, and the picture-perfect setting was topped off by the Rocky Mountains rising up in the background.

She knew the Diamonds came from old money, but hadn't ever really seen what that could look like up close. This was the family's private residence, not the state-owned governor's mansion. Realizing the level of wealth left her dumbfounded and wholly intimidated. Insecurity knotted in her stomach as she smoothed a damp palm past the hem of her T-shirt, over the hip of her jeans. Thankfully, she had Mae's dress to shore up her courage.

And if all else fails, just remember they put their pants on one leg at a time, too. Designer pants that probably cost more than her new monthly house payment.

On that note, she'd rather face Celia, Mrs. Diamond, and the governor in a dress rather than her jeans and tennis shoes, so time to get changed. Her hasty pivot almost knocked over one of the tall heat lamps dotting the outside edge of the patio every fifteen or twenty feet. Once lit, they would provide welcome warmth as the evening cooled, but realizing the threat of melted frosting, she wrestled the danger away from the dessert table before hurrying through the kitchen so she could retrieve her evening clothes from her car.

"Cakes all set, hon?"

She paused at the question from the woman who'd directed her where to go when she first arrived. Appearing to be about fifty years old and dressed in a sharp, figure-flattering uniform, the dark-haired, olive-toned Elena clearly ran the entire show as she directed and delegated while still monitoring the stove and the oven.

"Yes, thank you." She was about to ask where the nearest bathroom was located when Celia Diamond breezed into the kitchen wearing an emerald green dress similar to the one Honor had worn to the wedding the previous weekend. The one she'd almost worn tonight.

Marvelous Mae. You truly are a Godsend.

The bride-to-be's dark, sleek bob shimmered in the overhead lights, her brown eyes lit with excitement. "Guests are starting to arrive, Elena. And Honor! Oh my God, I just came from the patio. The cakes are *ah-maz-ing.*"

Relief turned her polite smile into a grin. Taking a breath to calm her nerves, she slid her hands into her back pockets and squared her shoulders. *No time to be modest.* "Thank you. I'm going to brag and say they taste even better."

"I can't wait—though it's going to kill me to cut into them."

She'd heard that a thousand times and always had the same answer. "That's what cameras are for. Cake is made to be eaten."

"My brother will take care of that," Celia assured her.

"The pictures *and* the eating. Cake is his kryptonite—especially if it has butter cream frosting."

The comment brought to mind her cake-loving neighbor, but she shoved his sexy, jerky mental image aside with a determined scowl.

A slight frown marred the other woman's brow as her gaze skimmed Honor's black T-shirt and jeans. "Aren't you staying for the party?"

"My dress is in my car. I didn't want to get it dirty. In fact, I was just going to ask if there's a bathroom I can change in?"

Celia's nose wrinkled. "Skip the bathroom. You can use my room."

"I don't want to be any trouble."

"I insist."

Honor relented with a grateful smile. "That would be great, then. Thank you."

"Of course." A woman's voice called Celia's name from the other room and her hair swished against her chin as she glanced toward the door, then started to back up. "I have to help my mom with the last of the flower arrangements, so just head up the stairs, and it's the third bedroom on the right."

"Oh. Um...o-kay." The last was spoken to an empty doorway.

From over by the stove, Elena shook her head with a soft chuckle. "I'll point you in the right direction, hon. Go get your dress."

Honor gave her the grateful smile this time, then hurried out to her car. When she returned with the dress and her duffle, the housekeeper pointed her through the same doorway Celia had disappeared and instructed her to take a right, go down the hall, then left up the stairs.

Not a single one of the small army of workers gave her a second glance as she threaded her way through to the stairs and gingerly sidled past a thick, satin rope barrier. The second floor was completely empty, as if she'd passed through some sort of invisible portal on her way up. The muted quiet soothed her nerves, until she realized if someone exited any of the doors lining either side of the wide hall, they'd wonder what the heck she was doing up there.

Which meant, time to get moving so no one had to wonder and she didn't have to explain. Mae had talked her into wearing her hair down, and her make-up was already done, so all she had to do was slip into the dress and then return her bag to her vehicle.

Moving to the third door on the right, she stepped inside the room, only to hesitate when she saw the navy blue and maroon accents. Glancing back out into the still deserted hall, she counted again. It was indeed the third door, but certainly not what she'd expected for a girl's room. Make that a woman—Celia was two years older than her.

Then again, *she* wasn't into soft and frilly, pink, or anything else pastel, so maybe she shouldn't assume the bride-to-be was either.

She shut the door with a quiet click and crossed the plush carpet to the king sized bed. As she laid her dress bag across the comforter and plunked her duffle next to it, a swift perusal of the room confirmed her old apartment could fit into this one room. But that didn't matter anymore, did it? Now, she had her own house.

A brief grin twitched her lips. It wasn't a mansion by the Diamond's standards, but it was *her* mansion.

Toeing off her shoes, she shot a quick glance toward the French doors leading to a second story balcony. This side of the house faced the backyard where the party would be held, but from where she stood, only the roof of the stables, and the fences and horses beyond were visible past the wrought iron railing.

Lingering nervous energy tickled her stomach as she opened the garment bag before stripping down to the black strapless bra and matching panties under her casual clothes. While sliding the dress zipper down, her fingers stroked the cool burgundy fabric. It pooled on the ground at her feet, and when she stepped into it, the soft, clingy material slid over her thighs and hips with a sensual caress that sent a shiver of decadence up her spine.

Between the mansion and the dress, she was beginning to feel like Cinderella.

Honor grinned at the thought and started to tug the princess-seamed bodice up over her bra. When the door swung open, a spike of alarm slayed her humor. She clutched the top of the dress to her chest as she jerked her head up with a gasp.

The sight of her equally shocked neighbor filling the doorway lodged her pounding heart in her throat.

"Whoa…hello."

Noticing his gaze focused much lower than eye level, she darted a hasty glance down to make sure her bra was covered. "What the hell are you doing here?" she demanded, making necessary adjustments while heat seared her cheeks.

"*I* am here for my parents' anniversary party. What are *you* doing here?"

Her jaw went slack for a second even as her stunned subconscious registered his tux and how devastatingly gorgeous he looked in the black and white. "Your *parents?*"

"Yeah." A brief smile ghosted over his lips. "I guess we haven't been formally introduced yet, have we?"

"No. You haven't taken the time to bother with that."

His head dipped with the slightest bit of acknowledgment of her pointed barb. "Asher Diamond."

Swallowing hard, she tightened her grip on the material clutched in her fingers. Trying to salvage some of her dignity, she asked, "And do you always walk into your sister's room without knocking, Asher Diamond?"

"Never," he replied gravely. "My room, however, always."

"Your room?" Her stomach dropped as she darted her gaze toward the bare dresser top. "But...you don't live here." Or did he?

"Not now, but I grew up here. It'll always be my room."

"Oh." The darker masculine colors and lack of anything girly made perfect sense now. Her embarrassment jumped another notch as she finally noticed the overnight and camera bags in his hand when he reached to set both inside the door. "Right. Well...Celia said her room was the third door on the right, and this *is* the third door on the right."

He leaned a shoulder against the door frame while sliding his hands into his pockets. She automatically followed the movements until she realized her attention was focused on the front of his pants, then she jerked her gaze back up. She wouldn't have thought it possible, but her face burned even hotter.

"She's the third *bed*room," he clarified. "The first room is a linen closet and staff bathroom."

Oh, hell, that's right. She did specify bed*room.*

But how was she to know about the linen closet-slash-staff bathroom? "I just assumed they were all bedrooms. Not all of us grew up with staff bathrooms, so it never occurred to me I would need to verify each room as I went."

"Understandable."

When she noticed his gaze had once more dipped to where she still had the dress in a death grip, a hot wave of prickly awareness swept from head to toe. Not fair, considering all he'd given her so far was a cold shoulder.

Also, why had he settled in against the door there like

they were going to have a neighborly little chat while she was only half-dressed?

She shifted with a twinge of impatience, the plush carpet squishy between her toes. "Okay, so…I'm sorry I mixed up the rooms, but can you give me a little privacy here? I only need a minute."

"Yeah. Sure." He straightened from the doorframe and pivoted to face the hall.

She grit her teeth when he didn't pull the door shut behind him, but seeing as his back was turned, she quickly shoved her arms into the short sleeves, tugged the material over her bra, and adjusted the folded, off-the-shoulder neckline before reaching behind for the zipper.

A full minute of struggle only led to frustration. Unfortunately, when she'd tried the dress on earlier in the week, Mae had been there to zip it up.

"You never answered my question," Asher said from the hall.

She cast his broad shoulders a swift glance. He'd canted his head slightly to the right, but kept his face trained away from the open door. She kept working on the stubborn zipper, sliding it down, then back up again, contorting her arms as she tried to make it go farther each time. "I was invited to the party."

"Yeah?"

Was that so hard to believe? She threw a couple of mental daggers right between his shoulder blades. "I was hired to bake the anniversary cake, but your mother also invited me to attend as a guest."

Now she couldn't get the zipper up *or* down. *Damn it.*

"Did she offer you a plus one?" he asked.

Something in his tone made her frown. "What?"

"A plus one. For you to bring a date, or…maybe one of your fiancés?"

Her entire body stilled. She lifted her head, tilted slightly to the side as she processed the terse question. Okay, she needed help, and she needed to see his face for this one.

She lifted the hem of the dress in one hand and moved to the door, her bare feet silent on the thick carpet. *"One of my fiancés?"*

He started slightly at the sound of her voice right behind him, then turned to face her, his amber gaze flicking down, then up. "You've been proposed to a lot since you moved in across the street."

Ohh. He'd seen both Jim and Bryan last weekend. That damn heat burned her cheeks again as she quipped, "Nosey much?"

His shoulders lifted in an unapologetic shrug. "Both happened outside of your house in plain view for anyone to see."

Yeah, if you were watching my house all day.

That should creep her out. Instead, her pulse fluttered with the idea he was interested enough to watch. Not to mention, Mae would be justified in calling her Kettle again, seeing as she'd checked out *his* house across the street an insane number of times.

"Two times hardly qualifies as a lot," she pointed out, trying not to get distracted by the yummy scent of his cologne. "And it's not—"

"In one week, two times *is* a lot. Not to mention you had a completely different date at the wedding."

He sounded annoyed—*looked* annoyed—but why the heck would he even care? If anyone had the right to be annoyed right now it was her. Unfortunately, she had to go through him to get out of his bedroom.

Speaking of which, if anyone had told her she'd end up in Hot Photographer's bedroom tonight, she'd have laughed. Now she just wanted to cry at the injustice of it all. The one guy in how long who got her engine revving and he turned out to be a Diamond—and her neighbor to boot.

She tried to see out into the hall, but his tall body and broad shoulders took up too much space in the doorway. She felt tiny in front of him without her shoes on, and even with them on, he'd still have more than six inches on her. "Is anyone else out there? Your sister maybe?"

Hopefully.

"Nope. It's just us." His brows drew together in a slight frown. "Relax. It's not like I'm going to do anything."

Unfortunately.

Oh, for crying out loud!

Thoroughly irritated with herself and him, Honor drew in a deep inhale and spun around to present him with her back. The skirt swirled and settled around her legs as her nose registered the contrasting layered scents of his cologne. Mint and lavender, spicy cinnamon and sweet orange blossom, and finally, vanilla and sandalwood.

Closing her eyes in a silent prayer of resolve, she reached up to drag her hair forward over her shoulder. "My zipper is stuck. Do you mind?"

CHAPTER 8

Seconds ticked by one by one. Acutely aware of each beat of his heavy pulse, Asher stared at the seductive allure of Honor Hartman only inches away. He clenched his fists at his sides while drawing in a deep, fortifying breath.

A combination of vanilla, butter, and almond assaulted his senses. *Oh, sweet heaven.* She smelled like cake. God hated him right now, didn't he? Or maybe this had all been set up by the devil.

Tempting him to sin with the forbidden fruit.

It had to be. The front view of her dress had been bad enough, with the unzipped material gaping enough to show glimpses of her strapless bra and the swell of her full breasts above sexy, black lace. The back view was downright torture with her shiny red hair pulled forward over her shoulder, exposing her spine all the way down to where the edge of her panties peeked above the zipper.

Can't stand here all night—and walking away a third time isn't an option either.

Well, not a good one, anyway.

He flexed his hands a few times, sucked in another mouth-watering breath to shore up his willpower, and finally reached for the zipper. It was stuck all right, with the burgundy material caught between the delicate teeth. He tugged gingerly to avoid ripping the fabric, breaking the zipper, or actually touching her.

It wasn't that he didn't want to touch. It was the wanting it too much that was the problem.

"Back in February, I was proposed to three times in one *day*."

Her shameless boast was accompanied by a smug smile over her bare shoulder. Her words turned into white noise when his gaze connected with her through-the-lashes upward glance. The setting sun lit her gold-flecked green eyes and gave her beautiful profile an angelic glow.

His fingers fumbled the zipper and his knuckles brushed against the warm, silky skin of her back. Her grin faltered, and she averted her gaze with a swift inhale that echoed his own.

Geezus, he'd give just about anything to lean forward and press his lips to the flushed hollow at the base of her neck. Then he'd tease that fluttering pulse of hers with the tip of his tongue...

His gut clenched with desire, and his hand trembled with the urge to strip off her dress, carry her to the bed, and explore every inch of her body with his mouth and his hands.

Unstick the damn zipper and get the hell outta here before you're the bastard who destroys some other guy's future.

The gold hoop earring dangling from her lobe swayed as she turned her head forward again. She trained her gaze across the room, throat muscles contracting in a hard swallow before she added, "Besides designing cakes, I have a proposal consulting business."

He stopped working the zipper, his gaze locked on her profile. "A *what*?"

"I help guys plan the perfect proposal for their girlfriends."

"Who needs that?"

"Lots of guys," she retorted, sounding slightly offended as her back stiffened.

Actual words from her comment a few moments ago finally registered. Three proposals in one day.

"In the past two years, I've facilitated twenty-three proposals."

"Anyone ever say no?"

"Once."

And from the wrinkle of her nose, she hated having that negative in her stats.

But wait a second…this could change everything. His pulse skipped a beat as the puzzle pieces finally fit together to reveal the complete picture. "So, the guys who proposed to you were what…practicing?"

"Exactly."

"You're not engaged?"

"Not even once."

Sounded pleased as punch about it, too. Interesting.

Asher got a better hold on the zipper, this time not worrying at all when his hands brushed against her back. She sucked in another breath, and his pulse kicked up a notch as well, sending a rush of blood straight to his groin.

He ducked his head slightly for a better view—of the zipper. "What about the guy at the wedding?"

"Sam? I was only there to make his ex jealous."

Hence the public break up scene Roxanna had told him about. "Did it work?"

Dumb question. Of course it worked. Look at her.

"They went out to dinner last night." Satisfaction filled her voice. "He texted this morning that it went very well."

"That part of your consulting business, too?"

"Just a favor for a friend."

The zipper finally let loose, shooting down a couple inches before he could stop the momentum. His hand brushed the curve of her butt when he grasped the material to pull it tight so he could run the zipper up in one smooth motion. It wasn't until his fingers fumbled to connect the teeny little hook at the top before he was able to step back and draw in a lungful of air—that still smelled like cake.

"All set." Relief and disappointment warred in his tight chest.

"Thank you."

The breathless words had him fisting his hands to keep from reaching out for her. All the more difficult to resist now that he knew she wasn't spoken for by another man —or three.

In the next moment, she flipped her hair back over her shoulder and crossed to the bed to grab the pair of black heels lying on the comforter. He traced his gaze over the enticing curve of her shapely ass when she bent to secure one shoe, then the other. They were nothing more than a sole and two little straps to secure them on her feet, but they were sexy as hell with her dainty red toenails peeking out.

He slid his clenched hands into his pockets to camouflage his growing arousal as she scooped up all her things, stuffed them into her duffle, and zipped it shut.

"All right, then. I'll get out of your way." She crossed the room with the handle of her bag slung over her bare shoulder and her gaze fixed about chest level. "Again, sorry about the room mix-up."

I'm not.

Definitely not in my way.

You can get naked in my bedroom any time you'd like.

Merit would've said any or all of those things out loud. Asher stood aside for her to pass with a quiet, "Not a problem. Can I carry that for you?"

"I got it, thank you. I'm going to put it in my car right away." She paused, shifted her stance while glancing toward the stairs, then gave his chest a quick smile. "I guess I'll see you down there."

"Yep."

Another brief curve of her mouth, a second of hesitation as her gaze dipped, and then she abruptly walked away. He released a low groan under his breath as he watched the subtle sway of her hips before a shift of the duffle blocked his view. When that flaming mane of hers disappeared below the top step, he remembered he'd come upstairs for more than the unexpected wardrobe assist.

That's right. He was supposed to put his bag in his room, make sure Shelby didn't still have her nose stuck in her veterinary books, and round up everyone to help greet the arriving guests.

He bent to pull his camera from his equipment bag when he saw Merit in the hall, walking toward him with a shit-eating grin. He met up with him in front of Loyal's room. His youngest brother's eyebrows rose until they disappeared behind the unruly mop of hair tumbling over his forehead.

"Never thought I'd see the day Angel Asher snuck a woman out of his room."

God, he hated that nickname. Roxanna's was ten times better and even then, he only tolerated it because it was Roxanna. "There was no sneaking going on."

"There you go. Own it."

Asher rolled his eyes, though reluctant humor did tug at his lips as he rapped on Loyal's door, then cracked it open to warn, "Mom wants us downstairs pronto."

"I can't tie this damn tie," his oldest brother groused as he came to the door in his tux.

"Ash got a quickie in with a sexy little redhead before the party started," Merit said with a grin.

"Help him." He shoved his loud-mouth brother toward the fashion challenged one before moving across the hall to Shelby's room. "And grow up, moron. Nothing happened."

Though, now that he knew Honor wasn't engaged or dating the guy from the wedding, he wouldn't have objected if it had. But not here. While their parents weren't stupid enough to believe their kids didn't have sex, 'shenanigans' were expressly forbidden on the second floor until they were married.

Merit worked his magic on Loyal's bow tie as he tossed over his shoulder, "Right. Nothing happened. You were just helping her put her dress back on for no reason at all."

Clearly, Merit had no problem breaking the rules.

Loyal cocked a questioning eyebrow and Asher shook his head. "She baked the anniversary cake, and Celia sent her up here to change. All I did was help with her zipper."

"That's your story?" Merit scoffed.

"That's what happened. Now drop it."

Shelby opened her door and stepped out in a little black dress and heels similar to Honor's. Geezus. When had his baby sister become a woman? He was used to seeing her in her vet tech scrubs and glasses. Even with her dark, signature Diamond hair pulled back into a smooth ponytail, her outfit, contacts, and makeup made her look much older than twenty-three.

She eyed the camera in Asher's hand with resignation. "Show time?"

"Yeah." He gestured for her to go first, then waited while the other two followed.

As they all headed toward the stairs, Merit asked, "Where's Mini-Mom?"

"Probably with Main-Mom," Shelby answered.

"That stopped being funny ten years ago," Loyal admonished.

"But it's still true," she shot back.

"So true," Asher confirmed. "They were rearranging the flower arrangements when I arrived."

As usual, the stairs had been cordoned off at the bottom to keep guests from the second floor, and Shelby and Merit turned to face him and Loyal for their usual huddle up before political shindigs.

"You all know Dad's announcing his senate run, right?" he asked.

They each nodded, and he took note of the mixed emotions on his siblings' faces. Shelby's lashes lowered to cover her dismay, but the downturn of her mouth gave it away. Merit was more than happy to welcome the spotlight, and the brighter the better. Loyal's stoic expression didn't give much indication of his feelings either way. Typical.

"All right, then," Asher said. "Everyone on their best behavior."

It was a warning meant for their younger brother, but the horn-dog just grinned as they each put their hands in for a quick pile and break. The first time they'd done it as a joke, but over the years it had become a secret little tradition he actually looked forward to. It grounded him, while at the same time reinforced they had each others' backs. It was nice to have Loyal back in the huddle tonight. He'd been absent for most of them the past four years.

"FYI," Merit said in a stage whisper, "I got dibs on the wine cellar after ten o'clock."

Loyal frowned. "Show a little class, Mooch."

Merit's gaze narrowed at the hated nickname. "You

should try it sometime. You might have better luck getting 'em to the cellar than the altar."

Their oldest brother's jaw clenched. "Fuck you."

Shelby backhanded Merit on the arm as Loyal stalked away. "I can't believe you said that."

He shrugged, and she shook her head as she left as well. He turned his mutinous gaze toward Asher. "No one can take a joke around here anymore?"

Except it hadn't been a joke, and they both knew it. Hell, they all knew it. "Like I said before, Merit. Grow the hell up."

Leaving him there, he made his way into the growing crowd of guests. Much as he loved his little brother, he'd had just about enough of him already tonight. Loyal had headed straight to the bar. When his oldest brother turned around with a healthy glass of his usual Black Maple Hill bourbon, he acknowledged Asher's silent concern with a tight nod. He nodded back, and eased back against the wall to fiddle with the settings on his camera.

Wine-red hair and a burgundy dress flashed in the corner of his eye. Just that one glimpse reeled him in like one of the Rocky Mountain spotted trout mounted on Grandpa Ira's wall. He raised his camera to zoom in on Honor talking with an older couple near the French doors leading out to the patio. The smile on her glossed lips lit up her eyes and rounded her freckle-dotted cheeks.

Time slowed even as his heart skipped and dipped before thumping so fast his breath caught in his chest.

She's The One.

The thought hit hard, and he swallowed hard as his pulse continued to race. From fear or excitement, he wasn't entirely sure, but then, he realized he'd felt an inexplicable connection to her from the moment he first laid eyes on her. Acting on it had been impossible when he thought she was engaged, but now, the impossible was entirely possible.

His heartbeat settled to a more normal rhythm as acceptance sank in. Followed by approval, and definite anticipation.

It was time he took a page out of Merit's book and went after what he wanted. Right?

Right. Difference was, he wasn't only looking for a one night stand or fifteen minutes in the wine cellar.

His feet itched to carry him to her side and jump right in. But the weight of what was at stake slowed his roll. As the song went, only fools rush in. Honor Hartman wasn't a woman he wanted to make a fool of himself over. Not in that way, anyway.

Forcing himself to take it slow, Asher gradually made his way across the room under the guise of taking pictures of his parents' guests. Unlike at the wedding where he used his camera to avoid her, tonight she was fully in focus.

CHAPTER 9

*T*he hair on Honor's arms prickled for the third time in as many hours, and it had nothing to do with the cool evening air. Even with her shoulders bare, the patio heating lamps provided plenty of warmth. No, this was something else entirely. Some*one* else.

While casting a surreptitious glance around, she raised her champagne glass to her lips. The bubbles were long gone, the sweet liquid now lukewarm, but holding the drink gave her something to do with her hands while talking to people.

Sure enough. In the middle of her pretend sip, her gaze landed on Asher's profile about three feet away as he snapped a photo of his father shaking hands with a nun. The governor left the woman with an ear to ear grin before placing his hand on his wife's back to guide her to a podium set up on a raised dais at the far edge of the huge patio.

It was crazy how awareness flared to life when the younger Diamond was within her vicinity, and yet when Celia made introductions earlier, there hadn't been a single tingle with either of his handsome brothers, or her fiancé,

Robert. The older brother had a solemn intensity about him, while the youngest one was an outright charmer she recalled seeing at the wedding last weekend. He'd seemed equally… charming…then, too.

By comparison, Asher wasn't even looking at her, and clear as day, she could picture his amber irises framed by thick, dark lashes. Her heart thumped hard in her chest as she recalled how she'd barely been able to breathe while he fixed her zipper. The graze of his warm hand on her back and her butt nearly had her hyperventilating.

It was a miracle she'd managed to walk away when the urge to turn around and press up against his tall body left her stomach quivering with the most intense longing. Hell, a move like that would've had her thinking of pulling him into the room and shutting the door. Undoing that perfect bowtie of his, stripping off his shirt, and seeing what he looked like lying on a bed for real instead of only in her late night fantasies. (And a few daydreams, too.)

Yep. It was an honest to God miracle she'd retained enough common sense to walk away.

When he'd come downstairs for the party, he'd circled close a few times while taking pictures, but they hadn't spoken again. She dreaded and anticipated the moment they were face to face because it seemed something had changed upstairs, after he'd learned she wasn't engaged—to two men.

Sheesh. He must've thought she was a real piece of work to accept a ring from two different guys while going to a wedding with a third. No wonder he'd given her the cold shoulder.

But now…now she had the distinct feeling if that had been what was holding him back, she was in trouble. Up in the doorway of his room, he hadn't even tried to hide the heat in his gorgeous eyes when she'd met his gaze over her shoulder. Just *thinking* about the moment made her body go hot and her breath turn shallow.

Governor Diamond called for his guests' attention from the podium. The older man was as dashing up there as his sons, and Mrs. Diamond looked like a movie star on the red carpet with her dark hair in an elegant up-do, diamonds sparkling at her ears and throat, and a long sleeved, floor length white gown hugging her svelte figure. As the governor thanked his wife, family, and staff for their hard work, Honor was able to lean against a nearby column and watch Asher while his attention was wholly focused on his parents.

So many wants and wishes ran through her mind. Unfortunately, whatever may have changed for him, nothing had changed for her. He was still her neighbor, and worse, he was a Diamond. No matter how fast the guy made her pulse race, she couldn't risk losing the commission from his sister's wedding.

But after the wedding—

No—*neighbor*.

The firm reminder made her sigh with disappointment.

"He's a great guy."

Honor started at the hushed female voice directly to her right. She turned her head to see the tall, willowy brunette who'd been with Asher at the wedding the weekend before. She'd seen them together tonight, though again, she got the distinct impression they were friends, not lovers.

The woman was probably close to her age, with a cascade of incredible curls that reached nearly to her waist. She wore a dark pair of wide-leg, tye-dyed silk pants paired with a sleek black halter top. Not many women could pull off such an outfit, but she managed to look exotic and elegant all at once. A quick downward glance had her thinking Mae would be so jealous of her black boots.

After offering a quick smile, Honor returned her attention back to the podium. "The Governor seems very nice, though I've only met him briefly."

The brunette tipped her head slightly to the right while she sipped some reddish-orange, fruity-looking drink. "I meant Asher."

She realized her sigh must've made her sound like a lovesick school girl. "We've barely met. I don't know him well enough to say if he's great or not."

"Well, I do, and he is."

Lucky you. With a sideways glance, she asked, "How long have you two been together?"

"Me and Ace? Oh, God no." The woman laughed softly while giving a delicate shudder. "That would be like dating my brother. Not that I have a brother, but I imagine that's what it would feel like."

The concrete confirmation sparked relief she had no business feeling. "Ace?"

"Just a nickname." She extended her free hand. "I'm Roxanna, by the way."

"Honor."

When she accepted Roxanna's handshake, the woman's grip tightened as her eyes widened. Then she jerked free, her sculpted eyebrows drawn down in a frown.

"Sorry," she muttered. "Static electricity."

Honor hadn't felt anything...but, o-kay.

"You're the wedding cake baker."

"I am. I did the anniversary cakes for tonight, too." Celia had made numerous introductions and provided plenty of networking opportunities.

"They're beautiful." The flat note of Roxanna's voice didn't match the complimentary words.

"Thanks." *I think?*

The conversation stalled, and she tuned back into the governor's speech. He'd moved on from thanking their guests to telling the story about his and Mrs. Diamond's first meeting. As he waxed poetic about their thirty-five years of marriage with their five children standing by, she couldn't help but think of her parents' seven divorces. Four for Mom, three for Dad. None of them amicable.

"I love their story," Roxanna murmured beside her. "It's inspiring to see love so lasting."

"They're an exception, not the rule," she commented with an absent glance sideways.

The woman's brown gaze narrowed defensively. "No. Diamonds don't divorce. It's like the golden rule of the family. The governor's parents have been married for fifty-five years. And each of Asher's uncles have been married at least twenty-five to thirty years, as well."

Honor shrugged. She didn't begrudge any of them their happiness, but the Diamonds' track records meant nothing to her. A few couples with long marriages were simply anecdotal no matter what type of 'rule' they deluded themselves with.

"Diamond men are in it for the long haul."

The statement sounded like a warning, but Roxanna's expression gave no clues, so she looked back toward the podium. Standing slightly behind the rest of the siblings, Asher's youngest brother flirted with yet another pretty female guest as the rest of the family listened to their father's speech.

"I doubt that one got the memo."

Roxanna grimaced. "Merit's a bit of a playboy, but trust me, Asher's the complete opposite."

As if to illustrate that point, the photographer shot his brother a glare over his shoulder that made the younger guy roll his eyes. He whispered something to the blond woman, then dutifully turned his grin to the podium as he slid his hands in his pockets.

Even from a distance, Honor could see the annoyed clench of Asher's jaw—until he glanced her way, and his expression softened. Her pulse skipped when he flashed a quick smile. It wasn't until after his mother stepped up to the microphone and he lifted his camera once again that she realized he'd probably been smiling at his friend, not her.

A sneak peek sideways brought her all the way around in surprise. Roxanna had faded back into the crowd as quietly as she'd appeared. Hmm. Honor faced the podium again, her mind replaying the past couple of minutes.

Odd as the exchange had been, and whatever the reasons for it, the brunette's comments reinforced the fact she needed to shut down her insane attraction for Asher Diamond.

He was a long haul guy. She was a short-term girl.

Diamonds didn't divorce; Hartmans *always* divorced.

Bottom line, neighbors, Diamonds, and long hauls were completely off-limits.

Another heat-inducing look across the room told her if presented with another moment similar to in the hallway outside his room, she wasn't so sure she could trust her willpower or her common sense. The only way of shutting down her body's magnetic attraction to the man was to leave now and avoid contact.

Mrs. Diamond's announcement confirming the rumors the governor was going to run for the United States Senate prompted cheers and applause from the guests. Honor set her warm champagne on the tray of a passing waiter and started toward the French doors.

"Honor!"

Celia's voice made her wince at her thwarted escape, but she halted and faced the bride-to-be with a warm smile.

"Mom would love it if you'd cut the cakes."

She hesitated, only to realize she couldn't say no. "Of course."

Trailing after her to the dessert table, she saw Asher standing off to the side with his brother, Loyal, youngest sister, Shelby, and Celia's fiancé, Robert. She purposely avoided looking their direction while waiting to greet his parents, all while cursing the familiar uptick of her pulse when she felt the prickling heat of her neighbor's gaze.

The woman ahead of her moved aside, and Honor stepped forward with a smile. "Happy anniversary, Governor and Mrs. Diamond. Thank you for inviting me."

"Thank you for staying after bringing those gorgeous cakes." The older woman surprised her with a quick hug. "But please, it's Janine and Mark. No need to be so formal when we'll be working together for Celia's wedding."

Her heart leapt with excitement at the confirmation the job was hers. Containing her grin was impossible as she stepped back and shifted her gaze to the governor. "Best of luck on your campaign. You'll have my vote, same as the last two elections."

He gave her a genuine smile that crinkled the corners of his golden brown eyes. "I appreciate your support."

Janine tucked an escaped strand of her upswept hair behind her ear as she leaned in as if to tell Honor a secret. "I know I should have some of our wedding cake, but the chocolate looks divine."

"Then you should have some of each," she whispered back.

"Brilliant idea, though this dress doesn't leave much room for indulgence."

"How about small slices?"

"Perfect. And can you add some of the Capitol on Mark's plate? The hummingbird spice cake is his favorite."

"Of course."

Honor moved around to the back of the table where plates, silverware, and four cake knives were laid on a rolling cart. Awareness prickled along the back of her neck as she made a few efficient cuts in the individual cakes to serve the couple of honor first. She fought the urge to glance over her shoulder at Asher and kept her focus on her task.

After she handed the cake plates to Celia and reached for the knife to cut more slices, a hard, warm body brushed up against her side.

Her swift inhale flooded her senses with the scent of Asher's cologne. Her heart lodged high up in her throat as he asked in a low voice, "Do I tell you what I want or just take it?"

Oh, sweet mother of—

"No!"

The alarmed cry jerked Honor's head up in time to see Roxanna lunge past Celia, toward the governor and his wife. Janine's start of alarm made the slice of chocolate cake tumble off her plate, straight down the front of her snow-white gown.

Gasps sounded all around them as Celia exclaimed, "Oh, Mom!"

Asher darted around to the front of the table. "Rox—what the hell?"

"I am so sorry, but I couldn't let you eat that," she said to his parents. "Neither of you can."

Janine stared down at her ruined dress as she asked, "Why ever not?"

"It's jinxed."

"It's *what?*"

But Honor had heard her loud and clear. So she hadn't imagined it earlier when she sensed the woman didn't like her work. She braced her knuckles on the table as she glared at the brunette. "Excuse me?"

"You shouldn't be baking anniversary cakes, and most certainly not wedding cakes," Roxanna accused. "Not when you don't believe in love."

From one breath to the next, it seemed like all the heat lamps had been cranked to high. "All I said was they were the exception, not the rule. I never said I don't believe in love."

Except you don't.

One sharp glance from Asher chilled her blood and turned her stomach. An apprehensive look from Celia fed the spark of panic. The rest of the family and nearby guests were avidly watching and listening, casting her smack dab in the center of a huge, blinding spotlight. Her belief in happily ever after—or lack thereof—appeared to be a major deal.

"Your cakes are jinxed." Roxanna shifted her gaze from Honor to Asher. "I told you something was off about them. I felt it when I touched her."

"Here we go," Loyal muttered.

Honor scoffed in disbelief at the brunette's crazy claims. "That's absolutely ridiculous."

"Ty and Jules. Carson and Hannah. Adam and Amy." The woman ticked off names two by two. "You baked their cakes and none of them are together anymore."

Lifting her hands in a *so what?* gesture, she argued, "I've baked hundreds of cakes for hundreds of couples. How is it my fault if a few of them split up? That's just the law of averages."

And totally par for the course anyway.

She shoved the cynical thought aside. She needed to refute the woman's absurd allegations, not reinforce them. Not even in her mind.

Governor Diamond murmured something in his wife's

ear, and Janine nodded while handing her plate to Shelby. "I need to go change."

The governor also passed his uneaten cake to their youngest daughter before ushering his wife inside. Celia followed, her red lips pressed together in a grim line as she avoided Honor's gaze. Sympathy edged Shelby's faint, apologetic smile as she set both plates on the table and brought up the rear.

Honor's heart sank with a heavy thud. *Annnd, goodbye Diamond wedding.*

She didn't even have to look around to know she also wouldn't be hearing from any of the potential clients she'd talked to tonight. She'd only given out her card if specifically asked, but no doubt they'd all be in the garbage before morning.

Resentment swelled as she fixed her gaze on Roxanna's profile, but the woman was too busy staring at Asher, biting her lip and looking like she was about to cry.

Like a brother my ass.

She was totally jealous. What other reason would she have for such a public attack?

Loyal stepped forward, his dark eyebrows drawn together over narrowed eyes. "That was uncalled for."

Yes, it was, thank you.

The tall brunette whipped her head around with an angry glare. "No one asked you."

"Tough shit. You humiliated Mom and her." He gestured toward Honor. "I'll say whatever the hell I want."

Asher moved between the two, a palm raised toward each of them. "Back off, Loyal."

Defiance hardened Roxanna's expression as she spoke in a low voice. "You'll thank me when they're together for another twenty years like your grandparents."

Honor's eyebrows rose. Did she really think a piece of

cake would have the power to break apart two people who'd been together thirty-five years? *Her* cake? The idea was ludicrous.

"My parents *are* the exception, not the rule," Loyal ground out. "For the rest of us, love is nothing more than an illusion that comes and goes." He jabbed a finger toward the dessert table. "And *that* is nothing more than cake and frosting, you frickin' whack job."

CHAPTER 10

*A*sher was pissed at Roxanna, but he wasn't about to let his brother go for her jugular. From the first day he'd introduced the two, Loyal scoffed at her ability to intuit things. After his second failed engagement, he'd been down-right hostile toward her. With that last comment, Rox would fight back like a cornered tigress, but underneath her bravado, the wounds would fester deep.

Seeing her furious expression, he knew he needed to stop any more poison-tipped barbs from finding a mark. Not to mention, he'd noticed one of the reporters his dad had invited watching from the sidelines with keen interest.

He moved closer to his brother, but spoke to the both of them. "That's enough you two, especially out here. Let's take it inside before this becomes even more of a scene than it already is."

"I'm not going anywhere where *he* is." Roxanna whirled around and stalked across the patio.

"Good riddance," his brother tossed after her back.

Asher clenched his fists as he lowered his arms, then forced his hands to relax. And here he'd have bet Merit would've been the one to cause trouble, not these two. Of all the times for them to knock heads.

He shot Loyal a dark look and turned to check on Honor, only to see a flash of her red hair as she slipped through the service doors leading to the kitchen.

Sonofabitch.

"Wow. That was all kinds of fucked up," Merit said in a low undertone. "You didn't have to be so hard on Rox."

Loyal brushed past him for the house.

Aware of the reporter still watching, Asher gave Merit a shove toward the patio doors, then followed both brothers inside. It didn't take but a second to decide he didn't want to talk to either of the two idiots, so he threaded his way through the inside guests to the kitchen so he could talk to Honor.

He should probably apologize for Rox's cake drama, and yet, there had been something in her startled expression—a flash of alarm—that had him wondering if his best friend hadn't struck a nerve with his sexy neighbor. But how in the world could a wedding cake baker not believe in love?

Roxanna had to have gotten her wires crossed some-where. Had to have. He couldn't fall for a woman who didn't believe in love.

A quick sweep of the kitchen revealed no sign of red hair. He paused near the prep island where he'd sat many Saturday and Sunday mornings as a kid. "Elena, the woman in the burgundy dress—"

"She went right through, *mijo.*" Their long-time house-keeper paused as she scooped a few leftover appetizers into a storage container and spoke over her shoulder while looking out the kitchen window. "*Prisa.* She's already in her car."

Crap.

By the time he dodged a couple of servers and dashed out the back service door to the driveway, Honor's vehicle was pulling out onto the street. He swung back toward the house with a soft growl of frustration, only to spot Roxanna in her Jeep. She sat with her head back against the seat, eyes closed, shoulders slumped.

Asher walked over and bent down to rap on the passenger side window. She jerked in surprise, big brown eyes wide when her gaze met his. Instant remorse filled her expression, and she unlocked the doors.

"I'm so sorry," she began as he slid inside.

"She's jinxing cakes?" he asked with a bit of accusation.

Rox looked like she was going to argue, but instead slumped back in her seat. "So maybe I don't know for sure she's *jinxing* them, but I panicked when I saw your mom about to eat some."

"Yeah. Clearly."

"She doesn't believe in love," she stated with a resurgence of defiance. "That I guarantee you. I felt it when I shook her hand."

His chest tightened at the idea that could be true, but he said, "That's a lot different than jinxing couples with her cakes."

"Well, she could be. I couldn't take that chance with your parents."

"I wish you would've." He ran his thumb along the crease in his dress pants before lifting his gaze to hers once more. "Especially tonight."

"Whoops. Sorry. Did I mess up your chance to screw the baker?"

"That's not it at all." Guilt twinged at her sarcasm, because it was a little. Not the screwing part—he wasn't Merit—but the opportunity to get to know her had been lost.

"Bullshit. Your aura's been simmering all night. It flares bright red whenever you're within five feet of her."

Sometimes he really hated that she could read him so

well. It made it hard to get her to see beyond the point she was trying to make.

"This was a big night for my parents, Rox. You know that."

Resentment glittered in her eyes as she tilted her head. "So I'm just supposed to pretend I don't know these things? Keep quiet and be *normal*?" Hurt filled her voice. "Now you sound like your jackass brother."

Damn it. Loyal had really gotten to her. She knew her being different was part of what he loved about her. "You're putting words in my mouth. That's not at all what I said."

"But it's what you meant."

"No." He took a breath to keep his tone level. "It's just, there's a time and place for what you do. My parents' anniversary party and Dad's Senate announcement is *not* it."

"Keep it in my shop," she bit out. "Got it, Loyal."

Asher consciously unclenched his jaw. "Rox—"

"No, it's fine." She faced forward, gripping the steering wheel with one hand while turning the key with her other. "You can get out now."

He recognized that stubborn tone. It wouldn't matter what he said, her mind was made up. He was the bad guy for now. Someone to take the brunt of her anger since the person she really wanted to tear into wasn't sitting in his place.

"Sometimes Loyal can be a jackass," he agreed quietly. "And I'm not excusing what he said, but you know where it came from."

She reached to jab the button for the radio and a popular pop station blared through the speakers.

He raised his voice to be heard over the music, hand fisted on his thigh. "You know his history, Rox. It wasn't personal."

"He called me a whack-job. It doesn't get more personal

than that." Both hands on the wheel now, she stared straight ahead, her chin set at a mutinous angle as tears glittered in her eyes. "*Get out.*"

Asher gave a couple of light, agitated fist taps on the door, then did as she demanded. "I'll call you tomorrow," he said.

When she didn't respond, he shut the door a second before she hit the gas pedal. He was slowly walking back into the kitchen when his phone buzzed in his pocket for an incoming text.

"Missed her?" Elena asked.

She was asking about Honor. He gave a distracted, "Yeah," as he pulled out his phone to read the text.

Rox: *Tell your mom I'm sorry about her dress.*

He frowned and started to type a reply when another one popped up.

Rox: *And tell your dad I'm sorry, too.*

He typed faster. *Are you texting and dri—*

Rox: *No. I pulled over to send this, so shut up.*

The tightness in his chest loosened slightly as he smiled, deleted, and retyped. *I will—tell them, that is (not shut up). And you're lucky.*

He pocketed his phone, then headed over to drop a quick kiss on Elena's cheek as a way to delay having to return to the party. "Awesome food tonight, *tia.* As always."

"Thank you. Now tell me what that was all about."

He reluctantly leaned back to glance out toward the main floor of the mansion.

"Your mom and dad came back down a few minutes ago," Elena advised. "Everything is covered out there."

Thank God.

"Come on, now. Spill."

He braced his hands back against the island and recounted the events on the patio as Elena multitasked, listening, scraping empty dishes, and directing servers passing in and out. Her brows quirked up when he got to the part about Honor's jinxed cakes, and then she *tsked* her disapproval of Loyal's verbal attack on Roxanna.

"It breaks my heart your brother is still hurting after all this time." She gave the spoon in her hand a vicious rap against the inside of the garbage. "I hope those exes of his get a taste of their bad karma someday."

"Yeah. Don't we all."

"I can see why Ms. Hartman departed so abruptly. Too bad you couldn't catch her."

"It'll get sorted out." At least he knew where to find her. He glanced toward the doors once more, then back to Elena. "You need some help with the dishes?"

"You just want to hide out, but far be it for me to say no to help. You'll need an apron."

He stripped off his jacket and slung it over the back of an island chair before removing his monogrammed cufflinks so he could roll up his shirt sleeves. Once the apron was tied behind his waist, he got right to work.

Elena bumped his elbow with her shoulder a few minutes later. "I miss this. Not the help per se, your mom makes sure I have plenty, but you kids here in the kitchen with me."

Combine him and his four siblings with the three Torrez kids and most times it had been pure chaos. The oldest son of Spanish immigrants who'd worked for his grandparents, Mr. Torrez managed the stables while Elena managed the house, and their family had lived in a guest house on the far end of the north pasture until the kids graduated high school. The eight of them had gotten into *a lot* of trouble together over the years.

"You miss that madness?" he asked in disbelief. "Really?"

"I really do," she confirmed with a nostalgic smile.

"Where is everyone these days?" All three of her kids had

joined the military after graduating high school. "Solana hasn't posted anything online in a while."

"She's been too busy. Her Quantico training starts next week."

"That's pretty awesome." The middle of the three at twenty-five, Solana was wicked smart, like his baby sister.

"We're very proud," she said with a grin.

"You should be. What about Reyes and Dev?"

"Reyes' four years are up in August, and he's not reenlisting, but Devante deploys again next month."

"Dev's in for the long haul, isn't he?" At twenty-seven, Dev was two years younger than him, whereas Reyes was the same age as Shelby at twenty-three.

"*Sí.*"

Her mixed feelings about her oldest son's career choice were obvious, yet he knew she was equally proud of him. He understood her worries over the danger of his Special Forces missions. He'd witnessed the relief on her face a few times after getting word Dev was back in the States.

Asher rinsed the dish in his hand and set it in the tray to drain. "Do you know where he's going this time?"

She shook her head as she scraped off another dish into the garbage. "It's classified. As always."

He gave her a nudge with his elbow when she handed him the platter. "We'll keep the prayers coming for his safe return." They didn't keep in touch on a regular basis, but whenever Dev came home, it was like no time had passed.

Elena pulled him down for a quick buss on the cheek with a murmured, "*Gracias, mijo,*" then did a quick sign of the cross before reaching for the next dish.

It was almost forty-five minutes later that he noticed through the window guests were starting to depart and reluctantly took off the apron to dry his hands. "I suppose I better go out there and say a few goodbyes with everyone else."

That is, if Loyal had decided to hang around and—he checked the clock—Merit wasn't down in the wine cellar.

"Thank you for your help," Elena said.

"It was entirely my pleasure."

"And everyone thinks Merit is the charmer." She stuck one hand on her hip, giving him a grin as he swiped his tux jacket off the chair and backed toward the party. "I'll save you a container of cake in the usual place."

Grinning, he crossed his hands over his chest as a silent thank you, blew her a kiss, and spun around on his way through the doors. His mouth watered just thinking about the decadent desserts and addicting frosting to go with each one. His pulse quickened just thinking about the delicious redhead who'd created them.

She doesn't believe in love.

The quiet voice in his head gave him pause, but a vivid recollection of her unzipped dress and bare back muted the cautionary reminder as he stifled a groan of longing. He had an overnight bag upstairs because he'd planned to stay the night so he could spend some time with Loyal, but even knowing the background behind his brother's outburst, annoyance still simmered for the shot he'd taken at Roxanna.

Better he go home tonight than stay and risk saying something he'd later regret. Tomorrow's family brunch would be soon enough to deal with Loyal again.

CHAPTER 11

$\mathcal{H}$onor vented her restless resentment as she viciously stirred her second batch of cupcakes by hand, her favorite ceramic bowl hugged against her chest while she turned to peer through the glass door of the oven.

Almost done.

She spun back to the island on the ball of her foot as a loud knock on her front door sounded over the music streaming from her portable speaker. She startled so hard, the bowl slipped in her arms, and she made a desperate grab to keep it from shattering on the floor.

Geezus.

She darted a glance at the clock on the wall. *1:13 a.m.* Who could that be at this time?

Her pulse stuttered, fingers tightening around the wire whisk handle as she debated ignoring the knock. Unfortunately, thanks to her lights and music, there was no denying she was home and awake.

She turned the music down a few notches before easing toward the door. A glance outside revealed no car in her driveway or on the street. Through the decorative glass panels on either side of the door, she could only see the shadow of the person on her front porch.

She stood on her side, too short for her peep hole, worrying her lip in indecision. She didn't have any pets because hair and wedding cakes didn't mix, but right about now, a great big dog sounded like a good idea.

Or a big, strong man. With dark hair and—

Nope. Give her the dog any day. A German Shepherd with a ferocious bark.

Another knock made her flinch before she barked, "Who is it?"

"Asher Diamond."

Surprise rocked her back on her heels, her heart suddenly high up in her throat for a whole different reason. A frantic glance down at her faded gray T-shirt and black leggings made her realize she was clutching the bowl of chocolate batter for dear life. Letting go of the whisk, she raised her hand to her hair. She hadn't even brushed through it when she got home. Just gathered it up into a ponytail and then twisted it into a haphazard bun. And she'd washed off all her makeup.

This was so not fair. He could be covered in dirt and grease and still be hot as hell. But of course, he wouldn't be after his parents' party, so it was doubly not fair.

"What do you want?"

"To apologize." There was a beat of silence, then, "Hopefully not through the closed door."

Man, come on!

"Please?"

Fine. She'd give him a few seconds to apologize, and then he could leave. Short and quick so there would be no time to drool over the man.

Or throw herself at him.

As she started to swing the door open, she caught a

glimpse of his dress shoes and black pants when the timer started beeping. "I'll be right back. I gotta get those."

Honor hurried back into the kitchen, deposited the bowl of batter on the island, shut off the timer, and grabbed her pot holders. In the middle of pulling the lemon blueberry cupcakes from the oven, the sound of her front door closing registered, followed by the unhurried tread of Asher's shiny black shoes on the hardwood floor.

So much for short and quick.

"It smells like heaven in here," he commented.

She turned around and nearly dropped both pans in her hands. Her breath caught in her throat as she took in six feet plus of *oh-my-God-I-want-him-now*. His dark hair tumbled over his forehead, he sported that rugged five-o'clock shadow, his tux jacket was gone, his bowtie hung undone around the unbuttoned collar of his snow-white dress shirt, and his sleeves were rolled up to reveal tanned, muscled forearms.

Annd, so much for not drooling.

He stopped on the opposite side of her kitchen island. "You do know it's after one o'clock in the morning, right?"

Recovering a fraction of her sanity, she set the cupcakes on the counter before reaching back to shut the oven door. "I could ask you the same thing."

"I just got home and saw your lights on."

Imagining him driving around in his Camaro made her mouth water even more. She turned back to move the individual cupcakes from the pans to cooling racks as she asked, "And it seemed like a good idea to walk on over?"

He leaned forward to rest his elbows and forearms on the island, putting the two of them at eye level. "I wanted to apologize for what happened. Since you were up, sooner seemed better than later."

She kept her gaze on her task. If she focused on busy

work, she wouldn't focus on him, because sure as shit, one look up and she'd get lost in his gorgeous eyes. "*You* have nothing to apologize for. I don't blame people for things that aren't their fault."

"Still. I am sorry. Rox went a little overboard."

"A *little?*" She scoffed and started stuffing empty liners in the pans for the next batch. "She accused me of jinxing my cakes and breaking up happy couples in front of everyone. Some of the guests had asked for my card—and then there's your parents and your sister. She *was* going to hire me for her wedding cake, but I can guarantee you that's not going to happen anymore."

A quick glance through her lashes caught the grimace on Asher's face.

"You don't know that," he said.

He wouldn't convince anyone with that weak argument, least of all her. "I saw Celia's face. No way she's going to hire me now."

"I'll talk to her."

"That's not the point. You shouldn't have to talk to her." Renewed anger surged as she finished the liners and reached for the bowl of batter. She set it down again with a thump and glared at him. "What the hell did your friend *Rox* mean when she said, '*I felt it when I touched her*'?"

He hesitated a few seconds. "She's psychic."

She snorted softly at that little gem, but then saw Asher's jaw tense. Recalling his defensive reaction to his brother's comments back at the party, her eyes widened. "Oh, wow, you're serious?"

And wow, he actually believed in that kind of hocus pocus?

"She owns a shop down on Aspen Street."

Honor saw the street in her mind's eye. "Lift Your Spirit?"

"That's her."

Her irritation faded slightly while she began ladling the chocolate batter into the liners. Roxanna owned her own business. So maybe not quite the whack-job his brother accused. "I've never been in there, but my sister loves that shop."

Glory and her friends met for coffee and then went to have their auras read every so often. Their mom had gone with her a few times, too.

"You should check it out sometime," Asher suggested.

She arched her eyebrows in disbelief.

He winced even as a hopeful smirk quirked his lips. "Too soon?"

"Way too soon. Besides, she might put a hex on me."

"She's a psychic, not a witch," he admonished, shifting to sit in one of her island chairs, his deliciously defined forearms still resting on the counter.

She noticed a scar on his left arm, thin, white, and jagged. A thought about how he got it quickly morphed to, were those gym muscles, or work muscles? Cameras weren't that heavy to give photographers that much of a workout, were they?

And his hands. Large, clean, with neatly trimmed nails. After a few peeks she still couldn't tell if they'd be soft or rough against her bare skin. The knuckle brush against her back as he'd zipped her dress earlier had left her fantasizing both possibilities.

"May I ask you something?"

That voice. Mmm. Yum.

But, his hesitant tone had her risking an upward glance. Her stomach flip-flopped at the unexpected intensity in his amber eyes. If it was going to be that serious of a question, she wanted to tell him no. Wanted to tell him to go home across the street, and yet she also didn't want him to go anywhere. The conflicting emotions were as messed up as her common sense right now.

Before she could think of a reply that didn't sound bitchy or cowardly, he asked anyway. "Was she right?"

Good. Not so serious. I can handle this.

"Of course not." Honor scoffed. "I definitely do not jinx my cakes."

"I meant about you not believing in love."

Well, crap.

His voice was serious again, and her heart thumped hard against her ribs. She kept her gaze downcast and kept ladling. "That's a pretty personal question, and we've only just formally met."

He pushed up from the seat to stand at the island as if preparing to leave. "You're right. Forget I asked."

"Who *doesn't* believe in love?" she said defensively. "I mean, I love my parents, and my sister and my brother. My two nieces." She gestured toward him with the ladle full of chocolate batter. "And my best friend and her son."

"Okay."

There was something that sounded suspiciously like disappointment in his voice. She finished filling the liners, set the batter bowl aside, and turned to open the oven door as she asked, "Would it matter? I mean, say…hypothetically… I didn't believe in *love* love. What would it matter?"

"It seems odd you'd choose to bake wedding cakes, of all things, if you didn't believe," he replied while she moved back and forth to put the second batch of cupcakes in the oven. "Hypothetically speaking."

"It's a business. I'm a designer first and foremost. What I believe shouldn't matter as long as I create what the client wants."

Closing the oven door, she pivoted back to set the timer. She pulled up short when she saw Asher had come around to her side of the island. Taken-aback, she watched his hand lift from her mixing bowl to his mouth. That drool she'd feared earlier threatened to make an appearance as he sucked chocolate batter from his finger.

"*Mmm.*"

"Hey." Her voice rang sharp out of self-preservation. "Only the baker gets to do that."

He lowered his hand, offering a sheepish grin that was way too cute and sexy at the same damn time. The only way she kept from smiling back was by reminding herself his crazy psychic friend had cost her his sister's wedding. But even then, it was a struggle when his gaze captured hers.

As seconds passed, the twinkle in his eye shifted and sharpened, turning burnt amber into more of a hot, melty honey brown.

"Sorry," he said.

Only he didn't sound at all remorseful. Didn't act it either when he reached to swipe inside the bowl again.

It was almost empty, so it wasn't like it was a big deal, but she'd just told him not to do it. She started to protest, but lost all ability to speak when he leaned in close to offer her his chocolate covered finger. Heat seared through her body at the dawn of his challenging, mischievous grin. Plus, he still smelled as amazing now as he had earlier in the evening.

When she didn't move, he pointed out, "You did say only the baker gets to taste test."

Oh, God, how she wanted to lean forward and lick that batter from his finger. Problem was, that would have her imagining licking batter off other parts of him, and thoughts like that were liable to make her combust right here in her kitchen.

And then who would take the cupcakes out of the oven?

Who the hell cares?

CHAPTER 12

*A*sher's heart hammered in his chest as he waited for Honor to decide if she was going to take his bait or not. It wasn't a smart move, seeing as she'd pretty much admitted Roxanna was right—*hypothetically*—but he couldn't resist getting closer, pushing her to surrender to the undeniable chemistry sparking between them.

She was simply too damn appealing with those skin-tight leggings, messy, just-out-of-bed hair, and her fresh scrubbed face with a dusty smear of flour camouflaging the freckles on her right cheek.

The chocolate batter slowly crept down toward his knuckle and she still hadn't made a move. The exact moment he started to lower his hand, she grabbed his wrist and leaned forward to lick up the drip, then wrapped those pretty lips around his finger.

Her tongue curled around the tip, her gaze locked with his the whole time. When she swallowed, the erotic pressure of her tongue pressing his finger to the roof of her mouth made him go from semi-hard to hard as steel in the space of one shallow breath. He pulled his finger from her mouth while lifting his other hand, then cupped each side of her face as he bent down to capture her lips.

She rose up to meet him, her mouth eager against his, her hands grasping his forearms while he walked her one step back to press her against the island. Her soft, breathy moan was barely audible above the music in the background, but he felt the warm sigh against his lips. He echoed the sentiment, then slid his tongue inside her mouth, licking deep, seeking her heat.

She tasted of chocolate, of course, but as he tangled his tongue with hers, he kept getting a hint of some decadent, elusive, irresistible sweetness that had him craving more. Just like the cakes she baked, one taste of the woman proved addicting.

He lowered his hands to her waist for a quick lift that planted her butt on the counter. His mouth smothered her small gasp of surprise as she gripped his shoulders. When he moved in closer, her knees bumped into his stomach. He ran his palms down along her thighs, then grasped above her knees to spread her legs and step between them.

All of a sudden, her knees gripped the sides of his hips, keeping him from getting too close. He bit back a groan of protest when she pushed against his shoulders. Her breath was as uneven as his as she drew her hands away from him to tangle them together in her lap. While shifting his weight back, he noted longing, dismay, and confusion chase across her face before her green gaze met his.

Resisting the animalistic urge to crush her to him, he gently flexed his fingers on her knees. "What?"

She smiled, but it faltered fast as she dropped her gaze to his chest. After a deep breath, she said, "We're neighbors."

"Yes, we are."

"Then you should understand why this isn't a good idea."

He frowned. "Just because we're neighbors?"

"Not *only* that, but it's a large part of it."

Asher slid his palms to the counter on either side of her legs and braced his weight on the heels of his hands. "Why?"

The question came out as more of a demand than he meant it to, sparking defensiveness in her expression.

"Because it is."

Softening his tone, he argued, "*Because it is* has never been a good reason why in the history of all reasons why, Honor. I'm going to need more than that."

She narrowed her gaze and stiffened her spine. "I don't owe you anything."

"You're right, you don't," he agreed. "But let's get something straight right away. I like you. I'm insanely attracted to you—have been since the first moment I saw you—and unless I'm way off base here, I think it goes both ways."

You were off base with Brianna.

Yeah, well, Honor was not Brianna. She was so far from that bitch they might as well be opposite poles of the earth. In fact, arousal still dilated Honor's pupils to the point the freckle in her right eye was barely visible. Interest like that couldn't be faked.

"Oh, really?" Her eyebrows arched. "Are you a jerk to all women you're attracted to?"

Reminded of how he'd walked away from her the first two times they met, he shot back, "No, just the one I thought was engaged. And while I will apologize for being an ass, it was the only way I could stop myself from kissing you when I thought you belonged to another man."

Her gaze dropped to his mouth as her tongue darted out to wet her lips. That insane attraction he'd mentioned ignited in a split second. The edge of the counter bit into his palms as he struggled to keep from moving in for another kiss.

She shook her head the tiniest bit, as if fighting her own internal desires. Then she drew in a deeper, more deliberate breath while lifting her chin. "None of that matters, because if we go too far now, it'll be too awkward living across the street from each other when things are over. This is my home now, and I don't want anything to mess with that."

"Why do you automatically assume—oh. Right." His chest tightened as if clamped in a vice. "Let me rephrase that. Why don't you believe in love?" He didn't even bother adding the hypothetical anymore.

"You really are nosey, aren't you?" She sat up straighter and gave a little shove against his shoulders.

He stepped back, and she slid down off the counter, then turned her back to him. Quick, efficient movements transferred dirty dishes from the counter to the sink before she snatched up the dish cloth and scrubbed the entire work surface with way more force than necessary.

Asher moved around her to plug the sink. Then he started the water running while reaching for the soap sitting next to the faucet. *Dishes, take two.*

"What are you doing?"

Giving the bottle a good squirt into the sink, he glanced over to see Honor's one hand fisted in the dishcloth on the counter, the other braced on her hip. A couple little soap bubbles floated up into the air between them.

"Isn't it obvious?"

"Well, yeah, but why? It's almost two a.m. Surely you'd rather go to bed?" Her cheeks flushed and she quickly added, "At your own house."

She didn't add *alone*, but her tone spoke the word loud and clear.

"Honestly?"

She hesitated, then grudgingly said, "Always."

"I'm hoping you'll send me home with a couple of these cupcakes as payment. After they're frosted, of course."

It was the truth, but not the whole truth. She'd been right

about the bed, but only if she joined him. Since that wasn't happening, he'd rather be here than there, even at two o'clock in the morning. He shut off the water and reached to take the dish cloth from her. The mere brush of their fingers sent a spark of electricity zinging up his arm.

Her quick little jerk told him she'd felt it, too.

"Didn't you have cake at the party?"

"One thing you'll learn about me, I can never have too much cake. And never *ever* have I heard of such a thing as too much frosting."

She rolled her eyes, but not before he thought he glimpsed a smile tugging the corners of her sweet, delectable lips. Geezus, he'd love to dive in deep for another taste.

"Fine, you can have some. In fact, you can take them right now. You don't have to work for them." She took two off the cooling rack, then scooped up a big triangle bag of frosting lying off to the side.

Damn. Looked like his time was running out. He started washing dishes anyway. "I don't mind—unless you do?"

"No."

"Good."

Her gaze bounced in his direction, then returned to the cupcake in front of her as she piped on a healthy dollop of butter cream. As if recalling his statement from a moment ago, she added a bit more.

Good Lord, I love this woman—and he was only half-joking.

"Now back to me being nosey." Because it only made sense to make the most of his limited time. "Is it because someone broke your heart? Is that why you don't believe in love?"

"*Now* I mind."

"I'm sorry," he said sincerely as he kept washing. "Must have been a doozy."

"It wasn't me," she huffed with exasperation. "More like, my parents have seven divorces between them."

Yeah...that could definitely skew a person's view.

"My parents have been married for thirty-five years," he countered. "And my—"

"Grandparents for fifty-five. And your uncles. Yeah, Roxanna told me all about them. And as I told her, they're the exception not the rule. In addition to *my* parents, my brother and sister are both divorced, too. The Hartman's don't have happily ever after in our DNA."

The hint of bitterness in that statement had him asking, "Have you ever been in love?"

"No, and I won't ever be."

The way she said it, all firm and matter of fact, made Asher snort. "Funny you think you get to decide that with your head."

She shrugged her shoulders and finished the second cupcake, then pulled the whole cooling rack over and started on the others. Absently noting those received half the amount of frosting, he began to suspect that maybe it wasn't so much she didn't believe in love, but more so she didn't *know* about love. What it was and how it worked.

His heart thumped with the idea he could be the one to show her.

"What about you?" she asked. "Have you ever been in love?"

"Once. Or so I thought. Bought a ring and everything."

"What happened?"

His shoulders tensed as he scrubbed crusty batter remnants off the bowl from her first batch of cupcakes. He hated admitting he'd been totally suckered by Brianna's act, but if he wanted Honor to be honest with him, he was going to have to do the same.

"Turned out she was only with me for the political

connections that come with the Diamond name. Her 'real' boyfriend was in local politics, and she was using me to make inside connections so he could set up a run at the state level."

"Wow. That's ballsy." She sounded offended for his sake. "Please tell me it didn't work."

Bittersweet satisfaction sparked a grim smile. "Not even close. He was handily defeated in the primary after word got around about how he ran his campaign. Last I heard, Brianna was no longer useful, and he dumped her after the election."

"That's karma for you. But it sounds like they both deserved what they got."

In total agreement, his shoulders relaxed again. He liked that even though she didn't believe in the elusive happily ever after, she had no problem voicing what she felt was right and wrong.

She stepped back two steps to check the oven, skimmed to the counter to exchange frosting bag for pot holders, then pivoted and opened the door to remove the two pans inside. Each movement was smooth and graceful, like part of a dance that made him want to take her in his arms and spin her around the kitchen. Why hadn't his parents had dancing at the party?

Honor set the pans on the empty cooling racks before picking up the frosting again. "If that doesn't make my point, I don't know what does."

After placing the final rinsed dish in the drying rack, Asher swiped a towel off the counter to dry his hands as she finished frosting the first batch of cooled cupcakes. "As I recall, your point was only hypothetical," he reminded. "And, you didn't make a point so much as ask why your beliefs would matter to your business."

She cast him a sideways glance, then set the frosting bag aside and turned to face him. "All right, then, let me ask you a question."

"Go ahead."

Her gaze shifted to the treats on the counter, then bounced back to him. "How can you believe in love after something like that?"

Fair question. He shrugged one shoulder and tossed the towel aside. "She wasn't the right one."

"The right one?" Her brow furrowed with what looked like disappointment. "Really? You believe in psychics *and* soul mates?"

He tilted his head at the question, considering how best to answer. "I don't *not* believe."

"What does that even mean?"

"It means…I believe…anything is possible." Deciding he'd rather leave her with that than give her a chance to argue, he gestured toward the frosted cupcakes. "I get two of those, right?"

She hesitated a moment, looking like she might have something more to say on their discussion, but then she turned to pull a plate from the cupboard. After arranging three treats in a center triangle, she offered it to him with both hands and a smile. Anticipation surged as he took it. Not because of his sweet tooth, but because she'd given him a plate he'd have to return. Was it a deliberate move, or subconscious?

Didn't matter. It was his open invitation to come over again.

Honor followed him to the door, stepping close to hug the edge after he swung it open. "Goodnight, Asher."

He paused on the threshold to reply, but one glance at her beautiful face and he couldn't resist lifting his free hand to cup the back of her neck while leaning down for another kiss. One more taste of heaven to get him through until he returned the plate.

Her lips softened under his, parting as his tongue sought

hers. As with each time he touched her, his pulse quickened and threatened to steal his breath. With the cupcakes in his other hand, and the door partially between them, he couldn't get as close to her heat as he'd have liked.

She'd risen up on her tiptoes, her free hand fisted in the collar of his shirt. His body urged him to dump the plate, sweep her up into his arms, and head straight to her room. Imagining the motions in his head spiked his already rapid heartbeat.

A low sound came from deep in her throat as she dropped back on her heels to break the kiss. Instinct sent him after her, but his name came from her lips in a husky whisper full of regret.

"Asher…"

He reluctantly lowered his arm and stepped back. She didn't have to say more. They were neighbors. She didn't want to do this.

Time to go home and give her some space.

But thanks to the glimpse of heated longing in her green eyes before her lashes lowered, it took every scrap of willpower he could muster to thank her for the cupcakes and make himself walk across the street to his own house.

He thought about how he had his work cut out for him, even as a cautious voice inside his head whispered he was setting himself up for the heartbreak of a lifetime.

CHAPTER 13

I believe anything is possible.

Honor shifted in bed as the memory of Asher's deep, husky voice made her insides flutter. She'd dreamed of his kisses most of the night, and woke up hot and bothered with that one line running on a loop in her head. His words gave her hope for something she never dared dream of, even though she knew the utter folly in believing their empty promise.

She groaned in frustration while rolling over to bury her face in the pillow. It wasn't even seven a.m. Her eyes burned, and each limb of her body felt like it weighed a hundred pounds as she lay there debating about getting up to get some housework done before getting ready for lunch with her mom and Glory, or trying to sleep a few more hours.

When the Scooby Doo theme song erupted from her night stand, she reached out to fumble for her phone without lifting her head from the pillow.

"Why are you calling so early?" she demanded of her best friend.

"It's after ten a.m.," Mae replied somberly. "I texted earlier, but you didn't reply."

Whoa. She must've dozed off again. "I was sleeping and didn't realize it was so late. I ended up baking and frosting until almost three in the morning."

"I'm not surprised. Are you okay?"

"I'm fine," she said, confused by the concern in her friend's voice. "Should I not be?"

"Um…you tell me. What happened last night?"

Asher Diamond happened.

And I want him to happen again—and again and again and again.

Immediately after those wanton thoughts, a flashback of the scene at the party jarred her memory—the whole reason she'd been baking half the night. A tiny knot of anxiety formed in the pit of her stomach as she rolled over and sat up. "How do you know something happened?"

"The headline on Denver Today's society blog."

"What headline?"

"*Local psychic claims wedding cake baker jinxes wedding cakes.*"

The knot in her stomach grew to the size of a boulder. "Are you kidding?"

"Why would I kid about something like that?"

She wouldn't. Honor flipped the covers aside and hurried downstairs to the living room where she'd left her laptop.

"What happened?" Mae repeated.

"Hold on." She typed the blog into the search bar and sure enough, there it was—with twice as many views as *Governor Diamond Announces Run for U.S. Senate.* As she skimmed the article, her heart pounded hard while nausea churned in her stomach.

"Not a witch, my ass," Honor muttered when she reached the last line of the bullshit post. "She *did* hex me."

"The psychic?"

"Yeah. Turns out she's friends with my neighbor."

"She's friends with the sexy jerk? Small world."

"It gets even better. My neighbor is Asher Diamond—Celia Diamond's *brother*. The governor's son."

"Oh, wow. It really *is* a small world."

"Tell me about it."

"Was he at the party last night?"

"Yeah, and he's actually not the jerk I thought he was."

"Do tell."

She explained about him thinking she was engaged and Mae laughed.

"He walked away because he was so attracted to you he didn't want to make a move when he thought you were engaged? Guy's got game."

Honor smiled. Asher definitely had game, and she so wanted to play even when she knew she shouldn't.

"Slam dunk on the wedding, then?"

"Not so much. Celia and her mother gave me a yes until this psychic chick messed everything up. She totally ruined Mrs. Diamond's dress, and as you can see, my reputation, too."

"They changed their mind that fast?"

"I haven't heard anything from them yet, but look at this shit." She gestured toward the laptop screen even though her friend couldn't see her. "Would *you* hire me for your wedding?"

"Of course I would," Mae insisted loyally. "I don't believe in that psychic crap."

"Well, unfortunately, a lot of other people who are not my best friends do believe in that psychic crap." Including Asher, apparently. She made a face as she recalled their conversation about love and soul mates at two o'clock in the morning. But with his genuine, *"I believe anything is possible,"* how could she hold it against him? No one was perfect.

Her phone dinged for an incoming voicemail. "I should probably let you go to see what kind of damage control I need to do."

"If there's anything I can help with, let me know."

"You want to take some cupcakes off my hands?" The three she'd given Asher hadn't even made a dent.

"How many batches did you make?"

Mae knew she was prone to going overboard when she was upset. "Just two, but they were double batches. I have almost four dozen here."

"I could take some for Ian's class tomorrow."

"You got 'em. I'm meeting my mom and Glory for lunch, so I'll drop them by on the way."

"Bring them by the office. I'm here until three."

"It's Sunday."

"The perks of being a CEO," Mae said with a wry laugh. "Ian's with my parents, so I figured I'd get some work done without feeling bad about taking time away from him."

"All right then. And I've got two boxes, so you'll have extras for the crew, too."

"I'll have hugs ready."

"Thanks." Her gaze shifted back to the headline on her laptop screen. "I'm gonna need 'em."

After they hung up, she read the blog post one more time, her anger rising at both the author and Roxanna Kent. Lift Your Spirit ended up with quite the nice plug, while Honor Hartman Cake Designs got creamed in the PR department.

The first voicemail she listened to was a cancellation for the end of June, and the second for a wedding in August. The knots in her stomach wound tighter when she clicked over to her email and found another June cancellation had been sent fifteen minutes earlier.

All the jobs had been on the books for more than six months, since many brides scheduled up to a year in advance. Usually she refunded deposits only if she was able to fill the slot with another bride, but she'd never strictly enforced the policy. She wouldn't have much choice now, though. Two jobs equaled more than half her mortgage payment.

Another email cancellation popped up on her screen, from a bride she'd recently agreed to fit in at the end of the summer. She'd been willing to work double hours that week for the extra income. Now, she might be left twiddling her thumbs with no work at all.

"I'm going to be bankrupt in days if this keeps up," she muttered.

After a few moments of wallowing and increasingly feeling sick to her stomach, she made a conscious decision to stop looking at the situation negatively and instead concentrate on a way to fix it.

Her insistence last night that Roxanna was wrong hadn't made a difference to the author of the blog post. The article was a load of hocus-pocus nonsense that didn't even tell both sides of the story. She needed proof that her cakes didn't jinx her clients. As she'd said, law of averages. Out of hundreds of couples, it was to be expected that some of them wouldn't last.

She pulled up her master client list and looked up the three Roxanna had named. Carson and Hannah Swanson. Adam and Amy Wilson. Ty and Jules Lambert.

Her stomach knotted as she dialed Jules' number. She was waffling between hoping for the woman to answer and praying for voicemail when a live, "Hello?" made her pulse skip.

"Jules? Um, it's Honor Hartman. I designed your wedding cake a couple of years ago?" Two years ago in June.

"Yeah…hi." Confusion colored her voice. "What can I do for you?"

"I…ah…"

Darn it. Should've thought this through better. It wasn't like she could blurt out something as ludicrous as, *"Did my cake ruin your marriage?"*

Drawing in a fortifying breath, she went with, "This may sound like a weird question, but are you and Ty still together?"

There was a brief, weighted pause. "No, actually, we're not."

"Oh." Dismay pooled in her belly. "I'm sorry to hear that."

"So am I." Sadness softened Jules' voice as she added, "But it is what it is."

Honor squeezed her eyes shut and forged ahead. "Do you mind me asking what happened?"

"Um…well, I guess not. *I* thought we both wanted kids. We never actually talked about it, but he's amazing with his nieces and nephews, so I had just assumed he'd want his own."

"He didn't?"

"No. We should've talked about it before we got married, but, again, I assumed…"

See? Right there. Lack of communication was to blame for their split, not her cake.

"Funny thing was, we were eating the top of our wedding cake that we froze for our first anniversary when I told him I wanted to start trying."

Well, hell. That sure as shit didn't help her case, did it?

"It was supposed to be a romantic gesture for us to someday tell our kids about the start of our family, but Ty looked at me like I was crazy and flat out told me no babies. He didn't want to be tied down with kids. We tried to make the marriage work for a little while after that, but neither of us were willing to compromise, and we were divorced by our second anniversary."

"Again, I'm sorry," she murmured with genuine sympathy. Her lack of faith in the institution didn't change the fact divorce could be heartbreaking.

"It's not your fault," Jules said.

Clearly she hadn't read the blog post on Denver Today. Yesterday, she would've agreed with the woman. Today, she wasn't so sure as guilt oozed in her gut.

Stop it. You did not jinx anything or anyone.

Honor made a few more calls before showering and getting ready for lunch, then carried two large bakery boxes of cupcakes out to her car. A quick glance across the street toward Asher's house made her pulse skip a beat.

It was now just before noon. Was he home? She wanted to go over and ask if he'd liked the cupcakes, but after those kisses last night, what she *really* wanted to know was, had he dreamed about her like she'd dreamed about him?

Maybe. After all, anything was possible.

CHAPTER 14

On her way to Mae's office, Honor glanced both ways at the stoplight for her right turn. A few blocks down on the left, she caught sight of the sign for Lift Your Spirit and narrowed her gaze. Roxanna Kent had managed to secure herself a prime spot. Honor would love to have a storefront in this area of Lakewood.

Someday.

"Or, maybe never," she muttered as she recalled the cancellations that had poured in over the morning.

After a moment of hesitation, she drove around the block and then turned left toward the psychic's shop instead of right to see Mae. Mom and Glory would understand if she was late. She parked across the street, then marched with one of her bakery boxes to the shop's front door.

Distinct musical tones sounded with her entry. As they faded, the muted overhead harmony of piano and flutes registered. Her nose twitched from an onslaught of competing essential oil scents, but when she moved past a display case of various crystals and mineral rocks, bold roast coffee took over her senses.

She would've thought tea to go with the new age Zen ambiance, but not far from the cash register counter in the back where Lift Your Spirit's owner stood, there was a full on coffee, cappuccino, and latte station with three small café tables and chairs. One was occupied by a trio of high school girls with cardboard to-go cups. Hmm. She hadn't realized Glory and her friends got their coffee and their auras read at the same place.

The store was much larger than she'd imagined from driving by over the last couple of years, especially since it didn't go all the way to the back. Behind the register was a small open, U-shaped area with a door on each wall. The door on the left was closed, the one in the middle she assumed was the exit to the back of the building, and she smirked at the long strings of colorful beads dangling from the top of the opening on the right.

Such a cliché.

A handful of other shoppers were scattered throughout, perusing a multitude of legit offerings besides magic eight balls, tarot cards, and fortune cookies.

Yes, she was being snarky, but it was better than being impressed by the soothing atmosphere and what looked like quality merchandise. Besides the oils and crystals, she noted candles, chimes, shawls, books, incense, clothes, leather sandals, Himalayan salt lamps, and more. A pretty, rust colored shawl caught her eye, but she forced herself to look away. The woman had sabotaged her business, no way she'd buy anything from her store.

Roxanna looked up with a welcoming smile as Honor approached, but it quickly faded. The brunette's long hair hung in a loose braid down her back, with a few soft curls trailing along the sides of her neck. She wore a stretchy, baby blue, V-neck T-shirt with a sunflower on the front, and a flowing navy skirt that brushed the floor.

Her gaze flicked down to the bakery box in Honor's hands, then lifted once more. From the remorse in her expression, she was well aware of the blog post. Not surprising, if indeed she really was psychic.

She's not.

Screw *hello* and *how are you?* Honor went with a bold, accusatory, "I've had five cancellations so far today."

Regret pinched Roxanna's features. "I'm sorry. I never intended that to happen."

"And yet it did." She plopped the bakery box on the polished wood counter and braced her hands on the cool surface while lifting her chin to meet the taller woman's gaze head on. "Did you know that Adam Wilson filed for divorce because he found out his wife was sleeping with his best man before *and* after the wedding?"

The frown drawing Roxanna's dark eyebrows together deepened. "I did not know that."

"And Ty didn't want kids, but Jules did. They never talked about it before the wedding, and afterwards, neither of them was willing to change their minds." She left out the part about what they'd been eating when they had that conversation. "As for Carson and Hannah, Carson got a huge promotion at work, but Hannah didn't want to give up her career to move overseas with him, and he refused to stay here. Their careers were more important than each other."

She had no clue if they had saved any of their wedding cake. If she was being honest, she'd been too afraid to ask anyone about cake after talking to Jules.

"Not every couple is going to make it," she finished. "None of those were my fault."

Roxanna lifted her chin, her expression set with resolve. "The Diamonds have been together for a very long time—"

"Thirty-five years," Honor confirmed in a tight voice. As if she needed to be reminded.

"I couldn't take the chance of anything messing with that. Not with what's coming."

"What does that mean?"

She looked like she'd said something she hadn't meant to. "I meant with the campaign."

"But who cares about *my* business, right?"

Roxanna still looked contrite, but her silence conveyed she was okay with the collateral damage.

Well, Honor damn sure wasn't. "You need to contact that blog writer and tell them you were wrong."

The woman's eyebrows rose. "I'm not going to do that."

"Why not?"

She glanced around before lowering her voice. "Because I wasn't wrong."

"I don't jinx my cakes." A flick of her wrist flipped up the bakery box cover. She took out one of the lemon blueberry cupcakes and thrust it forward. "Take a bite."

"I'd rather not."

"You owe me that much. Try it, and you will see I don't jinx anything. My cakes are amazing." It wasn't a brag, just a statement of fact after years of satisfied clients.

Roxanna's gaze narrowed before she reached out to take the cupcake as if it had cooties or something. She gingerly peeled the liner down, then took a bite. Her expression stayed passive as she chewed and visibly forced a swallow.

Then one sculpted eyebrow arched high. "Angry baking is a thing?"

"What?" Honor's stomach lurched. "No. Of course not."

Liar, liar, pants on fire.

"Whatever you say." The brunette turned and dropped the rest of the cupcake in the garbage behind her.

Her jaw went slack in surprise, but when Roxanna turned back to the counter, the psychic's gaze flicked to the chocolate ones on the other side of the box.

"Go ahead." She injected a note of challenge into her tone to hide her nerves.

One bite of the chocolate and the brunette's cheeks flushed. She closed her eyes with a low, throaty, "*Mmm*." When her long lashes lifted, her warmed gaze met Honor's as she licked frosting off her lips.

"Whew," she said around a second bite while fanning herself. "You definitely weren't angry when you baked *these*."

Heat flooded her face when she thought about who'd been at her house when the chocolate batch went in the oven. Before she could formulate a retort, a customer stepped up behind her and leaned forward to look inside the bakery box.

"Ooh, those look so good," the woman gushed. "How much are they?"

Honor shifted herself and the box to the right so there was room for her to place purchases on the counter. "Sorry, they're not—"

"Five dollars each," Roxanna cut in as she set aside the half-eaten chocolate cake in her hand. "And worth every penny."

Worth every penny? What?!

"I'll take two of each, please."

Honor cut her gaze to Roxanna, eyes wide in shock over her words of praise and the lack of hesitation in the customer's response. The shop owner simply reached under the counter and pulled out a brown gift box to put the four cupcakes in, then rang them up along with the woman's other items.

Once she left, Honor moved closer again. "You didn't seem overly concerned about selling her the angry ones."

"Your anger was specifically directed at me. It won't affect her." Roxanna opened the register and offered Honor a twenty.

"I don't want your money."

"They were your cupcakes."

Good point. Honor swiped the cash from her fingers. "Is this supposed to make everything okay?"

"I know it doesn't make up for what happened last night, but I have a license to go with the coffee bar, so I can sell them here whenever you want, to help make up for the cancellations. It's the least I can do."

"Oh, for sure it's the least," she retorted while stuffing the money in her jeans pocket. "The most would be for you to call the blog writer and admit you were wrong."

"I wasn't wrong." Roxanna gave her a sideways glance, then propped one hand on her hip, chin at a defiant angle as she faced her directly. "Tell me you believe in love and I'll call right now."

Aggravation shortened her breath as she stared at the stubborn brunette. What was with her and Asher insisting she answer that damn question? Like with him, she found she couldn't outright lie to his friend's face. She'd meant it when she'd told Mae she didn't believe in psychic crap, and yet the woman *had* eerily predicted her emotions for each batch of treats in the box. Her reaction to the chocolate was particularly unsettling.

Unless she'd talked to Asher. If he'd told her about stopping at Honor's house after the party, if he told her they'd kissed, then it wouldn't have been hard for her to make guesses about the cupcakes.

Taking a page straight out of his playbook, she replied, "Anything is possible."

Roxanna's scrutiny made her insides twitch. After a long moment, she said, "That's very true. And when *you* actually believe it, I'll be happy to make a new statement."

"What the hell?" Honor snapped in frustration. "Have you appointed yourself the Happily Ever After Fairy?"

"No. I am definitely not that." Dejection clouded her eyes for the space of one breath, then her expression hardened to stubborn again. "But I still stand by what I said."

Irritated frustration threatened to coil her fingers into fists. Instead, she flipped the top closed on the cupcakes with a muttered, "This was a total waste of time."

When she would've lifted the cupcakes to take them with her, Roxanna laid a hand on the box. "Leave them. I'll even pay you up front."

"These are for someone else." She jerked the sweets away and headed for the door. She'd talk to the damn blog writer herself.

On her way back to her car, she fumed at the woman's refusal to take back her accusation from the party. She knew why—it didn't take a genius to figure it out—but it still pissed her off. Roxanna didn't give a shit if Honor believed in love or not, she was only worried about her own reputation. Because who'd want to go to a psychic who made false predictions?

CHAPTER 15

*E*verywhere Asher turned, something reminded him of Honor.

The late morning sun hit the carafe of juice on the table, casting a rich, red shadow to almost match her hair. His youngest sister's gray sweatshirt was a couple shades darker than Honor's faded T-shirt last night. Seeing Celia and her fiancé steal a quick kiss at the door of the dining room had him daydreaming about his neighbor's sexy, sweet mouth all through Sunday brunch.

He'd wanted to knock on her door just to see her face this morning, to hear her voice. But it would've been a wasted opportunity with his family waiting on him before serving the meal. He needed to return the plate when he had lots of time, when they could talk and get to know each other, not drop it off and run. A move like that gave him no chance to finesse another kiss that was ten times better than her addicting frosting.

His mom and dad sat at one end of the twelve foot table, with his grandparents opposite. Celia, Robert, and Loyal filled in one side, and he, Merit, and Shelby the other. Currently, the baby of the family had asked their dad to go view a property she'd spotted for her future vet clinic.

"This is not part of the plan, Shelby."

"Maybe it's not part of *your* plan, but it is part of *mine*, Daddy."

She gave him a mutinous glare, and he frowned. The youngest Diamond was usually pretty easy going, but when she set her mind to something, look out.

"I don't like that location," Dad said. "The neighborhood is terrible. It's not safe."

"Just because it isn't in a rich neighborhood doesn't mean it's not safe. It'll be perfect for my clinic, and it has a full apartment upstairs, too."

"You have enough in your trust fund that you won't need to bother yourself with tenants."

"The apartment would be for me," she clarified. "I'm not living here after college."

"You don't want to mooch off Mom and Dad like Merit does?" Loyal asked with a smirk.

"Shut up, Loyal." Merit scowled at him across the table. "Celia only moved out a month ago."

"Celia had a full-time job the whole time," their dad snapped.

Asher held back a sigh for the direction the conversation had taken. At this rate, brunch was liable to drag on longer into the afternoon than he'd planned to stay. He hoped to talk Honor into having dinner with him before he had to leave for Pike's Peak later.

Thankfully, his mom held up a hand, her diamond rings flashing in the sunlight. "Let's not get into all that right now." She glanced at Shelby while refilling her coffee cup and their dad's. "You have another full year before you graduate. Now isn't the time to be distracted with moving anywhere. You need to concentrate on your studies, and we need to focus on your father's campaign."

"All she does is study," Merit interjected. "Geezus. Let her get a life and have some fun."

"Purchasing real estate isn't something you do for fun," Grandpa Ira admonished. "It's an investment to be taken seriously." As he would know—he'd doubled his own father's fortune in the real estate market forty years ago, and taught his son to do the same before he moved into politics.

Shelby sat up straighter in her chair. "I am taking it seriously, Grandpa. That's why I asked Dad to come look at the place with me. I'm planning ahead just like he preaches."

Their father shook his head and her face fell. "My entire week is booked solid between work and the campaign. Maybe you could go with her, Dad?"

"Sure," Grandpa agreed.

"I'll go," Merit offered at the same time.

"*You* should get yourself a job," their dad snapped.

Merit fisted the napkin in his lap and Asher bumped his knee against his brother's. It wasn't a bad idea for him to finally put his engineering degree to some use. He'd certainly be able to do a thorough inspection of the building. "You should both go. I'm sure Shelby wouldn't mind the extra opinion, right, Bells?"

"Forget it." Jaw set, their youngest brother tossed his napkin on his plate and shoved his chair back.

"Merit…" Shelby called after him as he strode from the room.

"Let him go," their father grumbled in a low voice. "It's what he does best. He needs to grow the hell up."

Asher agreed, and yet a split-second glimpse of Merit's expression had him wondering if there wasn't more bothering his brother than Dad getting on his case.

He couldn't find him after brunch, but he did catch

Celia in the kitchen. Without mincing words, he asked, "Are you still going to use Honor Hartman for your wedding cake?"

His older sister grimaced as she loaded plates in the dishwasher since Elena had Sundays off these days. "I don't think so."

"Why not? Just because of what happened last night?"

"Well, yeah. Didn't you see the Denver Today blog?"

"No. You know I don't pay attention to that crap."

"They did a write up about Dad, and another whole post about Honor's jinxed cakes."

His stomach sank for her sake even as annoyance flared. "That's bullshit."

Celia gave him a quick look. "You think Roxanna's wrong?"

Well, hell. He was damned if he did and damned if he didn't on that question. He forced a casual shrug and stepped up to the sink. "I talked to her last night. She doesn't *really* know for sure about the jinxing thing."

"Oh." His sister hesitated, then said, "Still...better not to take any chances, you know? I'll leave the first divorce in the family to Merit."

They always left the screw-ups to Merit. He did own most of 'em, but suddenly it didn't seem fair to always expect him to mess up.

Asher rinsed plates and handed them over one at a time. "I don't think it's such a big deal. And really, if you think a piece of cake has the power to jinx your relationship, maybe you and Robert shouldn't be getting married in the first place."

She huffed out a breath and paused. "Well, hell, when you put it like that..."

When she didn't add more, he prompted, "So...are you going to hire her or not?"

Celia gave him a longer, measuring look. "You *really* love her cakes, don't you?"

Oh yeah. And he liked the woman just as much. Maybe more.

Definitely more.

"All I'm saying is it seems kind of shitty to give her the job and then take it away again because of something Roxanna said. As Honor pointed out, a few divorces out of a couple hundred couples isn't exactly shocking. I'm sure the divorce attorneys at your firm can back that up."

"I get what you're saying, but I don't want to be one of the few."

"That's on you and Robert, not the person who bakes your wedding cake."

Shelby and Loyal walked in as Celia set the last plate in the rack. Asher shut off the water and reached for a towel to dry his hands while turning to lean back against the sink.

Loyal nudged their youngest sister's arm. "I told you they'd be done if we waited long enough."

She tossed him a grin, but Celia ignored the two as she met Asher's gaze and shrugged. "I'll think about it."

"Are you two talking about what happened with the cake baker last night?" Shelby asked.

"Yeah." Celia closed and started the dishwasher. "Asher's playing major defense."

Loyal's humor vanished in the blink of an eye. "He always defends that quack friend of his."

Asher stiffened, and he and Shelby said at the same time, "She's not a quack."

"Actually, he was defending Honor," Celia corrected. Her brown gaze fixed on his face. "This is more than you liking the woman's cakes. Come on. Spill."

Knowing they'd hound him for the truth, it was easier to fess up now than later. His neck warmed as he admitted, "She moved into the house across from me last week. I'm simply being neighborly."

"Right," Shelby scoffed. "I'm sure it has nothing to do with how pretty she is."

"She is very pretty," Celia agreed.

Whether dressed up for a formal event, or barefoot in her kitchen with no make-up and messy hair, she was stunning.

But then his youngest sister's eyebrows drew together. "You did hear Roxanna, though, didn't you? She said Honor doesn't believe in love."

The words came out like a warning. Because they'd all had it drummed into them for years; *Diamonds don't divorce.*

"Roxanna doesn't know everything," Loyal snapped.

Ignoring the dig at his best friend, Asher said, "Anything is possible once someone meets the right person."

His older brother gave a disgusted snort and strode from the kitchen.

Shelby frowned at his back, but Celia's gaze stayed on Asher. "You think you're the right person?"

He shrugged even as his heart answered, *Yes.*

Celia looked skeptical. "You better make sure Roxanna's wrong before you get in too deep," she warned.

Before he could respond, her fiancé leaned through the doorway. "You ready to head out, babe? I was hoping to fit in a few hours of work before the fundraiser."

Goodbye's were said, and Asher encouraged Shelby to still invite Merit along to look at her proposed veterinary clinic before ducking out himself. As he reached to insert the key in the ignition of his Camaro, he got a text from Roxanna.

Rox: *Did you happen to see your neighbor while she was baking cupcakes recently?*

A shiver snaked down his spine. No matter how many times she did that, it was still eerie as all hell.

Asher: *Last night. Why?*

Rox: *There is hope yet.*

He frowned at his phone. *What does that mean?*

Rox: *Nothing. Carry on.*

Except with her, nothing was ever *nothing*. Not that she'd explain more. She never did.

Asher: *Freak.*

Rox: *Love you, too.*

Asher: *So I'm forgiven, then?*

Rox: *You were forgiven last night. Am I?*

Asher: *Of course. I know your heart's in the right place.*

Rox: *Good. I think yours might be, too.*

Well, that was awfully cryptic. Typical Rox.

Despite the urge to hurry home, he made a quick detour onto Aspen Street and parked in the back of Lift Your Spirit shortly after one p.m. With Roxanna, face to face sometimes netted better results. Sometimes.

He used his master key to enter the back, an invite she'd extended from the day he'd purchased the building six years ago and offered her prime rental space. She looked up from the register and gave him a smile. Despite the recent text exchange, her welcome was subdued as he approached.

"How was brunch? Does everyone hate me?" Somehow, she sounded worried and mutinous at the same time.

He cast an absent glance at the three girls having coffee at one of the café tables. There were a couple other browsing customers, but that was it. Being it was a Sunday, Roxanna was the only one manning the store. Her two part-time employees, Tessa and Darcy, worked Tuesdays through Saturday so she could give readings in the back room.

"No one hates you."

Roxanna turned away as she mumbled, "Your brother does."

The misery in her voice made him frown. "You just have

to ignore Loy—*whoa*." He leaned over to peer closer at the top of the garbage. "Is that one of Honor's cupcakes?"

"Yes." Rox reached to the side and picked up a half-eaten chocolate one on the counter he hadn't even noticed. "And *Oh. My. God*," she stage whispered. "I now understand your mouth orgasms."

"Why is *that one* in the garbage?" Indignation sharpened his voice. He'd eaten two of the lemon blueberry already and no way in hell did something so equally orgasm-worthy belong in the trash. Knowing he had one more waiting on his counter had him wiping his mouth to make sure he wasn't drooling.

"Because it hates me."

Asher raised his eyebrows, but she took a bite of the chocolate in her hand—the flavor that hadn't been cooled enough for Honor to frost until after he'd left. But the batter had been divine.

He watched her chew, envious it wasn't his taste buds drowning in pleasure. "Why doesn't that one hate you?"

She gave a low hum of delight. "This one wants me. Better yet, it wants *me* to want *it.*"

Her evocative tone summoned the image of Honor leaning forward to suck the chocolate batter from his finger. His blood heated with the sensual memory. Now he wanted a taste of the baked version so bad he reached out to pluck the last bite from Roxanna's hand.

She moved faster than he expected, twisting her body to protect her treasure. "Keep your dirty paws to yourself," she growled before stuffing the rest in her mouth.

He snorted at her chipmunk cheeks. "How'd you get these anyway?"

She finished chewing before telling him about Honor's visit a short fifteen minutes ago, and her offer to sell the cupcakes to make up for the party fiasco. "I sold four while she was standing here, but all she did was storm back out as mad as when she came in."

"Can you really blame her?"

Rox shrugged.

Asher glanced at the garbage again. Could he pull that one out? It was just sitting on some crumpled packing paper. He was jonesing for some frosting since his mother had gotten rid of all the anniversary cake, *"Just to be safe."* God Bless Elena for saving the few pieces she'd sent home with him last night. But those were all the way at home, and this one was right here.

"Don't you dare," Rox warned. "Not in front of my customers."

He made a face and asked, "Why does this one hate you?"

"She was pissed off at me when she was baking that flavor." Her nose scrunched with distaste. "It was horrible. The frosting didn't even taste sweet."

"What? I had one last night and this morning and both were awesome—especially the frosting."

"This morning?" Roxanna's eyebrows sailed skyward. "Did you spend the night?"

I wish.

"No. I washed dishes and she sent me home with a plate of cupcakes as payment." *After two insanely hot kisses.* He gave her a mock glare for not sharing. "I didn't get any of the chocolate ones, though. She had just started those when I got there."

Her smug grin suddenly had him thinking back to what she'd said a moment ago. Honor was pissed off at Rox when making the lemon blueberry. And then he showed up for the chocolate—the flavor that made his psychic best friend groan with ecstasy.

He lifted his gaze to Roxanna's. "The chocolate wanted you, hey?"

"Yes."

"It wanted you to want it?"

"Oh, yes." Her grin widened. "Very much so."

He nodded and backed toward the door. Face to face had paid off with huge dividends.

"Where ya goin', Ace?"

"To get myself a chocolate cupcake."

And hopefully more.

CHAPTER 16

*W*ednesday night, Honor slipped beneath the covers, happy to be off her feet after another full day of baking. She reached for the lined, yellow slip of paper she'd left on her nightstand Sunday night and leaned back against her headboard to read it. Again.

Sorry I missed you. I'm leaving for a few days for work, but I have your plate. Call me to discuss my ransom demands.

There was a phone number, but no name. However, she didn't have to be psychic to know the strong, bold handwriting belonged to Asher. It was confident, sexy, and the whole darn note was oh so tempting.

Exactly like the man.

Four days ago, after her stop at Lift Your Spirit, she'd fumed through lunch with her mom and Glory, then made an impromptu visit to Mae's house on the way home that turned into dinner, a movie with Ian, and girl talk over wine after her godson went to bed. She'd come home after midnight to find the yellow paper taped to her door and was disappointed to have missed him. Since then, she'd reread his note a dozen times, a smile tugging at her lips every time.

She'd resisted calling him so far, but her willpower was wearing thin. On the one hand, she didn't want to encourage him. On the other, she wanted him bad enough to encourage the hell out him. He'd been right—the insane attraction went both ways.

The clock on her alarm clock ticked to 10:34 p.m. as her finger hovered over Asher's name in her contact list. It was nothing more than a phone call. She could handle a friendly conversation with her neighbor. Better than face to face, right?

Right.

He'd said he'd be gone a few days, and tomorrow was Thursday. If she waited any longer to call, he'd be back and standing at her front door.

Or she'd be at his. If that happened, all bets were off.

The moment she touched the screen to make the connection, her heart rate doubled.

"Hello?"

The gravelly rumble of his voice over the line robbed her of her breath. Honor managed a quick inhale as an involuntary smile curved her lips. The question in his greeting meant her name hadn't registered on his caller ID.

"I won't pay ransom without proof of life," she demanded. Or tried to. It was kind of hard to sound badass when she was smiling.

It only took about two seconds before his chuckle filled her ear. "Honor."

Happiness warmed his sexy voice and strummed desire deep in her core. Well, damn. This wasn't much better than face to face—and worse, she didn't have the option of reaching out to touch.

That's the point, dummy. Keep your hands off your neighbor.

"I gave up hope you'd call," he said.

"Well, it is just a plate," she teased.

"Oh, it's so much more than a plate."

It was an open invitation to see her again. While watching him walk across the street the other night, she'd declared her subconscious a genius. But to acknowledge that with him right now would be too encouraging. Even so, she was tempted.

The sound of rustling sheets sent her gaze back to the clock on her nightstand. "Am I calling too late? Did I wake you?" She wasn't completely used to her new schedule, so it still seemed early to her.

"It's all good. I have a sunrise shoot in the morning, but haven't been able to fall asleep yet."

Oh, boy.

That brought a familiar fantasy to the surface. Asher in bed. Shirtless. Covers riding low.

"The one good thing about a three a.m. wake up call is I'll be home before noon," he added.

"Three a.m.? That's less than five hours from now. I should let you go," she said, though genuinely reluctant to do so.

"Hell no. I want to hear your voice."

Those words had her fighting a giddy grin while snuggling down into her pillows. He might not be able to see her, but he'd definitely hear it if she let it loose. "Where's your shoot?"

"Pike's Peak. I'm doing the photos for a new sales brochure for a local climbing school."

"I love that area. Do you climb, too, or just stand back and take the pictures?"

"I climb whenever I get the chance."

"With ropes and stuff?"

"When I'm working, the ropes are necessary so I can get my shots. If I'm climbing for fun, I do a little freestyle here and there."

And *that's* where the muscled forearms came from. She closed her eyes and pictured him leaning on her island counter again, his defined arms tan against his white shirt sleeves.

"Is it dangerous?" The idea of him hanging onto a rock by nothing more than his fingertips made her heart thump with apprehension.

"I'm careful."

"I've never done anything like that," she admitted.

"Would you like to?"

"Oh, I don't know if I'm brave enough for that."

"Sure you are," he countered. "I'll take you some time and keep you safe. Better yet, I'm skydiving end of June for a job. Start there and everything else will be a piece of cake."

The thought of jumping out of a perfectly good airplane made her stomach drop right out from under her. "Yeah, that's gonna be a *hard* no."

"Why?"

"I'm not a risk-taker."

"I don't know about that. You started a business by yourself. You bought a house by yourself. You called me."

She smiled at that last part. "It took me four days to call you. As for the house and my business, depending on my skills didn't seem risky to me. I know I can depend on myself. The closest I want to come to anything like what you do is the proposal I arranged last year at the top of a mountain for a couple who were climbers."

"That wasn't the one *no* on your record, was it? Cuz that would've really sucked to get all the way up there and get shot down."

"No, it wasn't the *no*. Thank goodness."

Another low, sexy chuckle from him curled her toes.

"You are quite the contradiction, Honor Hartman."

"Why do you say that?"

126

"You supposedly don't believe in love, but you help people get engaged and bake their wedding cakes."

"Yeah, because it's what I do," she rationalized. "I get paid for it."

He made a noise that could've been agreement or not. "And that one *no* bothers you even though you had absolutely nothing to do with the woman's answer."

This time, she made the noncommittal noise, though it *did* bother her. A lot. Didn't mean she believed in love, though.

"Also, I heard you're baking cupcakes for Roxanna, but I thought you were mad at her."

"No, she's selling *my* cupcakes. It's the least she can do—especially since the blog writer isn't interested in what I have to say, and she still refuses to admit she had it all wrong."

Says the girl who one second ago silently insisted she doesn't believe in love.

That damn voice inside never knew when to shut up.

She quickly added, "Besides, it's a long way from making up for all my cancellations after that stupid post on the society blog."

"That bad?" he asked with a wince in his voice.

"Eight cancellations so far, and no new cake bookings or proposal consults."

"Ouch. Sorry."

She sighed. "At least the cupcakes are selling. Two dozen today, and she asked me to bring three dozen for tomorrow."

"What kind did you make?"

"Chocolate, and orange dreamsicle."

He gave an appreciative *hmm*. "That's what I want for ransom. Two chocolate ones."

"You know it's customary, and polite, to return a dish with a reciprocal offering, not demand more, right?" She wanted to be indignant, but once more she was smiling.

"Two chocolate cupcakes or the plate gets it."

And now she was laughing.

"Did you think of me when you made them?" he asked.

Her laugh faded under the force of her racing pulse. When she'd taste-tested the batter earlier, she'd relived the erotic feel of his finger in her mouth. And she'd leaned against the counter, eyes closed as she recalled how he'd cupped her face in his hands before he kissed her. The feel of his mouth on hers, the taste of him on her tongue, the strength of his body pressing hers into the counter...until the shrill beep of the timer jolted her back to reality.

"Honor?"

Her name in his husky voice was so much better than the timer.

Don't admit you were thinking of him.

Do. Not. Admit. It.

"Maybe," she whispered.

"That's a yes." A satisfied smile tinged his voice. "On that note, I will say goodnight, and I'll see you tomorrow."

"Really? That's goodnight?"

"Sweet dreams."

And just like that, he was gone.

She huffed out a breath of frustration as she dropped her phone on the nightstand. The man had a habit of winding her up and then leaving her wanting so much more. Pretty much guaranteed her dreams were more likely to be sexy than sweet.

She scooped up her sketch pad from the other side of the bed, and opened to a blank page to brainstorm ideas. An hour later, instead of a new cake design, she had an image of her newest recurring fantasy.

Asher in bed. Shirtless. Covers riding low.

CHAPTER 17

*A*sher checked the time and cursed the multitude of mishaps that had kept him from arriving home by noon. Hell, even five or six would've been better than nine at night. He was tired, bruised and sore, and his stomach grumbled at the mouth-watering aroma of pizza from the pie he'd grabbed at D'Angelo's after exiting the highway.

But the moment he turned onto Hopewell Lane and saw Honor's lights blazing, every ache and pain faded to the background. Eager anticipation raced through his veins and made it easy to give in to the urge to turn into her driveway instead of his. After being gone half the week, seeing her tonight was simply too tempting to resist.

He caught a glimpse of her through the window, working at the kitchen island like the other night. Her long, red hair was in a ponytail, and she wore a plain white T-shirt underneath a dark apron dusted with white powder. He hoped the counter hid bare feet and leggings again.

With the pizza box warming his palm, and a six pack of cold beer in the other hand, he stepped onto her front porch. His stomach pitched like when he'd lost his grip on the mountain face earlier in the day. Before he could knock, the door swung open and Honor's beautiful smile took his breath away.

"I knew it," she said, a note of excited awe in her voice.

His pulse skipped—until she walked right past him.

Well. Color me invisible.

The blow sent his ego to his knees as Asher slowly turned and followed her back to the driveway.

"This is a '69, right? Super Sport/Rally Sport combo?"

She slowly walked around the Camaro. The way her admiring gaze traced each line of the sleek body he'd restored made him jealous of his own damn car. He wouldn't mind one bit if she looked at his body like that.

"Yeah," he confirmed. "I'm impressed."

He was even more impressed by the fact she stood back instead of running her fingers all over his custom, dusk blue paint job. He hated when people did that. Especially women who thought their hands on his car would turn him on.

Then again, if he was being honest, *Honor's* hands on his car would definitely turn him on.

"I saw the back end of this baby in your garage the day after I moved in. Of all the classics, Camaros are my favorite."

She tossed him a quick grin as he recalled Mr. Collins' '57 Chevy catching her attention that first day he'd spotted her through his screen door.

"I love that you skipped the stripe and rear spoiler. It looks so much cleaner without it. Sleek and sexy, and the black interior is perfect."

She was perfect. Baked like a goddess, gorgeous as hell, and old car aficionado? There wasn't a whole lot more a guy could ask for. He decided he didn't care so much she wasn't looking at him. Then she ducked to check out the interior, and he ran his gaze over the curve of her perfectly shaped ass to where her leggings ended just below her knees, showing off toned calves, bare feet, and sexy red toenails.

Thank you.

"Ever see the movie *Better Off Dead* with John Cusack?" she asked over her shoulder.

"Of course. It's a cult classic."

"My dad rented it for us to watch when I was about fifteen. That's when I fell in love with this car."

"So you do have it in you," he teased.

"Well, I mean, with a body like this…"

He smiled at her joke, but he sure as hell understood the hot body argument.

She stepped back and ran her gaze over the Camaro one more time. He jerked his attention up when she did a quarter pivot to face him. His breath caught in his lungs when her gaze met his, her head tilted as a smile flirted on her lips.

"Any chance I can drive it sometime?"

If it keeps you looking at me like that, you can do anything you want, any time you want to.

"Can you drive a stick shift?" he retained enough common sense to inquire. But then the question had him thinking of some other stick she could shift.

Fuck. When did it get so hot?

Suddenly he wished he had a free hand to push up the sleeves of his Henley.

"I'm an expert at stick shift," Honor said seriously.

Asher valiantly tried to drag his mind out of the gutter and narrowed his gaze in mock suspicion. "How do I know you're not just saying that because my car seduced you?"

Her low laugh stirred his blood. "My dad taught me in his '66 Mustang."

Oh, man, that was one hell of a car. "Hardtop or convertible?"

"Fastback. Four speed manual transmission."

"Nice. All right, then, you can drive her." Those green eyes of hers lit with excitement, but he held up a hand as his stomach rumbled. "*Tomorrow*. Right now, I've got hot pizza and haven't eaten since noon, *and*...I want my two cupcakes."

Her wide grin told him she caught his adaptation of the *Better Off Dead* quote. "I hope you know you have to share," she warned on her way past. "I got caught up in work and forgot about dinner."

"I wouldn't have brought it in if I wasn't willing to share." He followed her inside, relishing her cake-scented wake as he watched the sway of her hips. "It's the least I can do for dropping in uninvited a second time in less than a week."

Every inch of the kitchen island and back counter was occupied by a large square cake, frosting bowl and pastry bag, and a multitude of tools that looked like they had nothing to do with cake baking. Asher shifted direction to set the pizza and beer on her kitchen table.

Honor brought over plates and napkins. "Is this going to become a habit?"

"Depends on if you mind."

"That depends on your pizza toppings."

"Pepperoni, sausage, and fresh mushrooms."

"I don't mind at all." She lifted the box lid, then closed her eyes as she inhaled the aroma with a low, "*Mmmm*."

Asher shoved his sleeves up to his elbows as he stared at her mouth. It took everything he had to not reach out and pull her into his arms. He craved another taste of those lips while every inch of her luscious curves pressed against him. He wanted her making that sound of pleasure because of him, not the pizza.

Reining in his over-zealous libido, he handed her a plate and offered a beer. A couple of bites into his first piece, he glanced at her island counter. "I can't tell if you're baking, doing construction, sculpting pottery, or landscaping."

She followed his gaze, then laughed. "I use the level to make sure one side isn't higher than the other. The pruning shears are to cut the dowel supports for each layer."

"And all the other stuff?"

Honor walked over to the counter to explain her use for the hammer, square, turntable and the rest of the tools while she finished her slice and he ate a second. After she washed her hands, she reached into the pastry box on the back counter before facing him with two chocolate frosted cupcakes that made his mouth water almost as much as she did.

He prayed she wasn't a stickler for the rules of this engagement. "I don't have your plate."

She drew back with an exaggerated gasp. "Oh, no, now what?"

He offered a hopeful lift of his eyebrows. "I'll bring it by tomorrow?"

"How do I know you're not just saying that because my cupcakes seduced you?"

When she scissored the treats up and down, he gave a bark of laughter. He was seduced by both sets of 'cupcakes' within his view. "I give you my word."

After one last teasing moment of consideration, she set the cupcakes next to the pizza box before returning to the island. As she started back to work, he swiped up half his dessert and took a seat on one of the stools to watch her process with keen interest.

His first bite of the chocolate cupcake brought forth a deep moan of approval. "This is *so good*...and the frosting... oh my *God*."

"Glad you like it."

Her pleased smile was directed down at her hands, and then she gave him a contradictory shy glance through her lashes that was so hot he gripped the edge of the counter and bit back another groan.

Her gaze flicked to the raw scrape on his forearm before she dropped it back to the cake. "How was your trip? You were home later than you said."

"Were you watching for me?"

"No."

That reply was so quick, he had to hide his grin with another bite of cupcake. After he swallowed, he gave her an abbreviated version that skipped the part about the fall that had him dreading how his body would feel in the morning. Especially his bruised shoulder. Even with the random surges of sexual chemistry, the dull throb of discomfort was starting to seep through again.

"I don't think that's the whole story," she said while transferring the frosted cake into a large refrigerator. She brought back two more naked ones a size smaller than the last, and proceeded to slice them in half horizontally with a tool that had wire stretched between two rods that curved up to meet on top. When he didn't reply to her comment, she paused to arch her eyebrows at him, her gaze lingering on his tender left cheekbone.

"A couple days with Rox and suddenly you're psychic, too?" he groused with a grin.

"No. But you're scraped and bruised. What happened?"

The concern in her too-perceptive gaze was like a soothing caress to his sore body. "A little slip, that's all. It happens sometimes." After the initial daze had worn off and he'd caught his breath, he'd been surprised to realize she was the first person he'd thought about while dangling from a rope nearly one hundred feet in the air. Had to make sure he got home to see her again.

She piped a thick border of butter cream frosting along

the top edge of the first cake layer as she asked, "You're okay?"

"I wouldn't be here if I wasn't," he quipped.

She shook her head and scooped a blob of frosting from a huge bowl off to the side. He reached to swipe his finger along the edge of the bowl, only to have her reach over and smack his hand with her spatula.

"Ow."

"Then behave. You have another whole cupcake over on the table."

"But the frosting is my favorite." He grinned at the smile tugging the corners of her mouth. As she smoothed out the top of the cake, he said, "Tell me about you being an old car genius."

"My brother, sister, and I worked on my dad's cars on the weekends we spent with him. I don't get much time to do that anymore, but the four of us still go to the Castle Rock Cruise In each year. Dad's cars have won a few trophies over the years."

"That's awesome. I haven't been to that one yet, but the Old Town Car Show in Fort Collin's is a favorite of mine."

"Old Town is fun," she agreed. "I haven't been since high school."

"Hard to believe the first weekend of June is next weekend already. We could go."

Honor grimaced. "Unfortunately, I have two weddings next weekend. All week is going to be crazy."

He pushed aside his disappointment. "Summer is your busy season, isn't it?"

"Usually. Though this summer is going downhill fast."

Because of all the cancellations. "Sorry."

She didn't miss a beat while placing the next layer of cake and repeating the frosting process from the first. "Again, not your fault. And Roxanna *is* trying to make it up to me. I don't see us becoming friends or anything, but the cupcake sales are making up for some of the lost cake revenue."

"She's not worried about you jinxing anyone?"

"I still don't think it's even a thing, but she claims it doesn't matter because I'm not making them for specific people, or for a specific event."

Made sense, he guessed. "Speaking of specific people, did my sister call you yet?"

"Nope."

He frowned. "Damn. I thought for sure I'd changed her mind."

One of her slim shoulders lifted in a shrug. "It is what it is. I may have to rethink my five year plan, but it's too early to see how this all plays out to give up."

Asher drained the last of his beer and slouched in the chair as he watched her efficient movements. "What's your five year plan?"

"My own specialty cake shop. I'll hire a couple of employees to help with the wedding cakes so I can book more, and maybe even branch out a bit. Kind of like *The Cake Boss.*"

"Why can't you do that now?"

"For a shop, location is key, and I can't afford that set of keys yet."

"And where is your key location?"

"Well, an area like where Roxanna's shop is would be perfect."

His heart gave a few fast beats and a squeeze of disappointment. Did she know he owned the building? Was she hinting? If she did, she was playing it super cool.

He frowned, not liking the instant flare of doubt in his mind—especially since it stemmed from Brianna, not Honor.

"Anything along or near Aspen Street, really." She'd

finished the layers and smoothed out what she'd earlier called a *crumb coat* over the whole cake before swapping that square at the fridge for yet another set of layers, another size smaller. "But I need to build up my savings again after buying this house. The initial setup for the shop will be pretty expensive."

He had almost told her he'd happily evict one of his tenants to give her space, but kept his mouth shut. First, that was his dick talking, not common sense, business sense, or even basic decency. And second, he'd been burned one too many times by someone wanting things from him, instead of wanting him. Honor hadn't given any indication she would use him like that, but the thought of things taking that route with her twisted his gut into a sour knot.

"What about asking your parents for help?"

"No," she stated with a firm shake of her head. "I'll do it on my own or I won't do it at all."

The finality in her voice raised his respect and eased his tension. With the noted exceptions of Rox and Elana's daughter, Solana, most of the women he knew were happy to live off Daddy's money. Even he and his siblings had taken stipends from their trust funds when starting out. The two youngest still cashed monthly checks, though in Shelby's defense, she was still in college compared to Merit having graduated almost two years ago.

"My best friend, Mae, built her construction company from the ground up, all on her own. No one gave her anything, and I want to do it the same way," Honor explained as she worked. "It felt great when I signed the papers for this house knowing it was all from my hard work. It's going to be that much sweeter when I see my name up above the doors of my shop."

He had the money to do that for her tomorrow. He'd do it, too, just to keep that gorgeous smile curving her lips. But her independence was to be admired and supported, not disrespected.

Before she caught him mooning at her like a lovesick puppy, he pushed up from the stool. "Mind if I use your bathroom?"

"It's right there." She pointed to a door on the other side of the patio doors leading to her backyard.

When he came back out, Asher swiped a second beer from the table and strolled around her living room. She shot him a quick glance, but otherwise was quiet over there in the kitchen. Having finished frosting the third cake, she'd rolled out a ball of white fondant and was using a metal cookie cutter to make flowers and leaves.

It looked like she'd be at it for quite a while yet, even though it was after ten. Exhaustion was beginning to edge in as he smothered a yawn before taking another pull off his beer. He knew he should go, and yet didn't want to leave. As simple as it was, he liked just being in the same room with her, observing, talking. He wished he had his camera in hand to catch the quiet beauty in her concentration.

After a brief perusal of the few pictures leaning against the wall waiting to be hung, he took his time looking at the framed photos on her mantle. "This your family?"

"Yeah. Mom and Dad, my brother, Josh, and my sister, Glory."

He'd been correct that the red-haired guy from that first weekend was her brother. He shifted his attention to a picture of her, and two gap-toothed little blond girls, all three of them dressed as witches for Halloween. "Your nieces are twins?"

"Yep. Annabel and Bailey are Glory's girls. That picture is from last year. I've gone trick-or-treating with them and my sister since they were babies."

He drank in her happy smile in the picture with her

nieces, wondering if she wanted kids of her own someday. He sure hoped so.

Don't get too far ahead of yourself.

"The picture on the right is my friend, Mae, and her son, Ian."

He recognized the pretty blond from last weekend, too. Honor had spun around pretty fast when he'd caught them watching him cut the grass, but her friend had offered a cheeky wave before going inside.

Shifting his gaze back to the family picture, he saw she took after her father in looks, but her sister was the spitting image of their mother. He recalled her parents had racked up seven divorces between the two of them. "Any half or step siblings?"

"There were a couple steps from my mom's second marriage, but they were adults already, and the marriage didn't last long enough for any of us to become close."

His brows drew down in a frown. "I can't even imagine that."

"Of course you can't. Your parents have been together for thirty-five years."

His pulse skipped as he glanced back over his shoulder at that, but her head was bent low while she rolled a tool with a metal ball on the end along the edges of one of the cut out flowers.

The wistful note in her voice told him she wanted the exact thing she claimed to not believe in. And if her heart longed for love to last a lifetime, then it was entirely possible she could fall for him like he was falling for her. As he'd told her, it wasn't like the mind had any say over what the heart wanted—no matter how many warnings were issued.

CHAPTER 18

*H*onor kept her head down as she thinned and waved the edges of the petals on the fondant flowers. Asher's drop-ins were something she could easily become addicted to. Pizza, beer, good company, awesome car, hot guy.

Sexy moans as he enjoyed something she created.

Yeah, he was some*one* she could easily become addicted to. Probably already was since she hadn't even considered sending him home when he'd pulled up in her driveway. Not to mention, she'd ensured even more time together when she'd shamelessly flirted so he would agree to let her drive his baby.

Mae would've laughed and called her a hussy, but that was only because she didn't understand the irresistible lure of the classics. She built things new. Tore down the old and replaced with new. Restoration wasn't her thing.

"You draw?" Asher asked from across the room.

"Some. Mostly I sketch out my cake designs," she answered absently.

Then it dawned on her what had prompted his question,

and she jerked her head up in alarm. Her sketch pad was wide open on the coffee table.

Her heart stuttered in her chest, heat flaring in her cheeks as he set down his beer and reached for the book. She'd been working on a client's cake earlier in the day, but the sketch of him sprawled in bed was only a few pages back. Granted, his body had been drawn based purely on the memory of being pressed against him during that kiss that still pleasured her dreams, but his face…well, there was no way he wouldn't recognize himself.

"Um…" She hurried around the kitchen island when he sat back on the couch, sketch book pulled onto his lap. He slouched down into the cushions, braced one booted foot on her coffee table, and leaned the book on his thigh to turn the page.

Thank God he was paging forward, not back.

Honor halted a few steps from the couch, bottom caught lip between her teeth, fists clenched at her sides. If she was lucky, he'd get tired of looking at drawings of cakes and set the book aside when he got to the front, or sooner. But if he didn't stop there, she didn't want to be sitting face to face when he saw the proof she'd been imagining him in bed naked, save for the sheet draped over his hips.

She spun on the ball of her foot and went back to her fondant flowers.

"I have been addicted to your cakes from the first wedding I ever tasted one."

She shot a quick glance at the top of his head, visible over the back of the couch. "How'd you know it was mine?"

"When I photographed the cake, I noticed the double H on the back. I like how you always incorporate that into each design without it being too obvious."

He'd noticed her initials? She could count on one hand the *brides* that had noticed her signature. It was something she did for herself, so she never felt the need to point it out. "How long ago was that?"

"Umm…I think about three years ago."

"Funny we never met before I moved across the street." She set another finished petal cutout aside to dry and started the next one.

Three more lined the drying rack when Asher's voice came from the couch again. "Technically, we met at Shawn and Meisha's wedding."

"If you're getting technical, that's only half-true. I didn't know who you were until your parents' anniversary party."

Paper rustled as he turned another page.

Please stay to the front.

"Yeah, I guess you're right," he agreed.

He sounded tired, and she glanced at the clock to see it was almost ten-thirty. If he had been up since his three a.m. wake-up call, plus a full day of climbing, she understood the rasp of exhaustion in his voice. She'd probably sound the same after working late tonight and getting up early to deliver the cupcakes to Roxanna's shop by eight. But the flowers had to dry before she could paint them, and she had fifty to complete before she could call it a night.

As she envisioned the cake in her mind and the next steps to complete tomorrow, the only sound was the crinkle of turning pages every two or three completed flowers. Then she realized even that had stopped.

"I didn't want to meet you, you know."

Asher's low, mumbled words stilled her hands. She lifted her head to watch the top of his. "Because of my multiple fiancés?"

"Nope."

When he didn't elaborate, she prompted, "Then why didn't you want to meet me?"

"'Cause."

She gave him a moment before saying, "*'Cause* is the worst reason why in the history of all reasons why, Asher."

After another prolonged moment, he said, "Your cakes are so fucking awesome, I knew if you weren't some little ol' grandma, you were going to star in every one of my erotic fantasies wearing nothing but an apron."

What?

Eyes wide, she stared across the room while lifting one hand to finger the neck strap of her apron as heat flooded her whole body.

"Turns out, I was right."

Was he drunk? She didn't think so off of two beers, but—

Oh—shit.

Her heart lodged in her throat as realization hit. He found the sketch.

Okay. Deep breath. That's fine. Clearly, the feeling is mutual.

Heart thumping in her chest, she gripped the ball roller as she waited for him to turn and look at her. One sultry invitation from his gorgeous amber eyes and she'd run over and jump him before he could say, *"I want you now."*

But he didn't turn. He didn't even say another word.

Was he waiting for her to make a move?

Probably. Especially since she had been the one to shut him down last weekend. *"We're neighbors. We can't do this."* Funny thing was, the more time she spent with him, the more she kept forgetting her own argument.

Or, maybe not forgetting it, but for sure not giving a shit about it.

As she debated what to do, a light snore sounded from the couch. In the blink of an eye, all her super-charged tension drained away. Another snore made her smile, and then she outright laughed at him—and herself—as she made her way over to the couch.

Asher didn't move a muscle at her laugh, confirming he'd fallen dead asleep.

Still smiling, she eased the sketch pad off his lap, flipped it closed on a cake design for next month, and set it on the coffee table. He shifted slightly, and she studied his face for a long moment. Even when asleep, he was panty-melting pretty.

The red scrape and underlying bruise on his cheekbone shifted her ridiculous disappointment that they weren't both horizontal on the couch at the moment to concern over how he'd gotten the injury.

He'd said it was a little slip, but once or twice during the past hour or so, she'd caught a wince on his face as he shifted. Her chest constricted at the thought of him being in danger. A *little slip* didn't result in a guy looking like he'd gone a round or two with a mountain and the mountain won. If he was sore now, he'd be hurting even more in the morning.

She glanced toward the living room windows that faced his house across the street. If she was smart, she'd wake him right now so he could go home and sleep in his bed. Better for his battered body, not to mention, what would their other neighbors think when they saw his car in her driveway in the morning?

Would he care?

Did *she* care?

She should, but didn't really. More so, she liked having him here in her house with her. She'd been drawn to him from the moment she'd seen him wrapping up the pieces of cake at his friends' wedding. Once he'd stopped being a jerk —and even she had to admit his reasons for that were actually quite decent—she'd discovered not only was the guy hot, he was genuinely nice and easy to talk to.

Plus, he had awesome taste in cake and cars.

She dragged a throw blanket off the back of the couch to

spread it over him. When she leaned over to tug it up his chest, she couldn't help a wistful glance at his relaxed lips.

Extra plus—he kissed like a god. And smelled delicious, too.

She looked back up just as his lashes lifted, and she was inches away from his beautiful amber gaze. Her heart kicked hard in her chest. Confusion flickered in his expression, so she drew up one knee and sank down on the edge of the couch beside him. "Hey. You fell asleep."

He blinked hard, then pushed up to more of a sitting position before drawing his arms out from under the blanket to flip it down over his lap. "Sorry."

She smiled. "It's all my fault. I should've warned you how boring cake sketches are."

"No, the sketches were great," he argued, the corner of his mouth tugging up. "I'm just wiped from the day. How long was I out?"

"Only a few minutes. In fact, I didn't mean to wake you."

When his gaze dropped to her mouth and lingered, her slowly calming pulse shot right back into high gear. It nearly exploded from her chest when he sat forward, but instead of fulfilling her silent yearning for a kiss, he braced his elbows on his knees while scrubbing his hands over his face.

His palm over his bruised cheek made him wince as he mumbled, "It's fine. I should go anyway. I was dreaming the second my eyes closed."

"About me baking in my apron?" she dared to tease. "And nothing *but* my apron?" Her words rushed out a little breathless at the end.

He stilled, his face still buried in his hands. "I said that out loud?"

"Along with, *'Your cakes are fucking awesome.'*"

He groaned and laughed at the same time. "I thought that was part of my dream."

"Nope."

He tilted his head to peer at her, his face in his palm. "I'm sorry?"

"Don't be. But for the record—I've never baked while naked."

His eyes warmed while his mouth curved into a slow, sexy smile that made her insides quiver. That sinful smirk contradicted her claim, even if it was only in his dreams.

"Too risky?" he murmured.

"Extremely risky." She drew in a breath and willed her voice not to shake as she leaned closer. Her breasts pressed against his arm with her whispered, "But, then again, maybe it could be fun."

The warmth in his eyes gave way for blazing heat. He shifted, lifting a hand to cup the back of her neck. She loved that. His hold conveyed possession and protection at the same time. As she started to close her eyes for his kiss, his grip suddenly tightened the tiniest bit, and he pulled back with a quick shake of his head.

"Before we do this, I want to take you to dinner."

Her pulse thrilled with the surety *this* meant more than a kiss, and she tilted her head toward the almost empty box on the table. "You brought pizza. And beer."

His other hand came up to palm her face. He ran his thumb along her bottom lip, his hungry gaze tracking the movement. "Not good enough. It has to be a real dinner. A real date. You dress up, I'll drive, we'll go to a nice restaurant, have dessert, the whole nine yards."

It sounded nice—great even—but her whole body yearned for his right now. She bit back a small hum of frustration. "Why?"

"Because I want more than sex."

So do I.

Honor swallowed hard at that voice in her head that kept

whispering things she knew better than to hope for. Except, lately, her foolish heart cheered the insolent little bitch every time.

The softened look in Asher's eyes made her suspect he'd read her mind, but before she could say anything, he closed the distance between them and captured her mouth with his. His lips were soft yet firm against hers, the kiss kinda sweet and a little cautious.

It was nice, but nowhere near as hot and passionate as the other night. Nice, but nowhere near as satisfying.

She leaned forward, pushing up onto her knees to get closer, winding one arm around his neck while threading her other hand through his thick, dark hair. She twined the strands around her fingers, loving the softness against her skin.

When she scraped her nails against his scalp, his low, sexy groan made her want more. With him, it was always more.

Tilting her head, she opened her mouth to deepen the kiss. He took the invitation and ran with it, his tongue snaking in to stroke against hers. Each parry and retreat built the heat between them, and he rose up with her before laying her back on the couch. With her knee drawn up against the back cushion, she moaned her approval when his weight pressed her into the cushions as he reclaimed her mouth.

Rock hard muscles branded her thighs and her breasts, and every inch in between. She hooked her leg over his hip, aching to get closer while she explored the planes of his back before sliding her hands down to the tight globes of his ass.

He tore his mouth from hers, his labored breath hot against her cheek. "I really should go."

But even as he spoke the words, his lips skimmed along her jaw, and he moved lower to nip her neck. A light suck and lick of his tongue shot red-hot desire straight to her core. She arched her hips up against the steel length of his arousal with a wanton whimper.

His guttural groan vibrated against her chest and neck.

"Fuck, Honor."

"Yes. Good plan," she panted.

He gave another groan. The scruff on his chin scraped the swell of her breast when he nuzzled the neckline of her shirt out of the way. "Geezus, you smell good enough to eat."

Yes.

When his teeth nipped at her skin, her core clenched hard. She reached back and underneath to unhook her bra, only to have him chase his hand after hers to stop it. Fingers gripping hers, he huffed out a breath as he laid his bristled cheek right over her heart. His thumped fast against her ribs in perfect sync.

"I meant what I said." Frustration roughened his voice. Or maybe it was regret.

It was her turn to huff out a heavy sigh. "I know you did. And I should be mad at you for it, but I can't be."

He lifted his head. "Why would you be mad?"

"Because you're going to leave me wanting more. Again." When his eyebrows rose in question, she said, "After that first kiss, after our phone call. *Now.* It's made for some very long nights."

He stared at her for a long moment, his gaze molten hot. "You don't do anything to…take the edge off?"

Heat flooded her face. "No." Though she'd thought about it. "Did you?"

"Um…"

She arched her eyebrows even as her body flushed at the thought of him stroking himself while thinking of her. "Each time?"

"Just after the phone call. It was late, and in my mind you

were baking. In your apron." She grinned as he added, "I was tired, and a cold shower would've woken me the hell up."

"You don't have to justify."

He shrugged with a cute little grin.

"Cold showers don't work the same for women," she complained, not quite sure what else to say as he still lay on top of her even though he was adamant *this* wasn't going to happen tonight. "At least I don't think so."

"Probably not," he agreed. He leaned down to kiss the tip of her nose, then captured her mouth in a long, slow, deep kiss that left her gasping for breath and writhing beneath him.

Damn his good-guy sense of honor.

He trailed his lips down the side of her neck, and she arched her head back to give him better access. As she struggled to fill her lungs while his lips and tongue erased the word *neighbor* from her vocabulary, his weight lifted from her body.

She moaned her protest, but then his hot breath against her ear sent a delicious shiver down her spine as he kneeled beside the couch.

"I know something that could work."

It took a moment for the husky words to register in her dazed brain. "Work for what?"

He nipped her earlobe and spoke with it between his teeth. "To take the edge off."

Her heart leapt as he traced the shell of her ear with his tongue while skimming his hand down over her belly to the elastic band of her leggings.

And just like that, she lost her breath all over again.

CHAPTER 19

*a*sher brushed his hand over the soft, silky skin of Honor's belly below her navel. The wide waistband of her leggings barred his access. Her stomach quivered beneath his touch as he swirled the tip of his tongue around the rapid pulse at the base of her throat.

"Yes or no?" he rasped against her skin, his breath short with anticipation.

Please say yes. Please.

He needed something to tide himself over until their dinner. Because he was a fucking idiot for not taking all she was offering right now.

Her breath came in shallow spurts as her fingers threaded through his hair. "I didn't say that to make you feel like you have to—"

"Oh, Honor, I want to," he interrupted. "I want to so *very* much."

"Then, yes," she whispered.

He rose up just enough to capture those delectable lips as he slipped his hand inside her pants. His dick throbbed when he felt how wet she was. Because of him. *For* him. The first graze of his finger between her folds drew a breathless gasp from her throat. He stroked his tongue deep into her mouth with each caress over her clit, all the while noting what moves elicited the best response.

As he increased speed and pressure, her hips bucked against his hand. A slight shift and he slid one finger inside her. When he added a second and rubbed his thumb over her swollen nub, her back arched on a low, drawn out moan, head thrown back.

"Oh…*God*…that feels good," she panted. "*So good.*"

The almost painful clench of her fingers in his hair turned him on even more. He stroked in and out, curling his fingers to hit just the right spot as his thumb played her clit.

"*Asher.*"

His name fell from her lips as a plea. It was the sexiest fucking thing he'd ever heard in his life. He couldn't wait to hear it again when he was buried to the hilt inside her.

One more circle of his thumb, a little extra pressure, and she detonated in his arms. He lifted his lashes to watch her come apart, and wondered again why the fuck he'd insisted on dinner first?

The answer was swift. Because with her, he really did want more than sex. She was worth the wait. She was worth the cold shower.

Oh, hell, who was he kidding? He was going to memorize this moment and use it as he took the edge off himself later.

Her eyes were closed as he withdrew his hand, smoothed her pants, and pressed a gentle kiss to her soft mouth.

"Wow," she breathed. The dark fan of her lashes lifted on her languid green eyes and a very satisfied grin curved her lips. "Thank you."

He gave a soft laugh. "You're welcome, and *thank you.* How's seven tomorrow for dinner?"

Regret drew her eyebrows down in a frown. "I can't do tomorrow. I have to finish this cake."

"Friday?"

She lifted a hand to palm his face, expression contrite. "I'm sorry, but I need every moment before I deliver the cake Saturday afternoon. But after *that*, I'm free for the evening, and all of Sunday before two-cake hell-week starts."

Holy blue balls, man. That was three whole days away.

"I'm really sorry," she repeated with a sheepish little grin tugging at her mouth.

"Don't apologize." He drew in a deep, fortifying breath and dropped a quick peck on her lips. "Saturday it is."

When he pushed to his feet and started to go, she flipped over and scrambled to her knees while reaching over the arm of the couch to catch his hand. "You're leaving?"

"Yes."

Her gaze dropped to his crotch and blood surged straight to his still-rock-hard erection. "You don't want me to—"

He leaned down and smothered her words with a hard kiss. If he heard that offer from her tempting lips, he'd be unzipping his jeans in two seconds flat. "Sweet dreams, Butter Cream."

"Butter Cream?" she sputtered as he strode away.

"Yep," he tossed over his shoulder while opening the door. "It's my favorite."

Frosting was not a satisfying substitute for sex, but by Friday afternoon, it was the best option Asher had since he didn't trust himself to go over by Honor's *and* keep his hands to himself. He'd texted both days since Wednesday night, because he'd wanted to let her know he was thinking of her, and each time she'd sent back cute replies. Cheeky replies. Replies that made him want to run across the street to see her smile and hear her laugh. Taste her lips and touch her in ways that made her entire body tremble in his arms.

So yeah, he was on day two of Operation Stay Away Until Saturday. Which meant after biking fifteen miles, cutting the grass, and finishing up the last of the digital photo edits for the climbing school brochure, he'd had to come down to Lift Your Spirit to get his sugar fix.

Normally, he'd say five dollars for a cupcake was highway robbery, but Honor's were worth every penny plus tax.

Over by the café tables, Darcy finished sweeping and wiping up, and picked up her cleaning supplies tote to carry to the back office. "All set here. Anything else before I go?" she asked Roxanna.

"Nope. Thanks, and I'll see you Tuesday. Have a good weekend."

"You, too. See ya, Asher."

With his mouth full of the last bite of fix number two, Asher gave the bubbly, part-time blond a nod and grin before turning back to Rox. He washed the cupcake down with a swig of coffee while she unpacked another Himalayan salt lamp from her most recent order. He'd been listening to her bitch and moan about her frustrations with office paperwork and her hatred of balancing her profit and loss sheets, but with Darcy gone, she gave him a sideways glance.

"Have you talked to your parents lately?"

"Not since brunch last Sunday. They've been busy with the campaign. Why?"

She carried the lamp to an empty display spot and plugged it in. "I was getting a weird vibe at the party."

"Wasn't that from Honor?"

"No, this was different."

Something odd in her tone set him on edge. Asher tilted

his head with a slight frown when she came back to get another lamp. "What do you mean?"

"It's hard to explain," she said. "I was just curious if you'd heard anything from your mom or dad this week."

"About what?"

"I don't know." Exasperation tinged her voice. "You know it doesn't work that way."

"Yeah, well, they would've called if I needed to know anything important."

"You're right." She met his gaze and offered a brief, reassuring smile before taking the lamp in her hands to the left side of the shop this time. "It was probably nothing. There was a lot going on that night."

"That there was," he agreed. And yet, his stomach gave another uneasy roll. Because nothing was ever *nothing* with Roxanna.

"So...dinner with Honor tomorrow," she said in an obvious change of subject. "Where are you taking her?"

"I have a couple places in mind," he said vaguely.

She twisted slightly to look at him. After a long moment, she turned back to adjusting the lamp. "Go with option number two."

He narrowed his gaze. "You have no idea where I'm even thinking of."

"I got a feeling. Just trust me."

"We'll see," he muttered. But he would trust her. He'd been leaning toward that one anyway.

The store's lone customer approached the counter, and having helped here and there in the past, Asher rang up the sale with a friendly smile, then pulled the last two lamps from the packing box and set them next to the register for Roxanna to take care of.

It was just the two of them again, so he boosted himself up to sit on the counter and took another drink of coffee to fortify himself for his change of subject. "I have some news for you."

Roxanna made a face as she joined him at the counter. "I don't want to hear this any more than you want to tell me."

Spot on.

"What makes you say that?" he bluffed.

She rolled her eyes as if he'd asked a stupid question. "Besides your voice being all ominous, your aura is all over the place, Ace. When I asked you about dinner with Honor, you were all light yellow optimism, and red sexual energy, with a little bit of lovey-dovey pink. But I could tell the moment you started thinking about your *news*. Everything shifted blue—and not the good shades."

"Damn, you're good."

"That goes without saying," she quipped with a smirk. "Just spit it out already."

"I talked to Loyal earlier."

The mention of his older brother brought forth a frown and muttered, "Explains the shitty blue shades."

"After he finishes his current audit project with our uncle's company in Texas, he's moving back to Colorado. Probably in time for Christmas."

With one hand on the counter, she braced her other on her hip. Her long, brunette curls slipped over her shoulder as she tipped her head to the right. "And I care about this why?"

He went for levity to try to ease the tension. "Well, for one, I know you have a thing for him, and two—"

"I do *not* have a thing for your jackass brother."

"Sure you do," he teased, waggling a finger in front of her face. "You're not the only one who can intuit things."

She batted his hand away and glared at him. "The only *thing* I have for Loyal is an intense desire to never see him again."

Asher cringed as he ran his finger along the seam of his cup. "That might be a little difficult."

Suspicion deepened her frown. "Why?"

"I told him he could use the second floor apartment."

"*This* second floor apartment?" She jabbed a finger toward the ceiling.

"Do you know of any others I own?"

Un-amused by his light joke, she huffed out a breath as her shoulders slumped. "But why in the world would he stay here? Why not with you, or your parents? Or a hotel, for that matter?"

Asher scoffed as he slid off the counter. "He's not going to move back home at thirty-one, Rox. And my mom would be hurt if he stayed in a hotel."

"Fine. Then tell him to buy his own place. It's not like he can't afford it."

"He will. This would only be temporary—if he even uses it at all. I just wanted to give you advance warning that it could happen. You know, in like six months. Maybe."

She made another annoyed face, then all of a sudden her eyes widened and relief filled her expression. "This is it."

"What?"

"This is the weird vibe from the party. I thought it was from your parents, but it was because of Loyal." Just saying his name brought back her frown. "God, he really is a jackass."

"You so want him," he teased.

Her fist slammed into his bicep. "Shut. Up."

"Ow." He rubbed his still sore shoulder—plus, she packed a wallop.

"I mean it, Asher. There better not be another word about it out of your mouth. Ever."

He'd been joking, but she sounded angry. Or maybe upset was the better word. He raised his left hand while using his right to draw an X over his heart in a promise of silence. Her fierce glare before she walked away had him wondering if she was protesting *too* much.

The joy that sparked when Loyal told him he was moving home made him realize how much he'd missed having him around the past four years. There had been a twinge of anxiety when he thought of the hostility between his brother and his best friend, but now he was left wondering if the hate Rox seemed to harbor for Loyal was hiding something else?

That worried him more than their animosity. Rox's capacity for love would make whoever won her over a very lucky man. He wanted her to find the happiness she deserved, but Loyal was more likely to break her heart than cherish it.

Speaking of which, how would Honor handle *his* heart? She hadn't used the argument about them being neighbors since their first kiss. In fact, she hadn't used any argument against them having a relationship since their first kiss, and tomorrow they'd go to dinner and hopefully more. Would she someday admit what they had could last, or was he leaving himself wide open for a world of hurt?

CHAPTER 20

"*A*nd then he just left?"

"Yep," Honor confirmed. "Walked out and hasn't knocked on my door since."

"Why am I just hearing about this three days later?" Mae turned her face into the breeze as she reached up to dislodge a strand of hair stuck to her lips. "We need to talk more often."

"We'd both have to be less busy." She leaned against the side of her friend's truck outside the house of her current kitchen remodel. With the sun shining down on their Saturday morning coffee break, her petite friend looked cute in her red company logo shirt, jeans, leather tool belt, and brown, steel-toed work boots.

"True, but you gotta call me with this kind of stuff. Especially if he starts ghosting you afterward." Indignation sharpened her tone.

"Oh, no, sorry. He's texted each day, but I thought for sure he'd stop by again."

Hoped he'd stop by, because it seemed her Asher addiction was a real thing. Expected him to stop by because, clearly, she was a *sure* thing.

"You'd think," Mae agreed, "but then again, you did tell him you had to work."

"I didn't think it would keep him completely away. Other stuff aside, it was fun talking to him while I worked." His sexy voice was ten times better than music.

"He probably doesn't trust himself not to sling you over his shoulder to ravish in your bedroom."

"Yeah, right." Though just imagining that scenario sent a giddy wave of heat through her body.

"I'm serious." Mae's smile softened. "He respects you. That's sweet."

"It is, but it's also frustrating when I know he fantasizes about me baking naked." Right now, she wanted the fantasy, not the respect.

No, you don't.

No, she didn't.

Well, she did, but she didn't. Yes, the man had rocked her world with just his fingers and his mouth, and in true Asher fashion, left her wanting more. But, his texts had been thoughtful, playful, and even the sassier ones had been kind of romantic. Every time her phone alerted an incoming text, her pulse sped up and her heart smiled. She was like Pavlov's dog expecting a treat.

"He totally gets points for not acting on that fantasy when you would've let him," Mae pointed out. "I will say though, as much as I want to hear these things, maybe keep the naked baking to yourself. That's an image I don't want in my head when I walk into your kitchen."

"I told you about the couch, and the *kitchen* is the image you don't want?"

Mae shrugged.

Honor laughed as she added, "If it helps, he said I'm wearing my apron."

"Nope." She gave a shudder. "That's even worse."

"How is that worse?"

"Because I just tried to figure out if the apron covers everything."

"It doesn't. I got curious myself."

Mae planted her free hand on her hip, nose scrunched. "Why would you tell me that?"

Honor fought a grin. "No secrets between friends?"

"Fine. If that's the case, I'm going to need to see your sketch of Asher."

"Oh, hell no. I'm not sharing that with you after you flooded my driveway with drool last weekend."

"Don't make me revoke best friend status."

Honor ignored the warning finger pointed in her direction. "You won't revoke anything. Dinner is tonight."

"Ooh." Her eyes brightened. "I'm going to need you to call me tomorrow with all the sexy details."

Honor arched her brows. "*Need* me to?"

"Hey, I told you, hearing about your sex life is the best I got these days."

"So far, it's only the potential for a renewed sex life," she cautioned.

"Please. If that man doesn't have *you* for dessert tonight I'll eat my work boot."

Anticipation tickled her stomach. "He's picking me up at seven. He said to dress up for the—and I quote—*whole nine yards.*"

"Nice. And then afterwards..." Mae waggled her eyebrows with a sassy grin.

Afterwards, neighbor-schmeibor and respect be damned. She was going to seduce him with her cupcakes—and not the ones she'd baked this morning. After the taste he'd given her Wednesday night, she wanted all of him tonight.

Every. Single. Inch.

Honor turned sideways in the mirror, smoothing her palms over her fluttery stomach as her gaze traveled the length of her classic black dress, down to her black heels. Sleeveless, with a high neckline, the dress was fitted in the bust, torso, and waist, and had a slight flare in the skirt that swirled around her legs just below her knees.

Asher had refused to answer her text asking where they were going, but unless it was some sort of formal event, this would suffice for pretty much anywhere. The evenings were still cooler for the end of May, so she grabbed her new, rust colored shawl from the dresser when she heard the faint sound of the Camaro's engine roaring to life across the street.

Her stomach went from fluttery to whirlwind as she made her way down the stairs. Of course, her mom would say to make him wait, don't seem too eager, but she'd been waiting to see him again for three days. Besides, making a man stand out on the front porch had always seemed rude to her—especially if they were on time.

Which he was.

Heart pounding hard, she walked to the door after Asher's knock and then promptly lost her breath when she opened the door to his gorgeous smile.

"Hey," he greeted.

"Hey back," she managed, surprised her voice sounded mostly normal. Then she just stared, taking in his stylishly mussed hair, scruff-dusted jaw, forest green dress shirt, black pants, and polished shoes. He looked so good. Better than—

A bouquet of yellow-orange Gerber daisies suddenly filled her vision, and she blinked to refocus her attention. She took them and lifted her gaze to his. The heat in his amber eyes warmed her from the inside out.

"Thank you," she murmured, stepping aside for him to come in. "I'll just put them in some water before we go."

When he drew even with her, she moved to close the door, but he caught her around the waist and tugged her against him from hip to chest. Surprise jerked her head up as his dipped and his mouth crushed against hers.

The door was forgotten as she wound her free arm around his neck and pulled herself closer. His tongue swept inside her mouth, searching and exploring, his teeth scraping and nipping until she whimpered with mindless pleasure and dropped the flowers to cling to him with both arms. Moments later, he pushed her up against the wall and leaned his forehead against hers. His palm gently cupped the side of her face as his thumb brushed her cheek.

Their labored breath heated the air between them as he whispered, "Sorry. I didn't give you much warning there, did I?"

"Hmm," she hummed, thankful his firm body offered support for her weak knees. "Never apologize for a kiss like that."

"I couldn't help myself. It was torture not seeing your beautiful face these past three days, and then you opened the door, and there you were, in this dress." He skimmed his hand from her face, to her shoulder, down over her ribs, to the curve of her waist.

Damn, the man was good.

Acutely aware of his hard length against her belly, she twirled her fingers in his hair at the nape of his neck. "Maybe you shouldn't have stayed away."

"I didn't want to bother you. You had a cake to finish."

"I did, but now it's all done and delivered."

"Will the bride and groom be happy?"

"Very happy. And you bothered me anyway."

"How?"

"I thought dirty thoughts of you every time I taste-tested the batter."

He growled from deep in his throat and his fingers dug into her hips, pulling her closer. "Why would you say that before we've even left for the restaurant?"

"Sorry."

"Never *ever* apologize for dirty thoughts of me. Now, let's spark some dirty thoughts of *us*."

She smiled as he tilted his head to capture her lips again. By the time he dragged his mouth from hers, she was ready to say the hell with dinner and skip straight to dessert. She had a small, leftover pastry bag of his favorite frosting in the fridge they could share in creative ways.

"I should not have done that before we left," he admitted, his voice low and rough. "But this right here is exactly why I had to stay away."

Heart racing in her chest, she reached down past his leather belt and palmed his erection through his dress pants. "Are you sure you're going to make it through dinner?"

His Adam's apple bobbed with his audible gulp. "My doubts are increasing by the second."

She arched her eyebrows in question, and he pushed away from her with a guttural groan. His hooded gaze swept down the length of her before he spun around and raised both arms to rake his hands through his hair.

"There's a reason why I wanted to take you to dinner first."

Honor stepped up behind him and wrapped her arms around his waist. "Tell me."

He quickly lowered his arms so his hands covered hers on his firm stomach. "Uh…gimmie a sec."

She loved knowing she made him this hot and bothered.

He thwarted her attempt to slide her hands lower by

threading their fingers together as he answered, "Romance. Respect. Seduction."

"You've already covered all three, Asher. Promise."

He squeezed her fingers. "I booked a reservation."

"Cancel it."

He hesitated long enough she thought he might agree, but then he said, "I want to do this right."

Of course he did. He was a long-haul guy. Ignoring the way her stomach bottomed out at that thought, she teased, "After Wednesday, I have no doubt you'll do it right."

"Geezus, Honor." He hung his head with a low, laughing groan.

After a deep breath, he turned around in her arms. She thought she'd convinced him they could skip dinner, until she met his gaze. Desire blazed hot and heady, but it was tempered by the uncertain frown drawing his dark eyebrows down over his amber eyes.

She sighed, then tilted her head as she stepped back. "You really want to go to dinner first?"

"At this precise moment, no." He shot a glance toward her stairs, then returned his turbulent gaze to hers. "But…"

"But you actually do." She nodded, oddly touched he was sticking to his guns even though her body buzzed with sexual frustration from head to toe. "Okay, then. Let's go."

"You're not mad?" he asked with a touch of suspicion.

"That you won't take me upstairs right now?" She laughed softly. "No, I'm not mad. However, fair warning. You will pay for turning me on and before taking me out. You've left me wanting more, Asher. *Again.*"

She pivoted with a swish of her skirt, then bent to pick up the flowers from the floor, making sure he had a bird's-eye view of her ass. His whimper-groan made her smile.

Asher Diamond was in a league of his own when compared to every single one of Honor's previous dates ever. Forget smokin' hot. He was honorable. Sweet. Smart. Fun.

Also, a complete gentleman well skilled at the subtle art of romance. He'd offered his arm out to the car, opened her door both in the driveway and at the restaurant, helped with her chair, and traced his finger back and forth across the back of her hand with the candlelight flickering between them as they finished their wine.

But most impressive by far, was the way he listened. She'd noticed it the other night while frosting the cake, too. His attention didn't waver, his eyes lit with interest, and he even asked follow up questions.

The entire night confirmed he wasn't just looking for an easy lay—he could've had that already. More than once. They'd both left their phones in the car, and with his undivided attention, she couldn't remember the last time someone had gone out of their way to make sure she felt special.

If she were of the foolish sort to believe in love, she'd be in real danger.

For once, that voice in her head remained mute. Instead of relief, the silence left an uneasy feeling in her stomach as the waiter dropped off the check and Asher reached to sign. No, it wasn't unease—it was the result of hyper-sensitivity to every single thing the man did in the low-lit, intimate atmosphere of the small dining room.

She'd warned him he'd pay for making her wait—and she'd had her moments of retaliation—but he'd upped the seduction level with each smoldering glance, the soft caress of his fingertips on her bare shoulder when she sat, and the side of her calf when he picked up her dropped napkin. Though, that one might have been as hard on him as it had been on her.

She took a final sip of her wine as Asher set aside the bill and lifted his warm gaze to hers. "All set to go."

The low, seductive tone of his voice shortened her breath with anticipation as she moved her napkin from her lap to the table. He came around to the back of her chair and draped her shawl over her shoulders. The gentleman. One hand settled on her shoulder, while the other trailed from her collarbone to the back of her neck, pulling her hair back so he could bend down to press a kiss at the crook of her neck. Now the seducer.

Cool air replaced his lips, and she shivered as he pulled out her chair. He rested his hand at the small of her back on their way from the restaurant to the bar. Suddenly, she was warm all over again.

She absently glanced toward the large television in the far corner of the bar as she said, "I'm going to use the restroom before we go."

"I'll wait here."

She felt the heat of his gaze until the door closed behind her. When she exited the stall, she took an extra minute after washing her hands to speed-brush her teeth and reapply her lip gloss. Back out in the bar, her gaze instinctively sought Asher.

He glanced her way, but then jerked his head back for a double take of the television. She noticed his entire body stiffen, and when she reached him, her pulse skipped at his ashen expression. He looked like he'd seen a ghost.

She moved closer, her heart pounding in trepidation as she followed his gaze to see a preview of the ten o'clock news playing on the TV. When she saw the image on the screen and read the headline below, her jaw went slack with shock.

CHAPTER 21

"*N*ews at ten—*Grayson Cole, the secret son Governor Diamond doesn't want his voters or his wife to know about.*"

Asher stared at the face plastered on the TV screen and kept staring even after the preview ended and some insipid reality dating show came back on.

What the ever-loving-fuck?

A soft touch on his arm made him flinch, and he looked down into Honor's green eyes wide with concern.

"Who was that?"

He saw the man's face in his mind's eye. The image on the TV had looked like Loyal. And he'd even seen some of his other siblings in the features, too. But he'd never seen the guy before in his life.

Honor's fingers squeezed his arm and he blinked to bring her face back into focus. He couldn't think here, surrounded by people and noise and all the questions whirling around in his head.

"Let's go." He took her hand and tugged her toward the exit.

She pulled against his hold once they were outside in the parking lot. "Asher."

The apprehension in her voice hit him square in the gut. When he realized she'd been trotting in her heels to keep up, he immediately slowed his stride. "Sorry."

"It's okay."

He shook his head. No, it wasn't. This was supposed to be a perfect first date for him to lay the foundation for their future. Instead, he was reeling from a bombshell he never saw coming and had no clue how to handle. He felt like an ass, but everything felt unreal at the moment.

It's not true.

And yet, he couldn't erase the guy's face from his memory.

When he opened the passenger door for Honor, she hesitated before getting in the Camaro. "Do you know him? Is he really your brother?"

"No." The curt, single word answered both questions.

Sympathy softened her gaze. "Do you want me to drive? Are you okay?"

He took a deep breath and attempted a smile. "I'm fine."

After one more moment of her gaze searching his, she slid into the passenger seat. His hand clenched on the door handle to keep from slamming it shut. It wasn't her fault, damn it. He didn't want to be a jerk to her. He strode around the back for the driver's side, confusion, anger, and uncertainty warring inside his chest as he rubbed his neck before yanking open his door to get in.

Silence sat heavy while he gripped the steering wheel. He wanted to focus on Honor, their evening together, and how much he liked her and wanted her in his life for years to come, but all he could fucking think about was that clip on the TV. Raw fear of the unknown had struck his heart cold when he'd seen that man's face on the screen.

Grayson Cole.

He looked like a Diamond.

Plenty of people have look-a-likes without any blood relation at all.

"Could it be true?" Honor asked softly.

"No," he denied roughly.

No fucking way I've got a brother I don't know about. None of us knew about.

That would mean his father cheated. That would mean his parents' marriage was nothing but a farce. That would mean they'd lied to him and his brothers and sisters for the past thirty-some years.

Diamonds don't divorce.

They didn't cheat either. Their love was true and lasting. His mom and dad *were* soul mates.

"Maybe you should call your parents."

He jerked his head toward Honor at the uncanny timing of her suggestion and saw her reaching into the glove box where they'd both left their phones during dinner.

"It's because of the campaign," he rationalized when she handed him his cell. His fingers clenched on it as he worked up possibilities in his head. "It's never been this bad, but my dad's opponents *have* done this kind of crap before. It's a common tactic these days. The other side feeds the media a lie to ruin his reputation, and they run with it without checking a single damn fact."

"Maybe."

He cut his gaze to hers. "Why do you say it like that?"

Her eyebrows pinched together as she bit her bottom lip. "The resemblance was—"

"No," he bit out. "Don't say it."

She didn't. But then again, she didn't have to.

The resemblance was uncanny. Especially to Loyal.

When her resigned sigh filled the silence, he fisted his

free hand on his thigh as he looked over at her. "Honor, I'm sorry. I don't mean—"

"Don't apologize," she cut him off with a shake of her head. "I get it. Everything is turned completely upside down right now. You need to call your parents and see what is going on."

He sure as hell did.

"Or, let's drive over there. They're only a few minutes from here, right?"

"I need to take you home first." As he said the words, he finally looked down at his phone and saw he had sixteen new texts in the past hour. Pretty much from everyone in his immediate family, Roxanna, and a few other friends.

"*Fuck,*" he whispered under his breath.

Honor reached over to grasp his arm. "Asher, let's just go to your parents' house right now. I'll call a ride service to get home. This isn't something that should wait."

He didn't want to agree, and yet at her insistence, he found himself starting the car and driving the couple miles to his childhood home. After passing a number of news vans out by the gate, he pulled up to the house to find numerous vehicles in the driveway. From his siblings'—excluding Loyal who was back in Texas—to his grandfather's, to the Explorer his dad's campaign manager drove. Then there was the red sedan that belonged to the head of the press team.

Someone was going to earn their salary tonight. Or get fired. Might be a toss-up as to which one.

He spotted Merit sitting on the brick half-wall of the formal front porch, tumbler in hand. Straight whiskey, no doubt. Shelby leaned against the brick next to him, a beer raised to her lips. His stomach knotted. Great. Merit was one thing, but if Bells was drinking, it was bad.

Both turned to watch while he parked and hurried around to Honor's side. She'd already gotten out and stood beside the car. She glanced at his brother and sister by the house, then tipped her head up to meet his gaze.

"Do you want me to stay? Is there any way I can help?"

His chest swelled at her offer. He stepped closer, grasping her free hand as the madness of the past fifteen minutes shifted sideways and she took center stage. "You've already helped. And I would *love* for you to stay, but I don't want the crazy in there"—he gestured toward the house—"to run you off before we have our second date, so it is probably best if you go home."

"Your family's crazy couldn't hold a candle to mine," she argued.

"I'm not willing to chance it."

He noticed the front door open and turned to see Celia and Robert step out to join the other two on the porch.

"You're sure?" Honor asked as they both stared toward the house.

"No, but yeah."

He returned his gaze to her and saw her lips curve up into a gentle, surprisingly understanding smile. Man, he wished he could just go home with her. Get lost in Honor and forget all this shit.

She squeezed his hand, then pulled away to swipe the screen on her phone. He stopped her by pressing the keys to his Camaro into her palm. Her lashes lifted, green eyes wide.

When she began to shake her head no, he insisted, "Yes. I'll get a ride home from Merit."

"I am not taking your car."

"You said you wanted to drive it."

"Not like this." She tried to give the keys back. "Not without you."

"I trust you, Honor. And I'll feel much better having you drive the Camaro home than riding with a stranger." They had a long moment of silent standoff before she finally gave in. Asher gave a subdued smile in victory. "The garage door opener is in the glove box, and then all you have to do is lock the service door on your way out."

"I'll be very careful with it," she promised.

"As long as you get home safe, that's all that matters." He walked her around to the open driver's side door.

Instead of getting in, she stepped forward and wrapped her arms around his waist while pressing her cheek to his chest. He automatically closed his arms around her, and then tightened his hold when her warmth seeped in to calm the rough edges of his frayed nerves.

"Let me know if you need anything," she said. "Pizza and beer, a piece of cake, a shoulder to lean on…"

Emotion swelled again and he pressed his lips to the top of her head. "I will. Thank you."

Up on the porch, Merit stood to give him a dark glare while he jerked his head toward the house.

He reluctantly released Honor so she could slide into the driver's seat. As soon as the door closed, he motioned for her to roll down the window, then leaned in to give her a quick kiss that lingered.

He eased back a few inches to meet her gaze, and she laid her palm against his cheek. "I mean it, Asher. It doesn't matter if it's the middle of the night or twelve noon."

After a single nod, he pressed one last kiss to her lips, then straightened and stepped back while sliding his hands into his pockets. "Send me a text when you're home?"

"I will." She cut her somber gaze toward the house as she rolled up the window. "Good luck."

He nodded and forced a smile as she left, but when he turned to face the house, it vanished in a blink. He was definitely going to need that luck—and a drink.

CHAPTER 22

*I*t was after three a.m. when Asher paid the cab driver and keyed his code into the lock box for the garage door. Merit had been in no shape to drive, not to mention, he'd had enough of his entire family for one night. The cab driver had been blessedly silent the entire ride, and he'd tipped the guy an extra ten.

As the door cranked up, Asher surveyed Honor's house across the street. Save for the porch light, the rest of her place was dark. Nothing like when she'd been up baking the other nights, or his house, where he'd noticed when the cab pulled up that she'd left the recessed lights in his kitchen on for his return.

Disappointment darkened his mood more as he turned away, though he knew it was for the best. He'd be horrible company after finding out the fundamental beliefs drummed into him all his life were lies. Turned out Diamonds *did* divorce. They lied. They cheated. And his dad had a kid that no one fucking knew about for thirty-one gol-damn years.

Betrayal came roaring back as he yanked open the door

leading to the kitchen and then slammed it shut behind him. Directly on the heels of the loud boom he heard a surprised exclamation and saw a flash of movement from his shadowed living room.

He stopped short when he recognized the figure sitting up on his couch, red hair spilling about her shoulders. The dim light from the kitchen barely lit her features.

"Honor? What are you doing here?" Confusion creased his brow even as his heart thumped hard with the sheer pleasure of seeing her. Anger drained away fast, leaving him feeling raw and oddly exposed in a way he'd never experienced before.

She hastily brushed her hair back from her face as she stood, then gestured toward his coffee table with a jerky motion. "I baked a cake. I was worried, and I couldn't sleep, and I bake when I'm worked up, so I made it and brought it over. I thought I'd wait for you to make sure you were okay, and I fell asleep."

He stared across the room at the dark shape in the middle of the table. "You baked me a cake."

"Yes." She smoothed her palms over her hips, then crossed one arm over the other on her stomach. "How did everything go? Are you doing okay?"

"No." There was a lump in his throat that made it hard to say more. Where the hell had that come from?

"Do you want to talk about it?"

Still staring at the cake, Asher shook his head. He needed a mental break from the past couple hours.

"Okay." She started to move away from the couch toward the front door. "Then I won't bother you. I'll—"

"No."

He raised his gaze to hers, emotion swelling in his chest, burning his eyes. Abruptly, he turned to grab two forks from the silverware drawer, then joined her in the living room and silently handed her one.

She took it and backed up to sit on the edge of the couch. He dropped his ass to the floor and leaned back against the seat cushion while digging in and scooping up a forkful of what looked like double layer chocolate. He shoved it in his mouth as Honor reached to do the same.

Decadent flavor exploded on his tongue—rich dark chocolate soaked in moist caramel with creamy chocolate frosting. It was the best fucking cake he'd ever had.

On the second bite, he raised one knee to rest his forearm between forkfuls. He stared unseeing across the unlit room while the frosting melted in his mouth, making his taste buds sing. His shoulder rested against her knee, his arm against the side of her leg. The physical contact helped ground him, slowing the thoughts whirling in his head.

Four bites in, he opened his mouth but instead of shoveling cake inside, words spilled out. "I have another brother. Or half-brother." That sounded weird out loud in his own voice. "His name is Grayson Cole. He's thirty-one. Lives in Boulder."

The information was coming out in bite size sentences. Bite, chew, swallow.

Choke. Not on the cake, but the words.

"He's three months older than Loyal, so technically, he's the oldest of us all." He ate another bite. "News flash—literally—my parents divorced a couple years after they got married. Just not officially *legally*. They were separated for six months and were *going* to divorce, but the night they signed the papers, my dad went out and got drunk and had himself a one night stand who ended up getting pregnant." His lip curled in disdain. "He said the next day, he realized he still loved my mom, and begged her to take him back, so they never filed the final papers."

On speaker phone from Texas, Loyal had argued it wasn't cheating since they'd been separated for so long and the papers signed. Merit agreed. Big shocker there.

He, Shelby, Celia and Robert were on the opposite side. Until the divorce was one hundred percent legal, the marriage vows were sacred. They'd all argued the semantics while Dad and Mom and the campaign staff were yelling at each other in the other room.

"Did he know?" Honor asked quietly, hesitantly. "Did either of them know about..."

He shook his head. "No. That news report was as much a shock to him as everyone else. The woman—*Vivian*—never told him." He spat the name out, his hand fisted on his upraised knee. "He said he never saw her again after that night. He didn't even remember her name until his press team read the details from the news."

"Wow. So, why now? I mean, I assume it's because of the politics, but your dad's been through two governors races, so why not then?"

"We've all asked that question tonight. Just don't have an answer yet."

After a moment of quiet, she murmured, "That is a huge secret for thirty-one years. It's crazy."

He barked out a humorless laugh. "I told you."

"I didn't mean it against your family," she said gently. "More so the fact this woman never told your dad about the baby, and didn't ask for child support or anything."

"The worst part is, I feel so bad for my mom. She's devastated." Because she'd been lied to for thirty-one years. His sense of betrayal was nothing compared to the pain he'd seen in her eyes tonight. "Now, she has to go through all this shit with the public watching and judging."

Honor's hand landed on his shoulder to give a gentle squeeze. "I'm sorry, Asher. This can't be easy on any of you."

That was an understatement.

"We knew the media scrutiny would be brutal with his senate campaign," he spoke around another mouthful of cake, "and it being a national seat instead of state, but none of us expected something like *this*. It changes everything. My whole family is going to be different from this."

His fork clattered when he dropped it onto the edge of the cake plate with an angry jerk. "Makes me want to punch something. Or someone. My dad maybe. The brother I should've known and grown up with, even though I know it's not his fault. His mother, because I *know* it's her fault, but of course, can't hit a woman." Hearing the sarcasm in his voice, he scrubbed his hands over his face, the scruff on his jaw abrading his palms. "Not that I ever *would* hit a woman."

Honor's hand shifted from his shoulder to the back of his neck, her fingers threading through his hair. "It's okay to be angry, Asher."

Ironically, her gentle touch soothed away the ragged edges of that anger, just like when he'd first laid eyes on her in his living room. He lowered his arms, closed his eyes, and leaned into her as the stroke of her fingers sent a warm tingle of awareness all the way down his spine.

In the silence, the clink of a fork sounded, and then he felt her move to sit directly behind his back with her legs bracketing his sides. Her hands landed on his shoulders and began kneading his tense muscles.

Asher let out a low groan and hung his head to his chest. Her hands were like magic, offering relief and comfort while quieting his mind enough to review the past fifteen minutes with her in his mind.

A few minutes later, he lifted his head with a quiet, "Thank you."

Her hands slowed, then stilled, then left his body. "Sure."

The uncertainty in her voice brought a wry smile to his

lips. He pointedly shrugged his shoulders. "Don't stop. The thanks was for being here and listening, and for the cake—which *is* fucking awesome, by the way."

He felt the tension in her thighs ease. Her soft laugh was music to his ears as her hands returned to resume their expert treatment. "Glad you like it."

This time, everything else fell away as his focus narrowed to only the woman behind him. The strength of her delicate hands, the warmth of her thighs against his arms, the ever-present scent of freshly baked cake mingling with the underlying hint of peaches and cream he'd noticed earlier at dinner when he'd brushed her hair aside to press his lips to her neck.

Reaching up, he captured both her hands and pulled them down in front of him. He held one over his rapidly increasing heartbeat, and the other he lifted so he could press his lips to her open palm. "The only thing better than your cake is you."

Her front leaned against his back, and then her warm breath fanned his ear. His breath caught in his throat as pure anticipation rushed through his body from head to toe.

"You think I'm awesome?" she asked in a teasing voice.

"No." He paused, then added, "I think you're fucking awesome."

The retaliatory nip she gave his ear shot an arrow of lust zinging to his groin. He reached up to grasp the back of her neck while turning his head to align his mouth with hers. The smile parting her lips allowed him to slip his tongue past her teeth, and he pulled her closer to plunder and explore without mercy.

She took it all and gave it right back, tangling her tongue with his as their teeth scraped and nipped, her eagerness escaping in a breathless whimper that had his pulse pounding with excitement and his own low rumble of need crawling up his throat.

When his neck began to ache, he maneuvered around until he knelt between her legs. The awkward jostling had them both smiling, until he crashed his mouth on hers in earnest. He splayed his palms on her back, caressing up and down, plastering her chest to his as her hands clenched in his hair in their joint effort to get ever closer.

Desperate for skin on skin, he grasped the hem of her T-shirt and dragged it up between them. They broke apart long enough for him to toss it aside, then came back together in breathless, sloppy kisses.

As he felt for the clasp at the back of her bra, she wedged her arms between them and started unbuttoning his shirt. "Bedroom?" she asked between gasps for air.

"Yeah," he agreed. "Hang on."

The moment she wound her arms around his neck, he surged to his feet with her in his arms. She lifted her legs to wrap around his waist, and he felt his way around the couch before heading for the hall. He buried his face against her neck, nipping and sucking at the base of her throat as her hair swished against his hands at her back with every step.

"Asher...wait."

His step faltered at the sudden dismay in her voice. He stopped completely, his heart high in his throat. "What?"

"I just..." She pressed her forehead to his in the dark hall-way, her breath hot on his lips as she whispered, "This isn't why I stayed."

Whooh. Shit, those words made it hard to breathe.

He dragged air into his tight lungs as he lifted a hand to cup her face. "This isn't why I asked you to stay."

Asher stared into her eyes, their breath mingling, hearts thumping in sync, the knowledge that they both still wanted it to happen heavy between them.

Nothing over the past five hours had made sense.

But this...Honor in his arms, slaying him to the soul as she offered more than she knew with those few vulnerable words?

This made sense.

CHAPTER 23

*H*onor felt the difference in his kiss when he laid her on his bed and followed her down. Still reeling from that moment in the hall, she told herself she was wrong. It was no different from the mindless, consuming lust that brought them to his room in the first place. She ignored the deafening boom of her idiotic heart and only allowed herself to focus on the physical.

It didn't matter how much she liked him, this was sex. Pure and simple—until her words came back to haunt her.

This isn't why I stayed.

She shoved them away and concentrated on the delicious sensation of his weight pressing her into the mattress. How it made her ache for him with every single breath. She shifted beneath him, spreading her legs to cradle his hips between her thighs. With the throb of his rock-hard erection against her core, she moaned into his mouth.

Yes. That's what I want. Now.

He rocked his hips against hers in time to the slow, deep, erotic strokes of his tongue into her mouth, and out again.

The simulation had her writhing, her hands searching to rip off the rest of his clothes.

The rest of his clothes? He hadn't even taken anything off yet.

She went straight for the remaining buttons of his shirt to remedy that situation, then shoved the material from his broad shoulders. He helped her wrestle his arms from the sleeves, and as soon as she tossed the shirt aside, she went for his belt. Asher shifted onto his side to give her room to undo the buckle and slide the zipper down. The press of her palm against his rigid length through his boxer briefs elicited a low growl as his lips left hers to trail down her throat to her chest.

She slipped her hand under the waistband to push the soft, clingy material down over the firm cheeks of his butt, but became distracted when he peeled her bra cup down and sucked her pebbled nipple into his mouth. At the same time, he cupped her other breast through her bra and pinched the tip with his thumb and forefinger.

The sharp clench of her core muscles had her gasping and arching her back for more. He flattened his tongue against her skin, then swirled it round and round her nipple before latching on for another hard suck. Her hips lifted off the bed as she dug her fingers into his buttock.

"Asher. Oh my God."

Her throaty purr of approval deepened when he hummed against her skin and did the whole thing again while she took her bra off faster than she'd ever done before so he could move to the other side. And when he palmed his free hand down over her belly to her leggings, she eagerly helped him strip them and her panties off, too. Anticipation tingled along her nerve endings as he skimmed his fingers up her calf, along her inner thigh, straight to where she wanted his touch.

But he didn't stop there, and she whimpered a protest.

He replied with one last suck on her breast, then trailed soft, wet kisses down over her ribs, and stomach, and lower, until he hit the spot she wanted him most. Like the night on the couch, he sent her soaring in record time, gasping his name as her orgasm hit.

"I could do that over and over again," he murmured, kissing his way up her body the same way he'd gone down.

"Not without you next time," she vowed after he'd pressed a lingering kiss to her lips.

"Good plan."

She grinned and reached up to gently brush his hair from his forehead. As their gazes connected and held, an unexpected hard thump of her heart in her chest knocked the wind right out of her. Her smile faded and so did his.

A shaky gasp filled her lungs again, and she quickly averted her gaze to his chest while lifting a hand to explore the hard planes with their dusting of dark hair in the middle that arrowed down to bisect his ridged abdomen.

Physical.

Muscles.

Hot, sexy body.

Long hard erection.

Honor pushed him onto his back and sat up to kneel beside him while grasping the waistbands of his pants and briefs. He lifted his hips so she could drag the clothes down his thighs and legs. She whisked them aside and then drank her fill of the sculpted male beauty before her. Her mouth watered at the sight of him laying naked before her, one hand behind his head showing off a bulging bicep as he watched her with hooded eyes.

Real life was so much better than her fantasy.

So. Much. Better.

She swung a leg over to straddle his and ran her palms up

his thick thighs. His erection bobbed as she got close, but she forced herself to keep going over his taut stomach, up to his chest.

Bracing her palms on his pecs, she asked, "You want to see just how good I am at handling stick shift?"

His surprised bark of laughter morphed into a choked groan, his gaze fixed on the sway of her breasts between them. He brought his arm down from behind his head and reached both hands to cup her flesh in his palms. "More than anything."

The squeeze of his fingers and rough pads of his thumbs circling her nipples sent off another spasm of desire deep in her core. She lightly rocked her hips against his hard length while dipping her head to kiss his parted lips.

He took her tongue into his mouth, then thrust up against her when she sucked his bottom lip between her teeth. Her breath caught in her throat. It would be so easy to reach down, grasp his thick length, and lower herself down until he was buried to the hilt.

She skimmed her hand between them to wrap her fingers around his hot, hard flesh. As she stroked up and down, the clench of his hands bordered on painful as her name wrenched from his throat on a growl.

"*Honor.* You're killing me here. I need to be inside you."

"Soon," she promised before pulling away to take her turn kissing her way down his body. His stomach muscles quivered beneath her lips, then his fingers tangled in her hair when she ran her tongue along the length of his erection before taking the tip of him into her mouth.

He groaned his approval, and she gave a soft hum as she took him in all the way to the back of her throat.

His hands fisted, pulling at her scalp with his sharp inhale. "*Geezus fuck*, that's good."

She lifted her head for a peek of his face through her lashes. "Better than frosting?"

His deep laugh jostled the bed beneath them. "Maybe. Give me another taste and I'll let you know."

"Sassy." But she grinned as she took him in her mouth again, this time swirling her tongue around his head before sucking hard.

His low, drawn out moan answered even before his words. "Yeah. Definitely better than frosting."

After that, she took her time, licking and sucking to keep him making those sexy, throaty sounds that turned her on more than she'd even imagined possible.

"If this is any indication, I assume you liked my car?" he asked between deep, controlled breaths.

"Yes. I absolutely *loved* your car, Asher."

Love you even more.

The words in her head caught her off guard, and she stiffened with alarm. He didn't seem to notice as he suddenly gripped her shoulders, pulling her up, rolling her over to lie on top of her while yanking open the drawer of his nightstand. He put on a condom in record time and then nudged her legs open.

When he hesitated and his dark amber gaze locked with hers, she squeezed her eyes shut to break the connection.

No emotion. Just sex.

She reached up to pull him down for an open-mouth kiss while lifting her hips to urge him inside her. He eased in, then out, then in a little deeper, his body trembling over hers with his restraint.

Damn it. She didn't need gentle right now. Didn't *want* gentle.

Digging her nails into his back, she planted her heels on the mattress and spread her knees wide. "Hard, Asher. *Please.*"

As if her words unleashed his control, he surged forward and buried himself deep in one thrust.

"Yes," she gasped. "*Again. Harder.*"

He complied with her request, and when she felt her climax begin to build, she arched up, urging him faster with each thrust of his hips. They lost rhythm as they both plunged over the edge.

He collapsed on top of her while they both caught their breath. "Hmm," he hummed when he finally eased his weight off to the side. His hand rose to brush her hair back from her forehead, and her heart tripped as his gaze met hers. "Your cake is great, Butter Cream, but yeah, I'll take you driving my stick any day."

She laughed and lightly backhanded his chest, relieved for the levity. "I'm not sure I like that nickname, *Ace*."

He propped his head up on his elbow, amber gaze narrowed. "What'd Roxanna tell you?"

"You tell me and I'll let you know if it matches."

"I'm not falling for that one." He dropped a kiss on her lips before pushing up to walk toward the open door of his master bath.

"You aren't going to tell me?"

"Nope."

He wasn't the least bit self-conscious of his naked body, and she rolled on her side, unashamedly enjoying every step until he was out of sight.

In the following moment of silence by herself, she real-ized she wanted to stay when he got back.

She never wanted to stay.

Her heart started pounding, and her breath shortened. She shouldn't want to stay now, either. Swallowing hard against the sudden flip-flop of her stomach, she cast a quick glance at the bedside clock while getting up to search for her clothes.

She found her bra and leggings, and then her underwear, which she quickly slid back on. Recalling her T-shirt was out on the living room floor, she scooped up Asher's dark green shirt. After she shoved her arms into the sleeves, she criss-crossed the open sides over her chest and was heading toward the hall when his voice came from the bathroom door.

"You're leaving?"

She jerked to a stop at the door, bra and leggings clutched in her hand, heart still hammering in her chest. Guilt flushed her cheeks as she stumbled over her words. "I, um, I was just going to…grab my T-shirt."

He stared at her for a moment, then walked across the bedroom to swipe up his briefs. Seeing him still semi-hard made her want him all over again, even after he pulled the underwear on. Suddenly she didn't want to leave anymore, but wasn't sure what to do.

He shoved aside the covers and bent one leg as he sat on the bed. "You don't have to stay if you don't want to, Honor, but I'd rather you didn't sneak out."

"Hard to sneak out when you know where I live." The joke earned her a smile, but it faded fast. "If I stay, what would the neighbors think if they saw me in the morning?"

"This neighbor wouldn't mind in the least. He'd even make you breakfast." He looked over his shoulder at the clock. "In a couple hours."

Honor hesitated as she took him in, sitting there on the bed. Rumpled hair, sexy scruff, gorgeous eyes, generous lover. Her heart said *stay*. Her mind still said *run*.

"You've been here a lot longer than me. You don't care what your neighbors think?"

"Only the one that lives across the street."

Slow footsteps carried her back to him, and she dropped

her clothes on the floor beside the bed. "I guess I'll get my shirt later, then."

This time, his smile stayed. He reached out to grab the edges of his shirt and tugged her closer. She rested her hands on his shoulders, then her breath caught as he slowly parted the material and slid his hands up to cup her breasts, his expression reverent. When he leaned forward to suck the tip of one in his mouth, his whiskers scraped against her skin. Her knees went a bit weak as she recalled the feel of that scruff against her inner thigh.

"Fair warning." His amber gaze met hers as he flicked her nipple with his tongue. "Breakfast is going to be more like brunch."

Honor twined her fingers in his hair and let her head loll back. "I'm good with brunch."

CHAPTER 24

*A*fter a quick shower to avoid looking like sex warmed over on her walk across the street, Honor paused in the bedroom doorway for one last lingering look at Asher sprawled in the rumpled sheets. It had been almost five a.m. when he'd returned from tossing the condom the second time, and they'd both fallen asleep the moment he slid beneath the covers and snuggled against her side.

It was almost ten-thirty now, and she figured she'd let him sleep a bit longer before having to face the upheaval in his life again. Out in the living room, she carried the platter of partially eaten cake from the coffee table to the kitchen, considering the bombshell of discovering a half-brother you never knew existed.

Had Grayson Cole known? Or had his mother kept a whole loving family secret from him, too? Either possibility was downright shitty.

Would Asher's parents make it through this? Having celebrated thirty-five years together, even she had to say, it would be a shame if they didn't. Seeing the whole family together the evening of the anniversary party, it was clear they were close. She hoped they worked it out and weathered the scandal for Asher's sake—and his brothers and sisters.

After covering the cake, she smothered a tired yawn, located his coffee, and started a pot to brew. While waiting, she couldn't help replaying bits and pieces of them together, only a few short hours ago. The more she thought about everything, the more her heart and her mind struggled over the awesomeness/folly of her decision to stay.

The sex was great—lust she could reconcile with her mind. But wanting to stay and just be near him—that was her heart talking all the way. She needed to keep it purely physical, but how in the world was she supposed to do that when she liked him more than she'd ever liked anyone?

Her head was starting to hurt when she spotted a loaf of bread on his counter. Seizing the distraction, she checked the refrigerator to confirm he had milk and eggs, then whipped up a large batch of French toast while mentally prioritizing her upcoming week.

One cake had to be delivered Saturday, the other on Sunday morning, but both had a ton of elaborate add-ons, so she needed to start the detail work ahead of time before baking on Wednesday and Thursday. There was enough to do that she could even start tonight, despite the fact it was supposed to be her day off.

Lifting her coffee mug for a sip, she flipped the last slice of bread in the pan. The scuff of footsteps from behind alerted her Asher was up, but before she could turn, his arms slid around her waist. He pressed his warm lips to her neck, his scruff-covered chin scraping her skin. She tilted her head, giving him better access as his solid heat at her back woke every cell in her body in a way coffee never could.

"Good morning." He sucked in a deep inhale against her neck. "Something smells good."

"That's the French toast."

"No, it's you," he murmured. "But what's the deal here? I was supposed to make *you* breakfast."

Her first instinct was to tell him he could make breakfast next time. Instead, she checked herself and lifted the shoulder his chin wasn't resting on. "I was up."

His hips nudged her backside. "So am I."

"I noticed," she said with a smile. It was a heady feeling knowing how much he wanted her.

When he lifted a hand to turn her head so he could cover her mouth with his, she blindly set her mug on the counter, then spun around and wrapped an arm around his neck to lose herself in his kiss.

Mmm. He smelled all male while tasting minty fresh. Better yet, he was hard and warm and mostly naked in his black boxer briefs.

His touch roamed up and down her back, pressing her close as if he couldn't get enough of her even though he'd had her not that long ago. One hand palmed her ass and tugged her hips tight against his erection.

Her body throbbed in anticipation as she nipped at his bottom lip. "You're insatiable."

"I told you, I can never have enough cake."

"Oh, is that what you're calling it now?"

His other hand rose, cupping the back of her neck while his thumb brushed her face in that way that made her feel so special. "*You* are the cake, Honor. Not sex."

"I thought I was frosting?"

"You're that, too. Basically, you're anything and everything that's good."

Her heart thumped hard at the warm look in his eyes. A girl could get used to this.

But what happens when I get used to it and then it's gone?

She stiffened in his arms a second before a knock sounded at the front door. His hold eased, a frown drawing his dark brows down as his gaze held hers for a heart-stopping moment before shifting toward the sound. Honor pulled her arm down from around his neck and turned back to the stove.

"Um…you're going to need to get that," he said.

She half-turned toward him. "It's your house."

"Well, if I go, whoever it is will think I'm *really* happy to see them."

Honor glanced down, then couldn't help a grin when she saw his briefs left absolutely nothing to the imagination. Okay, yeah, she probably should answer his door for him.

She reached to set the spatula on the counter when another light knock sounded as the door opened.

"Asher? You home?"

Roxanna's concerned voice was only one second ahead of the brunette rounding the corner into the kitchen. She pulled up short when she saw both of them by the stove.

"Oh. Hi."

"Hi," they said at the same time.

Her gaze bounced from Asher, to Honor, and back again. Then her eyes widened, and she held up a hand while turning her head. "Geez Louise, Ace. Put that thing away."

Honor smothered an amused snort at the reaction.

Asher crossed his arms over his bare chest and widened his stance. "You're the one who walked in uninvited."

"I knocked. Twice. And if you'd answered your texts, I wouldn't have had to come over to make sure you're okay." Her profile turned pink as she added, "Although, I can see now why you didn't bother with your texts."

"Yeah, pretty obvious, isn't it?"

"Too obvious. Go put some damn pants on."

He didn't speak for a long moment, then finally huffed out an annoyed breath and strode toward his bedroom.

"Take a cold shower while you're at it," the psychic called after his back.

"Or you could just leave," he hollered back before the bedroom door slammed.

Honor watched Roxanna's grin fade in the awkward silence that fell when it was just the two of them in the kitchen. They had come to tolerate each other over the past week or so. Their last exchange when she'd dropped off cupcakes had bordered on friendly. Barely.

She gestured to the platter of food and plates on the island. "There's plenty of French toast if you want some?"

"I don't want to intrude."

"Too late." She tempered the words with a wry smile.

"Yeah, sorry."

The tall brunette contradicted the words by grabbing herself a third plate and fork—from the correct cupboard and drawer, without having to search for the items like Honor had. Witnessing her familiarity with Asher's home and realizing she must have a key to have opened the front door sparked a twinge of jealousy.

"I get his mail and keep an eye on the house when he's gone for work, that's all. I told you, he's like a brother to me. Yeah, he's hot, but no way do I want to ogle him in his briefs."

The reply stood the hairs of her arm on end as she shot Roxanna a glance, but the woman's head was hidden behind the pantry door. She emerged with syrup and powdered sugar and casually set them next to the plate of French toast, as if answering someone's private thoughts was perfectly normal.

Then she darted a furtive glance toward the living room before leaning on the counter to ask, "How's he doing?"

Still somewhat unnerved, Honor arched her eyebrows. "Seems like you should already know that."

A smile curved her lips. "That last thing was a woman

thing, not a psychic thing. If I spent the night with a guy and his female friend just walked right in, I'd want to know why she had a key, too."

That made sense—though, she could've totally used it to shore up her psychic claims instead of giving Honor ammunition against them by confirming it was a lucky guess.

"I don't have to prove myself to anyone." Roxanna faced her and held out a plate, inviting her to eat even though Honor had done the cooking. "You're either open to believing, or you're not. *You* get to decide that, not me or anyone else. Only you."

Her pulse stuttered as she stepped forward to take the plate. Not only had Roxanna correctly guessed her thoughts again, but she got the impression the woman was referring to more than belief in her uncanny abilities.

"The thing is," Roxanna continued, "this is really huge. I don't know how he's playing it, but I do know he went to his parents' house last night after the news broke, so I stopped to make sure he's doing okay."

"He was upset when he got back last night," Honor admitted, her chest tightening with the memory of his anger and confusion. "He didn't want to talk about it much, though I don't think he knows a lot of details yet, either. Then again, even if he did tell me anything, it's not my place to repeat it."

The other woman looked up from her plate, a glimmer of respect in her brown eyes. "Right. Of course. Thanks. I'm glad you were here for him."

There was no resentment in her words, only genuine gratitude that Honor had helped her best friend.

Okay. So maybe she could be friends with the psychic, too.

She nodded to Roxanna and selected a slice of French toast as Asher rejoined them. The smile he gave her warmed his eyes before he headed for the coffee pot to pour a cup.

Breakfast forgotten, her mouth watered as she raked her gaze from the top of his damp hair to his bare feet, appreciating his snug, black T-shirt, and a pair of faded jeans worn and ripped in all the right places.

She was glad she'd been here for him, too. Glad he'd wanted her here.

But how long will that last?

The question hit hard, undermining her happiness after the night they'd shared. The warning thoughts were coming more often now. And with Roxanna's comment about how big this whole situation was for Asher and his family, she needed to seriously consider...how long before she became an afterthought for him?

Relationships didn't last. She was well aware of that fact, and letting herself even hope for anything different was opening herself up for heartache.

She snuck a glance at Asher from beneath her lashes and caught him watching her over the rim of his coffee cup, his expression pensive. Was she the reason for that serious look? Did he still want more than sex, or was he realizing that this could get too complicated? Was she reading too much into his somber expression, or did he sense her inner turmoil?

Maybe the brooding had nothing to do with her at all. Could be he was thinking of his family.

Of course he's thinking about his family! And she was being a complete idiot obsessing over something so little.

Stop over-thinking things!

Tossing him a quick smile, she ducked her head to concentrate on her plate. But then, while cutting up the slice of French toast into bite size pieces, she realized her problem.

She was looking at him different than any other man she'd dated. What she needed to do was simply let go of her uncertainty and enjoy each moment solely for the moment. Enjoy *him* solely for him.

Forget the future, because they didn't have one.

No qualms about hoping for more when she already knew it wasn't going to happen.

When it was over, it would be over, and as long as she kept *that* front and center in her mind, she'd have nothing to worry about.

Other than the fact her silent little pep talk made her want to cry.

CHAPTER 25

*A*sher couldn't shake the feeling something wasn't right. Rox's arrival may have provided Honor with a convenient cover, but he'd felt her pull away *before* the knock. And while he'd been thrilled by her eager perusal when he returned to the kitchen, he still sensed her pulling away.

Maybe it was the family bomb that dropped last night. *He* didn't even want to have to deal with it, so was it fair to expect her to? Probably not. But he didn't like the idea of her putting distance between them after last night. Especially not after he'd had to convince her to stay.

One night down, a lifetime to go.

He carried his coffee over to the island to dish up a couple slices of the delicious smelling French toast and caught Roxanna's smirk from where she sat on an island stool next to Honor.

"That was a quick shower, Ace."

"Cold ones always are," he shot back.

The moment the words were out of his mouth, he felt like his face slammed into the mountain all over again. Was Honor creating distance between them because of his friendship with Roxanna? Did their closeness bother her? He wasn't used to filtering their exchanges.

No, hold up. She'd pulled away before they knew it was Rox at the door. And, right now, her humor-filled gaze transferred from him to his best friend.

She certainly didn't seem upset as she leaned forward to ask, "He won't tell me why you call him Ace."

"It's really not that big a deal," he said.

Rox laughed, her brown gaze twinkling. "It isn't. He just sucks at poker and doesn't like to be reminded that I took him to the cleaners the night we met back in college. I gave him the nickname so he'd never forget."

Asher grimaced while pouring syrup over his food. "Yeah, well, I didn't know I was playing with a psychic."

"I read people, not cards," she defended, syrup dripping from her raised fork. "It's not my fault you have numerous tells."

"Ooh, do tell," Honor joked.

She took a breath to speak, but Asher fixed her with a glare. "Rox."

Lucky for her, she ate her food and kept her grinning mouth shut. Finally, he stabbed a chunk of his French toast. "Shouldn't you be at the store?"

"Tessa's covering for me today."

"Oh." He raised a bite, but another knock from the front door jerked his head around. Plunking down his fork, he got up from his seat with a muttered, "Of all the mornings. It's like Grand-frickin'-Central here today."

As he left the kitchen, he heard Roxanna say, "We'll talk later."

"Better not," he hollered on his way through the living room. Roxanna talking to Honor scared the crap out of him at the same time he loved the idea of the two of them becoming friends.

A shiny black SUV he didn't recognize was parked next to Rox's ancient Jeep. He opened the door and blinked in surprise when he saw Loyal on his porch. "Hey. I didn't know you were coming back."

"What the hell did you expect with all this shit going on?"

He stepped aside for him to come in, then eyed the overnight bag in his hand. "Staying a while?"

"Just a couple nights. You okay if I stay here? I don't think I can handle the house right now."

Normally, he'd have no problem with his brother staying a few nights. But after last night with Honor, he had to bite his tongue to keep from suggesting he find himself a hotel. "Yeah. It's fine."

"Do I smell coffee? And food?"

Loyal's bag thumped to the floor as he headed straight for the kitchen. His step faltered when he saw Honor and Roxanna at the island, and Asher bumped his shoulder on the way past. Honor gave his brother a welcoming smile, while Rox sat stiff and refused to even look at him.

Recalling their conversation the other day, Asher kept an eye on his best friend as he said, "Loyal, you remember Honor Hartman from the party."

"Yeah. The cake baker. Good to see you again." His narrowed gaze moved between her and Roxanna on his way to the coffee pot. "You're awfully forgiving."

Honor just smiled, but Rox's lips thinned as she pushed up from her stool. "I'm going to get going."

Loyal leaned back against the counter, a smirk lifting the corners of his mouth. "Roxanna, please. Don't leave on my account."

His brother's smug grin grew as she pointedly ignored him, thanked Honor for breakfast, then added, "Asher, I'm here for you if you need anything."

"I know." He gave her a one-armed hug, grateful she cared

enough to come by, even if she had interrupted his morning. "Thanks for checking in."

"Always."

"Always good to see you, Roxanna," Loyal called after her.

After the front door slammed, Asher spun around and shot him a dark look. "Why do you antagonize her?"

"What? I was polite."

He shook his head as he slid onto the stool next to Honor once more. "You really are a jackass."

Loyal snorted while grabbing a mug to pour some coffee. "You find out anything more this morning?"

"Man, I haven't even had a chance to eat the breakfast Honor made me." And it was starting to piss him off.

"Speaking of, do you mind? I didn't eat before catching my flight." He gestured toward the last three slices on the plate.

Asher threw up a hand. "Hey, yeah, why the hell not?" He inhaled a deep breath and turned to give Honor a tight, apologetic smile.

Loyal paused mid-reach for the plate, his gaze bouncing between them. "I'm sorry. Am I interrupting something here?"

Asher arched his eyebrows in disbelief, but before he could explode, Honor swiveled on her stool and slid off the other side. "Don't worry about it. In fact, I should probably get going, too."

No!

"I know you guys have a lot to talk about. I don't want to be in the way."

"You aren't in the way," he denied.

"She knows about the other brother?" Loyal asked at the same time.

"National news, remember? Everyone knows about the other brother—plus, we were at dinner when I found out."

Asher turned a pleading look toward Honor. "Please don't let him run you off, too."

"I really need to get started on the cakes for this week."

"I thought you had the day off?"

"Not after I figured out everything I have to get done."

He sighed his disappointment and got up from his stool again. "Fine. Come on. I'll walk you home."

"I can make it across the street on my own."

"I know, but I'm still going to walk you." He wasn't taking no for an answer. If she was going to be as busy as she'd said, he wouldn't see her much this next week. At least he sure hoped her telling him how busy she'd be was all about work, and not her giving him the brush off.

Her smile made him think she was pleased at his insistence, but she turned away before he could be sure.

"All right. See you around, Loyal."

His brother nodded and smiled with a mouthful of French toast, and Asher rolled his eyes as he followed Honor out the door. A couple neighbors on the left side of his house were out in their yards, and he lifted a hand in greeting, not caring one bit what they thought of him and Honor together.

He took her hand in the driveway, and held tight on their way across the street. "I'm sorry about this morning. It was nothing like what I'd envisioned when I promised you brunch."

She laughed. "It was definitely interesting. And kinda fun."

"Sure. Right." He squeezed her hand. "Hey, um, you know Rox and I are just friends, right?"

Her sideways glance met his through her lashes. "Yes."

"Friends only. That's all it's ever been, all it'll ever be."

She swung their joined hands between them while facing forward again. "I admit, after what happened at the anniversary party I did wonder if she might be jealous, but today erased any last notion of that."

"It did?" And here he'd feared the opposite.

"A woman would have to be either completely blind, uninterested, or a lesbian to not even *try* to sneak a peek of you in all your glory."

"That doesn't even sound right," he protested with a laugh. "I was wearing underwear."

"They weren't hiding much."

He bumped her shoulder with his arm as they approached her porch. "Sounds like *you* snuck a peek."

She bumped back. "I did more than peek, big guy."

He laughed again, loving that she'd looked and wasn't shy about admitting it. His ego was exceptionally pleased with the *big guy*. "So...I know you're going to be busy this week, but you take breaks for lunch and dinner, right?"

"Short breaks."

"Mind if I stop by sometime around break time?"

She stepped up onto her porch, then spun around to rest her hands on his shoulders. He lightly grasped her hips as she said, "Depends on what you're stopping by for."

"To see you, of course."

"Not for cake?"

"Well, I mean, if *you* offered cake, I wouldn't say no."

Her head tilted, humor shining in her pretty green eyes. "And when you say cake, you mean...?"

He waggled his eyebrows and tugged her closer.

Her gaze narrowed to a glare but the effect was totally ruined by her grin and the way she melted against him when he buried one hand in her hair and wrapped the other arm around her waist. She opened her mouth beneath his, and he savored the faint taste of sweet syrup on her lips as he angled his head to deepen the kiss.

A long minute later, it took everything he had to break

away and wish her a good day. He hooked his thumbs in his front jeans pockets and walked backward while drinking in her unexpectedly shy smile before she turned for her front door.

"Hey, Honor."

She spun around. "Yeah?"

"The cake was fucking awesome. Both times."

Her mouth formed a surprised O before she laughed with a slow shake of her head from side to side.

Asher spun around, grinning as he hummed the entire way back across the street. She made it easy to forget the shit with his family…until he walked through his front door and Loyal looked up from his seat on the couch with a slice of Honor's chocolate cake on a plate in his hands. Possessive jealousy flared in less than a second.

"You and the cake baker?"

"Yeah, me and the cake baker." He stalked over and yanked the plate and fork from his brother's hands. "*This is mine.*"

"Getting laid should put you in a better mood."

"Shut the hell up, man." He went into the kitchen and dropped the plate on the counter. "Sometimes you're worse than Merit."

Loyal followed him with a laugh, then sank down onto one of the island stools, forearms braced on the counter. "You're really not going to share your cake with me?"

Fuck no.

"Roxanna sells her cupcakes in the shop every day now. Go get one of those."

Loyal's lip curled with distaste. "You couldn't pay me to set foot in that place."

She'd be happy to hear that. Or relieved, if it meant his brother didn't take him up on his offer to stay in the empty apartment above her shop.

He shot him a glance and grabbed his breakfast plate to warm his cold French toast in the microwave. "You know, you really should be nicer to Rox."

"Just because you're friends with that woman doesn't mean I have to be."

Asher opened his mouth, then snapped it closed as he transferred the dirty pan and spatula from the stove to the sink while his food warmed. He'd promised he wouldn't say a word, and Rox would kill him if he even *hinted* at anything. Besides, she hadn't actually admitted a single thing. Right now, he was going off his gut feeling.

"All I'm saying is it wouldn't kill you to not be such a jerk when she's around."

"I was perfectly nice when she was here. *She* wouldn't even say hi to me."

It was like trying to reason with a two year old. He sat at the counter with his plate and finally took his first bite of breakfast. He closed his eyes and telegraphed a silent *thank you* across the street to Honor. With his second forkful, he asked, "What are you doing back, Loyal? There's not much we can do until dad's team sorts things out."

"I want to go see him."

His brother's solemn gaze stilled his hand. "Grayson Cole?"

"No, the Pope." He shoved up and stood straight. "Of course Grayson Cole."

Asher was totally on board with that. He'd been contemplating the same move despite the conversation at their parents' house last night. Speaking around another bite, he advised, "The campaign team said they needed to check into everything before any of us did anything rash. By their definition, contacting Vivian or Grayson Cole would be rash."

"Fuck the team. What did Dad say to that?"

"He didn't like it, but he's going along with it for now. He doesn't want to give the tabloids more fodder."

"And Mom?"

Asher rested the tines of his fork on the plate. "Mom wasn't saying much at all by that point."

Loyal paced toward the living room, then spun to come back. "None of this has been sitting right with me since the moment I heard it, so—"

"Join the club."

"—I found a PI willing to work through the night to start digging into these people."

He raised his eyebrows. "And?"

"It's all about the campaign."

"I could've told you that for free, Einstein."

Loyal shot him a *shut up* glare. "Dad's had two successful governor's races and *this* is when some secret, illegitimate child first comes out? If you look at it from the money angle, this woman had eighteen years to ask for child support. She'd have to be living under a rock not to know who Dad was all this time, what the family's worth, yet she didn't even try to blackmail him to keep her silent."

"You'd have preferred blackmail?"

"No. You're missing the point." He thumped his fist on the counter. "These people don't have money—haven't had money. So, the only reason this woman would've chosen *now* to 'reveal' her little story is because it's not true. The opposing party found a guy who looks like us and paid these people a shitload of money to fake a scandal so Dad will lose. They're desperate to win the party majority in this election."

The last part was one hundred percent true, but the rest had holes. Unfortunately.

"Except Dad admitted to the affair," he reminded. "And they have a DNA test."

"Oh, please. You know Dad never gave permission for

that test. We can't trust the results of a test done by the same people who paid for the story. My midnight PI guy proves everyone has a price, so I say before we believe anything, we need to investigate *and* have our own test done."

"Dad's lawyers are putting in a request for a second test today. But, Loyal, come on. You saw the news."

"Yeah, so?"

"This guy doesn't just look like us, he could pretty much be your twin."

Annoyance twisted his features as he shook his head and turned away. Rubbing the back of his neck, he stared out the window for a long moment, and then his shoulders slumped as he blew out a rough breath.

When he faced Asher again, resignation filled his grimace. "I still want to go see him. I don't give a shit what Dad's decided to do."

"I'm totally with you on that part." Asher stood and deposited his empty plate in the sink. "When were you thinking?"

"Today. Now."

"Fine by me. What about Celia, Merit, and Shelby?" Like any family, they had their differences, but when it came right down to it, they always had each others' backs. It only seemed right they include them in this, too.

But Loyal shook his head. "I want to get answers from this guy, not ambush him. Five of us at once will only make him defensive."

CHAPTER 26

"Shit," Asher muttered as they approached Grayson Cole's driveway and saw two unmarked vans parked across the street. "We should've borrowed Roxanna's Jeep. You know that's the press."

He switched his visor to the side window as the sliding door of the closest van opened and a camera man jumped out.

"Hang on." Loyal took the turn fast enough to fishtail between the plastic *Private Property* and *No Trespassing* signs on either side of the gravel driveway, then gunned the gas. Thankfully, it appeared the guy's house sat a decent distance from the road with trees in between to block the view.

Asher twisted to look out the back window. "Think they'll obey the signs?"

"They fucking better."

No one looked to be following, so maybe they wouldn't make the news. He exchanged a look with Loyal as his brother parked his Audi Q8 rental next to a rusty, faded red F-250 a little after one p.m. Located ten minutes southwest of Boulder, the place was neat and clean, but no amount of tidiness could hide its age.

He ran his gaze over the weather-grayed boards on the small house while shutting his door to join Loyal in front of the vehicle. There was an uneven, moss-covered brick walkway leading to the front porch, but the echo of a hammer striking iron from the backyard drew them around to the back of the house. With each step they took, the quicker his pulse beat.

"Looks like he could do a lot with an influx of cash," his brother groused in a low voice.

Asher cast him a sideways glare. "Probably not best to go in with accusations."

Loyal didn't bother with a reply.

On the other side of a rustic, chest-high fence, a tall, dark-haired guy in jeans and a T-shirt swung a sledge hammer against a metal stake. After a couple more blows, he side-stepped a few feet to start another, his movement disturbing a large, black and tan German Shepherd lying on the patchy grass.

As soon as the dog spotted them, it started barking and bounded across the yard to jump at the fence. They each took a cautious step back as Loyal called, "Grayson Cole?"

Without turning around, the guy let the hammer hang by his leg, and tipped his head back in obvious annoyance. "I already told you people I've got no comment, so take your stupid interviews and shove 'em up your ass," he hollered over the barking dog. "Now get the fuck off my property before I call the cops again."

Noticing Loyal's hands fisting at his sides, Asher laid a hand on his arm. "We're not reporters," he called. "Just wanted to introduce ourselves."

"Call off the damn dog," Loyal growled.

The guy turned around, his expression hard as stone. The

moment he saw them, the sledge hammer slipped through his fingers, and the iron head thudded on the ground. After a moment, he bent slightly to grip the handle again, then adjusted his grip to the base by the steel head as he crossed the yard.

"Remy. Quit. Heel."

The dog immediately stopped barking and trotted around to his left side. When he stopped by the fence, the dog obediently sat next to him.

Saying Loyal and him could pass as twins was an understatement. Discounting Grayson's trimmed beard being a bit longer than Loyal's scruff, they both had the same angled jaw, stood about the same height, and had the same pissed-off-at-the-world look in their dark, brown eyes.

Asher reached a hand over the fence. "I'm Asher. This is my, ah, brother, Loyal."

The guy's eyes narrowed, and his mouth pressed into a thin line at the word *brother*. Still gripping the sledge hammer in his fist, he ignored the handshake offer, and Asher pulled back when a low growl lifted the dog's lips.

"I know who you are," Grayson said brusquely. "What the fuck do you want?"

Asher blinked in surprise at his continued hostility.

Loyal bristled beside him. "That's how you're going to play this?"

"What?" He turned his free hand outward, palm up. "Did you expect a fucking hug or something?"

"Of course not," Asher returned. "Basic manners would suffice."

Loyal crossed his arms and braced his stance. "Why should he bother? The story is out. The check is probably clearing the bank right now. His job is done."

Grayson lifted his hand to jab the head of the hammer in

their direction. "I haven't taken a dime from those vultures, nor do I plan to."

Fury roughened his voice, tension radiating from him in waves as the dog's growls intensified.

"You expect us to believe you weren't on board with this plan your mother concocted?"

"Remy, quit." The animal quieted as the guy glared at Loyal. "What the hell are you even talking about?"

"We know this is all a setup to derail our father's campaign so he loses the election."

"I don't give a shit about *your* father."

"Interesting." Loyal shot Asher a cynical glance. "He's not even trying to back up the story. What happened, did your mom cut you out of the deal? Is that what's got you so pissed off?"

"There is no deal. I'm pissed off because this whole shit-show has been a nightmare since last night. My phone won't stop ringing, and I had an army of reporters knocking on my door last night and this morning. I had to call the cops to get rid of them."

"You should've known they'd want follow up interviews."

"And how the fuck would I have known that?"

"Common fucking sense," Loyal snapped. "When you chum the waters to ruin the reputation of a respected governor running for Senate, you're gonna attract the sharks."

"You're talking like a fucking idiot," Grayson accused.

Asher almost laughed at that comment. He even sounded like Loyal. "Surely, you had to know once the story broke the press would want to hear directly from you."

"You assume I knew what the hell was coming, but that fucking news report last night came out of nowhere. At least in Afghanistan I expected there would be I.E.D.s to blow everything to kingdom come," he grumbled.

Asher's frown now matched his brother's—and his half-brother's. "Your mother didn't tell you before she sold the story?"

Grayson's jaw clenched. "My mom didn't sell any damn story."

"You're saying you didn't know the governor was your father before last night?"

"My father is dead." Deep creases lined the guy's forehead. "I've known that from the time I was old enough to ask."

And yet, he didn't sound like he was stating a long known fact. It was more like he was repeating the words to convince himself what he'd been told all his life was still true.

Hearing the confusion mixed with frustration, Asher was inclined to believe he hadn't known the shit-storm—as he aptly described it—was coming. Last night, before he'd talked to Honor, he'd resented the hell out of this guy. And then on the drive, Loyal had him doubting the few facts they did know.

But now, he realized maybe Grayson was going through the same emotional grinder they all were.

Loyal crossed his arms, clearly unconvinced. "That's an interesting way to play it."

"I'm not playing anything."

"Plausible deniability. I think now that the story is actually out there, you're scared. Because the truth is going to come out about the lies you and your mother told to ruin our dad's reputation." He leaned forward to jab a finger in Grayson's direction. "And believe me, we're going to make sure you're all exposed."

The dog rose up with a sharp bark, and Loyal jerked back.

"Here's a truth for you," Grayson growled. "I don't want anything to do with a single one of you fucking entitled, pretentious pricks. I don't want your money. I don't want to know you. I don't even want to know *about* you. Now get the *fuck off my property."*

Loyal took a breath to speak, but Asher turned to face him while stepping between the two. "Let's go," he said quietly. "This isn't helping."

He looked like he was going to argue, and when Asher put his hand on his chest to back him up, he knocked it away. He started to back up, but leaned to the side for one last warning. "The truth will come out. You can take *that* to the bank."

A stop at their parents' house on the way home left a cold knot in Asher's stomach. Mom had packed a bag and left without a word to anyone where she was going or when she'd be back. Dad was out doing damage control on the damn campaign, and Celia was rattled enough that she and Robert were discussing postponing the wedding.

He and Loyal had discussed telling everyone about their visit with Grayson, decided not to, but then Asher spilled when guilt got the better of him. After the past twenty-four hours, the idea of keeping a secret from any of his siblings didn't sit right.

Not only were Celia, Shelby, and Merit now pissed off at the both of them, but Loyal wasn't happy with him, either. His brother had gone for a long run when they got back to Asher's place and was currently in the shower, while Asher was doing his best to distract himself with work.

To no avail. He set his laptop on the coffee table and paced from his living room to the kitchen. On the ride back, Loyal had voiced the possibility of their parents following through on the divorce they'd averted all those years ago. Asher shut him up. It was way too soon to even be thinking they might go that route, and yet since the thought had been planted, it niggled annoying little wormholes in the back of his mind. He couldn't imagine their parents calling it quits after thirty-five years.

Restless energy had him pulling a fork from the silverware drawer. He lifted the cover on the chocolate cake, but after two bites, he tossed the fork in the sink and headed back to the living room. It was still the best cake he'd ever had, but it was no substitute for what he really wanted.

Maybe he should go for a bike ride. Exercise it out like Loyal. Standing in front of the window, he raked a hand through his hair and gripped the back of his neck. Screw the bike ride.

What he really wanted to do was go across the street and be with Honor. Despite the earlier teasing about cake, he'd settle for simply being in the same room as her. Even when sexual awareness had his entire body humming, something about her presence calmed his spirit in a way he craved more than her actual cake right now.

Problem was, it had dawned on him earlier that she hadn't actually answered if it was okay for him to stop by. He didn't want to push too hard and drive her away. Grimacing, he returned to the couch and picked up his computer again.

Done with his shower, Loyal tapped the back cushion on his way to the kitchen. "Beer?"

"Sure."

He came back with two bottles, then sat on the opposite end of the couch and pulled out his own laptop. Silence reigned as they drank and worked—or Asher pretended to work in between morose stares over the top edge of his screen.

"Are you lusting after the girl or her frosting?"

Loyal's question jerked his gaze sideways.

His brother's mouth quirked at the corners as he pointed

his beer at him. "I'm guessing the girl since you already have her frosting on that cake you're selfishly hoarding."

"Can you blame me?"

"No. The one bite I had was fucking awesome."

His choice of words sparked a reluctant smile. "I was talking about the girl, though I do agree on the cake." He met his brother's gaze as he finished off his beer. "She could be the one."

What's with the could? *She* is *the one.*

Loyal's expression remained impassive as he stared at him for a long moment. "Did you learn nothing from Brianna?"

"Yeah," he snapped. "That she *wasn't* the one."

"And some chick who doesn't believe in love is?"

He arched an eyebrow. "Thought you didn't believe a word Roxanna says?"

"You know what? Forget it." He slammed his computer shut and surged to his feet to swipe up Asher's empty bottle. "Be an idiot," he muttered on his way to the kitchen. "But don't say I didn't warn you. Just look at Mom and Dad."

Jaw clenched, Asher locked his gaze on his laptop screen. "They'll work things out."

"You don't know that. None of us know that, and clearly, thirty-five years is no guarantee."

Because of his brother's sore past, nothing he said would change the direction of the discussion, so he dropped the subject. When Loyal offered a second beer, he declined and reached for his phone instead.

A few minutes later, his brother groused, "You've got nothing to eat around here besides that damn cake."

"There's a bar not far from here that has good burgers. We can order take out."

"Or just eat there."

He didn't feel like going out, but sitting here wasn't any more appealing. "Yeah. Fine. Let's go."

Down at Nick's Pub, they squeezed in at the corner of the bar where Loyal ordered a beer and Asher requested a soda while they waited to order their food. His brother scoped out the place while he took out his phone to send Honor a text asking if she'd eaten dinner yet. Her reply came less than a minute later.

Honor: *Not yet. I'll break for a bowl of cereal in a bit. How has your day been?*

Asher: *Crazy. Do you like burgers?*

Honor: *Sorry on the crazy. And who doesn't like burgers?*

Asher: *Loyal and I are at Nick's. Want me to bring you one on our way home?*

Honor: *Nick won't mind you stealing one of his burgers?*

He'd forgotten she was still new to the neighborhood.

Asher: *He'd call the cops if I stole one, but since I'll pay for it, we'll be good. Nick's is a pub, Butter Cream.*

Honor: *Ah. Got it, Ace. You don't have to do that...but on the other hand I'm starving, and I do love a good burger. Medium. Extra pickles and tomatoes, mayo and BBQ sauce. Please and thank you.*

The positive response prompted a grin. She didn't mind if he stopped by. He responded he'd be there in about a half-hour, then tucked his phone in his back pocket and asked Loyal, "You mind if we take our food to go after all?"

"Let me guess, the baker is offering more frosting?"

"Her name is Honor," he said pointedly. "And, I'm going to bring her a burger for dinner. She's been working since she left this morning."

Loyal fished the rental keys out of his pocket to drop them on the bar. "I'll call a cab to get back."

Damn. Now he felt like he was being a shitty brother, ditching family for a woman. "You're welcome to eat with us, if you want." The support Honor had expressed about his family so far left him pretty sure she wouldn't mind. And since she'd already stressed her breaks had to be short, they wouldn't stay long.

"Oh, God, no. You bit my head off when I tried to eat some of that cake. I'm afraid of what you might go after if I talk to her and she falls for me instead of you."

Asher snorted and socked him on the arm as the waitress approached. "Never gonna happen, bro."

The unexpected teasing broke the uneasy tension between them since their trip to meet Grayson. They put in their order, then talked easily until their food arrived. Asher fisted his to-go bag in his hand and stood.

"You're sure?" he asked one last time as he stole a fry from Loyal's basket.

"I'm sure, you romantic sap. Go get your damn heart broken."

CHAPTER 27

*A*s Honor chewed her last bite, she noticed Asher was only just starting the second half of his burger. He'd been busy recounting the trip to meet Grayson Cole and the stop at his parents' house after. Conflicting emotions deepened his voice as he spoke, and her chest had tightened for him when he said the guy didn't want anything to do with them. Seemed Loyal and Merit agreed with Grayson wholeheartedly on that one point, while Asher and his sisters weren't sure how they felt.

"Loyal still isn't convinced he's your half-brother after meeting him?" she asked.

"Not so much. I think he's just in denial."

She reached for a French fry from the cardboard basket between them. "Sounds like you're not."

His shoulders lifted. "I don't doubt that the right amount of money could buy a fake DNA test, but the problem with that is they have to know if we did our own, that lie would be exposed. And they have to know we'd demand to do our own."

"And, your dad did admit to sleeping with his mother."

"Yeah. That, too."

In a moment of silence, Honor returned to the one thing that blew her mind. "I can't believe she lied to him that his father was dead. What a shitty thing to do to your kid."

"Right?" He rested his forearm against the edge of the table and grabbed a fry. "I don't get how that's better than him knowing about my dad and our family. We've missed knowing him for thirty-one years."

She crumpled her empty burger wrapper and stood. Her leg was warm where his had rested against it, and when she passed behind him on her way to the garbage, she gave in to the urge to rub her palm across his hunched shoulders. What she really wanted to do was wrap her arms around him in a tight, comforting hug. But then she wouldn't want to let go.

Before she could get one step away, he reached back and caught her hand. His strong fingers gave hers a light squeeze. She understood the silent thanks, and yet that one touch sparked the banked desire simmering between them from the moment she'd opened the door.

If he tugged her back to his side, she'd forget all about taking a short break and peel that soft cotton T-shirt over his head right here in her kitchen.

When her second reluctant step toward the island put pressure on his grip, his fingers tightened for a second, but then he released her. She bit back a sigh of disappointment.

Suck it up and get your ass back to work.

She tossed her garbage and turned on the faucet to wash her hands. "The PI your brother hired said Grayson and his mom didn't have money, right? So, is all this about making money off the story, or sabotaging your dad's campaign?"

"Both most likely. Loyal texted me just before I got here and said it appears Grayson's mother's ex-husband sold the story to the opposition."

"The ex-husband? Was it a recent divorce?"

"Yeah. They were only married a couple of years."

"Maybe that's why it's coming out now."

"Could be."

"What a jerk. Though, his mother kind of is, too, for lying and keeping that secret all those years."

"I still can't wrap my head around why. They didn't have money back then or now. From what the PI has said, they both live in small houses and drive older vehicles, she's a waitress at a tourist restaurant, and he joined the military right out of high school instead of going to college. He's been self-employed doing odd jobs since he got out a couple years ago."

She leaned her hip against the island counter as she grabbed a towel to dry her hands. "What does any of that matter? Not everyone can afford college, or, he might not have even wanted to go. I went straight into designing cakes out of high school."

"I guess I'm coming from the angle parents are supposed to want better for their kids, so why would his mother struggle all those years when she could have received child support from my dad? He would've supported them both if he'd known."

Honor rested the towel on the counter. "Maybe she was afraid."

"Of my dad?" he asked with disbelief.

"Of losing her baby. If your family was as well known then as it is now, she knew your dad had a *lot* more money than she did. He would've been able to afford a whole team of lawyers to gain custody and take him away."

Asher's brow furrowed as he swiped a napkin across his lips and met her gaze. "My dad wouldn't have done that."

"You don't know that any more than Grayson's mother did."

"I don't believe this." He swiveled in the chair to face her. "Are you seriously taking her side?"

"No." Her voice rose in response to his. "What she did was completely wrong. All I'm doing is offering a possible reason why. You've never had to worry about money, Asher. Never had to worry about what it can and can't buy."

He stared at her for a long moment, as if taken aback by her words. For the first time since they met, she saw him as the rich guy born with a silver spoon in his mouth and realized they'd been raised worlds apart. Yet, she'd never felt that from him. Not once, until she had to be a jerk and point it out.

"I'm sorry," she said quietly. "I didn't mean—"

"No. It's fine," he said. "You're absolutely right." After a long beat of silence, he added, in a low voice, "But I guarantee you, my dad would not have taken the baby away."

"Okay." She held up her hands, then reached for her sealed bag of fondant. "I understand that you *do* know your dad better than her, but you've spent almost thirty years with him. She was with him for one night—and you know they didn't spend that time learning about each other's character."

He made a sound of disgruntled dismay as he turned back to the table. "I really don't want to think about that."

"Sorry."

He shook his head and picked at his food. Not quite knowing what to say, she focused her gaze down, kneading a chunk of the fondant with the heels of her hands, softening the icing so she could roll it out.

"What would you do?"

Honor glanced up in surprise to see Asher had once again turned in his chair to face her. His intense gaze made her pulse skip a few beats, and she lowered her lashes. "About what?"

"Would you tell me if you got pregnant, or would you be too afraid?"

Wow. This was not the direction she would've expected this conversation to take. Then she realized her heart had given a little thump of...giddiness...at the thought of having his baby. Not just *a* baby, but *his* baby.

What the hell?

Now her heart was racing like a runaway freight train. She drew in a calming breath before answering honestly. "Yeah, I'd be afraid, but I would tell you."

"Do you really think I'd try to take the baby away from you?"

She shook her head at his wounded tone while working her roller back and forth. "No, not that. I don't think you would do that any more than *you* think your dad would. I guess it's more that I'd be scared because a baby is a huge thing. It changes your entire life."

She'd witnessed that reality when Mae had Ian, and even experienced it a bit herself on the fringes. There's nothing she wouldn't do for her godson.

"Would you want it?"

Asher's follow-up question lifted her gaze without hesitation. "Yes, I'd want it. The alternatives wouldn't even be an option for me."

Relief flashed in his eyes, and she saw his shoulders relax when he shifted back and reached for the last of his burger.

Tilting her head slightly, she asked, "Would you?"

"Oh, hell yes," he said around a mouthful of food. "No other options for me, either."

His unhesitating enthusiasm was heartwarming and sexy in a way she never could've imagined with food in his mouth. She smiled to herself as she picked up her cookie cutter to start the petals. Her skin prickled when she sensed his renewed scrutiny, but she ignored the heat in her cheeks and kept her gaze down.

He finished eating, drained the last of his beer, then rose to gather together what was left of their mess.

"Do you want kids?" he asked somewhat casually. "Like in general, not because of some *oops*."

Her pulse skipped at that question. She loved kids, but never allowed herself to go there in her mind or heart. After all her parents' divorces, she'd vowed years ago no kids without a husband. Marrying someone she didn't love wasn't an option any more than not taking responsibility for an 'oops', but did she really need to explain that when Asher already knew how she felt about love?

"That's not an easy question to answer," she stalled.

"Sure it is. You say yes or no."

"It's not that simple."

"From right now to how you end up with them isn't that simple, but whether or not you *want* them is."

She needed to say *no*. "Yes."

Damn it.

"Someday," she quickly added to combat a second swell of hopeful giddiness.

"Me, too."

His affirmation sparked another excited leap of her pulse. Her clients, Jules and Ty, had gotten married and divorced because they'd never had the kid conversation, yet here she and Asher had just had it, and she didn't even believe in love.

This was getting way too dangerous. And yet resisting him, denying herself…both were impossible.

From beneath her lashes, she watched him toss the garbage, then he walked around her to swipe the dishcloth from the sink to clean the table. When he brushed unnecessarily close on his way back, a heady rush of awareness surged forward with even more force than before. All their talk of babies had her thinking about how to create one in the first place.

Thinking about making a baby with Asher had her body lighting up and tingling in all the right places. A fortifying breath kept her from tossing the cutter and throwing herself at him. Barely. But she had to summon some self-control or she'd shuck her apron and everything else right there.

Imagining *that* scene made her think of Mae saying she didn't want that image in her head, and she choked on a giggle.

"What?" Asher asked.

She pressed her lips together and shook her head. Nope. Not admitting those x-rated thoughts out loud. His gaze narrowed, and she quickly asked, "What do you have going on this week?"

"A couple of standard shoots for the Colorado Conservationist. Another one for the botanical gardens."

"No travel to an exotic land?"

"Not until end of the month, and only then if you consider Wyoming exotic."

"Is that the skydiving?"

"Yes."

"Exotic enough."

He leaned a hip against the counter and braced his hand on the sink. "The offer still stands for you to come with me."

"And my answer is still definitely no," she retorted.

"Worth a try." His slight smile fell as he watched her cut out a half-dozen petals. "I suppose I should go and let you get your work done."

She cast him a sideways glance. "Or you could hang out a bit—unless you're mad at me for what I said earlier."

"I'm not mad at you. I appreciate you listening and your input."

Thank God. "Is your brother waiting back at the house?"

"Loyal's a big boy. He can entertain himself—if he's even back yet."

"Then stay."

He eased closer along the counter. "There's one small problem with that."

"What's that?"

"If I stay, I'm going to want to touch you. If I touch you, I'm going to want to kiss you." His voice went all rough and husky in a way that made her stomach flutter like crazy. "And if I kiss you, I'm going to want to do so much more."

By the time he finished speaking, his hard chest pressed against her arm, and he slid his hand along her back to grasp her hip. Honor's breath caught in her lungs, and it took everything she had to keep making cutouts of the rolled out fondant. It was just for show, though. She wasn't going to do a damn thing with any of the petals before her lips were on his, and after that, by the time she made it back, they'd be dried out and worthless.

"What makes you think that's a problem?" she asked breathlessly.

"You were very adamant about short breaks."

"Oh." She feigned disappointment. "Yeah, I was, wasn't I?"

"Mm-hm."

She made a show of looking at the clock, tipping her head sideways in blatant invitation. "Well…I've got about five minutes left. How quick can you be?"

He chuckled at her teasing. "I refuse to be that quick."

Good answer.

His fingers flexed on her hip as he leaned closer. When his lips grazed the side of her neck while his other hand rose from the counter to cup the side of her face, she gave a shaky sigh. "You'd have had more time if you'd touched me when I opened the door."

"I wanted to."

His warm breath on her sensitive skin weakened her knees with anticipation, like earlier when she'd first opened the door to his rakish grin. "Why didn't you?"

"I didn't want your food to get cold," he rumbled.

Another good answer, and yet she forced a laugh as his mouth journeyed from her neck, to the underside of her jaw, to her chin. "You were just hungry."

"That, too." His lips curved against her skin. "I'm still hungry."

"Want me to get you some cake?"

"All I want is you, Honor." His mouth hovered a hairsbreadth away from hers. "Only you."

Best answer ever.

As his lips crushed against hers, she twisted into his arms and forgot all about the sugar flowers on her counter.

CHAPTER 28

*a*sher carried the tray he'd found in Honor's kitchen up to her bedroom. She was sleeping on her stomach, red hair spilled across her navy blue pillow case. He stood for a moment, gaze tracing the curve of her bare shoulder in the early morning light as he remembered her soft skin beneath his hands and mouth, her alluring scent, and the addicting taste of her on his tongue.

Loyal had told him to go get his heart broken. After last night, that was entirely possible, because she had his heart in the palm of her hand. He loved spending time with her as much as he loved loving her in bed. Even when their conversation had gotten slightly heated, he loved hearing her take on the situation. Well, more so he loved that she wasn't afraid to speak her mind, even though she'd immediately apologized.

And he loved that she wanted kids, even if it was *someday*.

A glance at her nightstand clock had him moving forward. She stirred when he braced one knee on the mattress, and his heart swelled when she rolled over and gave him a shy smile.

"Mmm, morning."

Her sleep-husky voice made his dick twitch behind the zipper of his jeans. The temptation to strip down and crawl back into bed with her rose up hard.

"Hi."

She pushed up to sit, pulling the sheet with her to cover her breasts. As she brushed her long hair back from her face, her lashes lifted, her green gaze rising along his body until it met his. He bridged the tray across her legs, and leaned over to give her a soft kiss.

"You're not staying?" she asked.

The moment the question was out, he noticed her lips press together, as if she wished she hadn't let him hear her disappointment. But he was thrilled she was unable to contain the emotion.

"Unfortunately, I have an appointment I can't miss."

She nodded and lifted the bowl he'd improvised as a plate cover to peek at the breakfast he'd made her.

"Scrambled eggs," he supplied. "I hope you're good with that?"

"I'm great with scrambled eggs." She lowered the cover and lifted her gaze again. "You didn't have to do this."

"I figured it was better than a note on the counter."

She tipped her head to the side with a subdued grin. "You're a smart guy."

"I have my moments," he agreed. Though right now, he was kicking himself for not rescheduling his meeting the second he woke up beside her. He hated the thought of giving her more time to over-think things between them. "I gotta get going, but I'll text you later."

"Okay."

He leaned in one last time to press his lips to hers. Before he could pull back, her hand rose the back of his head, fingers threading through his hair as she opened her mouth and drew him in with the sensual glide of her tongue against his.

His heart rate spiked on a hot surge of desire. He buried his hands in her hair and pressed her back into the pillows, but then had to break the kiss before he lost the ability to walk away.

Resting his forehead against hers, he brushed her cheek with his knuckles. "Any chance I can bring you dinner again tonight?"

After a moment of hesitation, she shook her head with a negative hum.

"Not even five percent?" he coaxed past his own disappointment. "Cuz I can work with that."

Her breath fanned his lips with her laugh. "I'll make something for us."

His pulse leapt with joy even as he protested, "But you have work to do, Butter Cream."

The roll of her eyes was accompanied by a smile. "I have an easy chicken chili recipe I can throw in the slow cooker. Takes me five minutes and then it cooks all day."

"You're sure?" *Dumb ass. Take the offer and run.*

"Positive," she affirmed. "It'll be ready anytime after six."

"I will see you then."

He couldn't resist one more taste of her delectable lips, then got his ass out of her bedroom before he completely tossed being professional out the window and stood up his client.

Back across the street, he discovered Loyal had come home at some point and left again with his rental. The unmade bed in his guest room told him his brother had likely left that morning, though Asher hadn't seen his departure while he'd been cooking Honor's breakfast.

He showered and headed out to his appointment, then detoured over to his parents' house by late morning to check on his dad, who hadn't gone into the office for the first time in years.

Celia had sent a group text to all the siblings earlier that Mom had gone up to the St. Julien Hotel and Spa in Boulder. The location prompted a flurry of speculation if she'd gone to see Grayson or his mother, Vivian, but Celia didn't have any other details beyond their mother's express desire to be left alone for the time being, and to not tell their father where she was staying.

Then she had to sign off for court, and Shelby had class, while Loyal, and Merit surprisingly, reported they were helping out at campaign headquarters for the day.

Elena gave him a hug when he entered the kitchen. "How are you doing, hun?"

"Okay. How's everything here?"

She lifted a shoulder. "About as good as can be expected. Your father is working through a bottle of scotch in his study."

Asher arched his brows.

Her expression was grim as she nodded. "He told Eugene off first thing this morning. It wasn't pretty."

Yesterday, he'd been wrapped up in damage control, and today he was telling his campaign manager to bug off? Not good. He hadn't talked to his dad since the night the news broke two days ago, so he made his way into the study after asking Elena to make them a fresh, strong pot of coffee.

His father sat behind his desk, chair turned to face the window, his hair standing on end from the fingers currently threaded through the silver-tinged strands. In his other hand was a tumbler half-full of scotch, with the half-empty glass decanter within reach on the desk. His tie was crooked, top button undone, and he hadn't shaved. His father always shaved.

"Hey, Dad."

The governor glanced in his direction before raising his glass for a deep swallow.

Asher's chest constricted with sympathy for the pain in his red-rimmed, brown eyes. He snagged another tumbler from the side bar and walked over to pour an inch of the amber liquid. He sat in a chair and held the glass without raising it to his lips. It had been something to do, but on second thought, he didn't want a drink.

His dad, on the other hand, emptied his in a couple of swallows and poured himself more.

"What's the plan, Dad?" he finally prompted.

"I don't know."

His gruff voice sounded as defeated as he looked. His dad always had a plan. He'd taught his kids to always have a plan. That way when life threw you a curve ball, you assess the plan, adjust, and keep moving forward.

Celia, Loyal, and Shelby were big on the plan Plan. Merit's plan was no plan at all. Asher's had been to bury himself in his career and someday find the right woman to share his life and start a family. Not much of a concrete roadmap, he realized, but after meeting Honor, it couldn't have been more perfect.

It might take time to convince her love—everlasting love —was something she could believe in, but he had time to show her just how good it could be.

A leather squeak across the desk drew his attention to see his father reaching for the decanter again. Asher surged up and snatched the alcohol from his hand. "If you don't have a plan, then it's time to figure one out. But you gotta be sober."

His dad slumped back in his chair. He'd aged these past two days, looking a good ten years older than his fifty-six years. The disparity of his father's weary, dejected image layered over his happy, optimistic thoughts of Honor had his gut knotting with guilt and unexpected doubt. He'd been in his dad's position before, but more so out of humiliated anger over Brianna's duplicity, not heartbreak.

Honor could break his heart.

If he continued down the road he was on, she could shatter it in a million pieces and have him looking exactly like this tomorrow. Because hell, if his parents could split up after thirty-five years, what chance did he have with someone who made no secret over her lack of faith in love? Who was he to think he could be the one to make her believe?

A stab of fear was bowled over by guilt for his selfishness. He was here for his dad, not to think only of himself. And his parents were *not* split up. They were taking time to work through a hundred and five mile-per-hour curveball.

He set aside his own worries and asked his dad, "Have you talked to Mom since Saturday night?"

A slow shake of his head barely stirred the gray strands sticking up from his scalp. "She won't answer my calls. Won't text me. Nothing. I don't know where she is or if she's even okay."

"She is okay," he started. His dad's gaze jerked to his, and he held up a hand. "She texted Celia, but you gotta give her some time, Dad. That's step one of the plan."

He rubbed a hand over his face, his palm rasping over the gray stubble on his chin. "I should've told her. All those years ago, I should've told her what happened. What I did."

Asher didn't know if he agreed or not, so he simply listened as his father continued, the words tumbling drunkenly from his mouth.

"But I was afraid she'd change her mind and file the divorce papers, and I'd lose her forever. But then...I think that if I *had* told her, maybe I would've found out about this boy, this *man*, who is my son. I hate that I haven't known him all this time. That you kids didn't know your brother. But, if

I'd told your mother what I did and she'd left me, I wouldn't have any of you kids, and I can't bear the thought of that either."

The forlorn guilt in his father's rough voice as he went back and forth put a lump in his throat. If he'd ever doubted his dad's love for their mom or the family—which he hadn't —his heartbreak right now reinforced his absolute devotion.

Asher blew out a sigh as he rose to go set his glass and the decanter back on the side bar. He'd originally been angry with his father, but having considered the situation further, he could understand Loyal and Merit's view that if the divorce papers were signed, as far as his father believed, it was over. If he'd been as heartbroken then as he was now, he could understand him getting drunk and making a stupid mistake.

Hell, he could even understand Vivian not telling his dad about Grayson if Honor's possible explanation were true. He didn't like any of it, but he could understand the potential fear that would have motivated the woman's decisions back then.

Returning to the desk, he said, "I think things happened the way they were supposed to happen, and even if they didn't, you can't change it now."

"I can't bear it if she doesn't come back."

"Mom will come back, Dad." She would, wouldn't she? Of course she would. After thirty-five years and the family they had, he couldn't imagine his mom throwing it all away. "You just need a chance to talk to her again. And when she's ready for that, you can apologize."

"I apologized a hundred times already."

He knew that. Just like his father had apologized to him and all his siblings Saturday night. "Then you'll apologize again. As many times as it takes."

"I don't think she'll forgive me for this. And I can't really blame her. I beat myself up over it for years before I finally convinced myself we were happy, we had a great life, a great family, so that one night didn't really matter. It was nothing after all." His brow furrowed in a deep frown. "A nothing that led to a baby."

"You not knowing about Grayson isn't your fault, Dad."

He shook his head, the exaggerated movement revealing the effects of the alcohol. "I know that, rationally I know, but it doesn't matter in here." He pressed his hand to his chest, face twisted as if it hurt. Tears filled his eyes, and his head lolled forward toward his chest as he mumbled, "I should've told her."

A quiet knock turned Asher to the door, and he rose to meet Elena halfway across the room. He gave her brief smile as he took the tray loaded with coffee, cups, and a couple of sandwiches. "Thanks. Good call on the food."

"You guys okay?"

"We will be."

She gave an understanding nod and a light squeeze on his forearm. "Anything else, just let me know."

By the time his father drank some coffee and ate half the sandwich, he'd rebounded enough to stop wallowing. Asher directed the conversation to positive actions until Loyal and Merit arrived an hour later with campaign stuff. The four of them worked into the afternoon, and after four, Celia and Shelby joined in. It felt like old times, if they didn't dwell on the fact Mom didn't bring in afternoon treats. They all noticed, but none of them spoke it out loud.

It was almost six p.m. when Asher pulled Loyal aside. "Honor's making dinner. You guys got this?"

"Yeah, we're good. I'll see you later." He raised his eyebrows and clapped him on the shoulder. "Or, maybe not."

Asher grinned on his way out the door, sent Honor a text he was on his way, then spent the next fifteen minutes unaccountably nervous on the drive home. He thought of his mom again, and used voice command to call her cell phone.

It went straight to voicemail, and he left a quick message as he pulled into his garage. "Hey, Mom. I hope you're doing okay. First off, know that I love you, and I'll love you no matter where any of this ends up. Dad's pretty wrecked right now, and that's not to make less of what you're going through, but just to let you know he loves you more than anything. When you're ready, I hope you will give him a chance to talk before you make any decisions. And if you need to talk, or if you need anything at all, please know we're all here for you. Love you."

He ended the call and shut off his car to make his way across the street. Just like the first time he'd gone to Honor's the night after his parents' anniversary party, his pulse raced with a combination of nerves and anticipation. He was doing his best to keep the sliver of doubt from earlier in the day from rearing its ugly head when his phone buzzed a text notification.

Honor: *Door's open.*

Realizing she must've seen him, he tried for a glimpse through the kitchen window but saw she'd drawn the curtains. The door handle easily twisted beneath his hand, and he called out, "Hello," as he stepped inside.

"In here," she replied from the kitchen.

All it took was the sound of her voice to make his heart leap with excitement. As he shut the door, his gaze snagged on a pair of charcoal gray leggings lying on the floor near the entry, and with his next step, he saw a pink T-shirt crumpled near the foyer wall. Curiosity took him around the corner, and his brain registered a bra and panties scattered halfway between him and the kitchen island at the same moment he lifted his gaze.

His instinct to confirm what he'd seen on the floor was

instantly overridden by his stunned double take when he saw Honor next to the island holding a pastry bag of frosting— wearing nothing but her apron. Her hair was down, the luscious red curls spilling over her shoulders and down her back, but it was the sight of her bare breasts, the outer edges of her dusky pink areolas peeking out on either side of the apron, that robbed him of his breath and sent a jolt of heat fizzing through his veins.

"How do you feel about dessert first?" she asked in a slightly unsure voice.

He forced his steps to be slow and deliberate while raking his greedy gaze down the length of her luscious body and back up to her beautiful, flushed face. "I'm always up for frosting."

Right now. Literally.

Her gaze dropped below his waist, then lifted, and the tremulous smile she gave him wiped away any doubt festering in his mind. Or his fear of it anyway.

She still looked a little nervous when he moved in for a kiss, but she raised her arms to loop around his neck. He crushed her close, devouring her mouth, relishing her sweet scent and savoring the unique flavor of her on his tongue. His restless hands slid down past the apron strings at the small of her back, and he groaned against her lips when he cupped her bare ass to tug her against his arousal.

"Best dessert ever," he declared, his voice rough.

"You've barely gotten a taste," she breathed.

"Hmm." He walked her around to the side of the island next to the sink and hoisted her onto the empty counter. Empty save for a condom. "As of right now, I have a new rule about dessert."

"What's that?"

He captured her gaze as he took the bag of frosting from her hand. "Take my time and savor every bite."

Her throat muscles worked in a hard swallow, but her heated green gaze never left his as she reclined on her elbows and shook her hair back over her shoulders. The movement jostled her breasts, spilling them farther out the sides of the apron. He moved in between her spread legs and piped frosting around the tip of each exposed nipple, his hands trembling with need.

Her breathing had gone shallow by the time he was done, and her low moan of pleasure when he bent to suck the first one clean made his body throb hard. Urgency tensed his whole body, but he honored his new rule and took his time, making her climax twice before sheathing himself to thrust deep into her welcoming heat right there on the counter. Afterward, her warm lips tickled his throat as she murmured his name against his sweat-slick skin.

Right then, he knew it didn't matter how long they had together. No matter the risk, his heart was indeed hers, and he would cherish every minute with her—be it a week, a month, or thirty-five years.

He prayed for the thirty-five and more.

CHAPTER 29

"*T*his is getting serious." Mae selected a white chocolate raspberry swirl cupcake from the bakery box on Roxanna's coffee counter and joined Honor at one of the café tables. "You've never been with a guy this long."

The second part was true. Unless she counted her boyfriend the summer between junior and senior year of high school—which she didn't. If 'real' love didn't last, then teenage love definitely didn't last. And it hadn't even been love with Derek, just him trying to get into her pants.

The first part appeared to be equally as true—which scared the living daylights out of her more each day. It had been a little over three weeks since Asher had brought her a burger, stayed the night, and then woke her up with breakfast in bed. She'd returned the favor by surprising him in the kitchen wearing only her apron. She'd nearly chickened out, but was so glad she hadn't after he gave her the best sex of her life in the kitchen, and again later upstairs.

Since then, they'd been spending time together every day, learning about each other, their lives, and their families.

They talked—sometimes argued—about anything and everything while she baked and he worked on his laptop. Sometimes he stayed overnight at her place, sometimes she walked across the street to his—after Loyal returned to Texas.

They'd eaten dinners together, gone for walks, drives in his Camaro, and even mountain biking a couple times. He took that shit as seriously as cars and cake, and she'd still had fun despite sore muscles later.

He'd helped her deliver cakes, and in return, she'd played camera assistant on a couple of his jobs. She discovered she loved watching him work. His concentration, attention to detail, and the instinct he had for getting the perfect shot made him an exceptional photographer, no matter if the subject was plant, animal, landscape, or person. She'd even found herself his subject on more than one occasion, both while working and playing.

Things seemed perfect. She was happier with Asher than she could ever remember being, which was the exact reason her mounting anxiety was becoming harder to brush aside. Chest-tightening panic had struck a few times in their quiet moments together. Emotional moments. He always managed to say or do something just right to make her smile, or laugh, or turn her into a mindless puddle of desire, but when she was by herself, fear, doubt, and common sense would resurface with a vengeance.

Seeming perfect wasn't perfect, and something this good couldn't last. All she had to do was look at his parents. His mother had returned home last week, and while she put on a good public face with the governor, Asher had told her they were still not speaking in private. The household was positively glacial as they awaited the results of the second DNA test Grayson had finally consented to have done.

Honor toyed with her coffee cup, watching her best friend peel the wrapper from her cupcake, while Roxanna poured steaming water over a tea bag in her mug and reached for a honey stick. Mae was still working her remodel job a few blocks away, and she'd taken to popping in for a coffee break when Honor brought fresh cupcakes each morning.

Mae and Roxanna had clicked right away, while Honor and the psychic had moved from toleration to tentative friendship.

Her best friend's revealing comment about her having never been with a guy this long exposed her worries in one succinct sentence, and she found herself revealing, "He asked me to go to Wyoming with him next week."

The brunette store owner paused mid-reach for a spoon. "He did?"

She nodded, her stomach tightening at the surprise in Roxanna's voice. "The first time he asked, he joked about me skydiving with him, so I didn't think much of it."

Mae jerked her attention up from the treat in her hand, her blond hair swaying about her shoulders. "You? Jump out of a plane?"

Honor laughed at her wide eyes and arched brows. "I know. I told him it was never gonna happen." Spending three weeks with him was the riskiest thing she'd done in years. Or ever. "But this morning, he suggested I still come with since I haven't filled the cancellation for the last weekend in June."

Mae licked white chocolate frosting swirled with raspberry from her finger. "Are you going to go?"

Her stomach clenched again, knotted in an unsettling combination of anticipation and anxiety. "I'm not sure. I want to go, but I'm a little scared it'll ruin everything."

More like a lot scared.

Roxanna sat down with her mug. "How would it ruin everything?"

Indecision held her tongue. Much as she wanted her

input, there was the whole best friends factor. What if Asher ended up hearing all about this little chat-fest?

"I wouldn't betray your trust, Honor. I promise, whatever you say is between us."

She scraped her thumbnail up and down the seam of her cup while the psychic stirred her tea. "I'm afraid he'll read too much into it."

In fact, Roxanna's earlier surprise was a perfect indication the concern had merit. If the invite wasn't standard operating procedure for him, then maybe it was as big a deal for him as it was her.

He was an amazing guy—and the sex was equally so. But in the back of her mind was the ever-present nagging reminder of the psychic's warning the night of his parents' anniversary party. Asher believed in love, and all the stuff they were doing together pointed to him settling in for the long haul. She'd never let herself get in too deep before and couldn't help worrying about allowing herself to now.

"Maybe *you're* reading too much into it," Mae said.

"Really?" She frowned at her friend. "You think so?"

"It's just a couple days away, right?"

"Yes, but you're the one who said it was getting serious."

"Forget that." She waved her free hand and then tucked her blond hair behind her ear. "Forget serious. Put it all out of your head and just relax and have fun. Take your own advice, you know?"

"I am having fun." More so than she ever had with someone before. But it was hard to put it out of her head when even that made her nervous. She kept expecting the feeling to go away, or at least fade, but each time she saw him, her pulse still leapt like the first time she'd spotted him at his friends' wedding almost six weeks earlier.

"When you think about it," Mae continued, "maybe this

has been the longest relationship you've ever had, but in guy-time, you two have been together for like two minutes."

Together. Relationship. Hard to forget *serious* with those other two words added to the mix.

Roxanna arched an eyebrow. "Guy time?"

"Yeah. A month or so in, most guys are stuck in the having fun-slash-hanging out phase."

Honor cocked her head. "And you're basing this off of what, Miss I Haven't Had Sex in Six Years?"

"Hey—you don't say that out loud." She looked around, but the closest customer was at the front of the store.

Roxanna pantomimed zipping her lips shut and tossing the key over her shoulder. Honor flipped her palms skyward. "It's a fair question."

Mae made a face before answering. "Jen and Becca each waited over three years for their engagement rings. It took my brothers five and seven years to propose. And what about the guys you consult for proposals? Are they promising *'til death do us part* after barely a month?"

"No."

"There you go, then. Stop over-thinking this thing and let yourself live in the moment for once. He's going to be working half the time anyway, so just go with him and have fun." She lifted the last bite of cupcake as she looked at Roxanna. "Don't you agree?"

Honor's pulse picked up speed as she waited for the brunette's response.

"Yeah, definitely."

The indifferent agreement didn't settle Honor's anxiety, but Mae didn't seem to notice as she rose to her feet and picked up her coffee. "See? And if you ask me, I think you should skydive, too."

"Well, I *didn't* ask you."

She grinned and headed for the door. "Let me know when you're leaving."

After the chimes faded back to harmonious flutes, Honor met Roxanna's somber gaze. Her stomach flipped over as she asked, "What do you really think?"

"Skydiving could be fun."

"You know that's not what I meant."

Roxanna's soft sigh confirmed she did. "I think…if you're in this…*relationship* with the expectation it's going to end, then you'll *find* a reason to end it. That doesn't seem fair to Asher or you."

After a moment, Honor realized she was right. It wasn't fair to him at all. She didn't want to get hurt, but hurting him would be worse. Letting this thing between them go too far would be much worse.

The voice in her head tried to speak it was far too late, but she drowned it out with a goodbye to Roxanna and turned up the radio on her way home.

CHAPTER 30

*A*sher unpacked cartons of Chinese take-out on his coffee table and glanced at Honor sitting to his right on the couch. She'd appeared apprehensive when she first arrived, but then she'd melted into his kiss hello in that way that always melted his heart. Yet, once again, when she stepped away, something seemed to shift, and it had felt like an end to more than their kiss.

Unease formed a knot in the pit of his stomach that refused to go away. Everything had been going great, especially the past couple of days. This morning, they'd slept in and then snuggled in her bed with coffee and croissants. They'd parted with a long, lingering kiss...so, what had changed from then to now?

"Everything okay?" he asked carefully.

She shot him a quick sideways smile while reaching for chopsticks and a carton of chicken and broccoli. "Fine. How was the shoot?"

Last thing he wanted to talk about right now was work when she wouldn't look him in the eye. "Same old routine. I can't wait for next week."

Her fingers tightened on her chopsticks, and he recalled Roxanna's earlier text. *Don't push too hard.* When she'd refused to elaborate, he'd been stuck wracking his brain as to what she meant. Honor's texts through the day had seemed normal, but what could really be judged from texts?

Seeing her tension now at the mere mention of the Wyoming trip, he was pretty sure he'd figured out what not to push too hard about. "Speaking of next week," he began.

"I can't go," she blurted out. "I'm sorry."

"Don't be sorry." He forced himself to sit back casually with his food when he really wanted to take her hands and kiss her and seduce her into saying yes. The tactic had worked well the past few weeks whenever he sensed her head getting in the way of her heart. "If you don't want to go, you don't have to go. It's not that big of a deal."

Her gaze met his for a long second, then shifted away. "It's just that even though I don't have a wedding cake client, I still need to make cupcakes for Roxanna's. I need the sales to make up the difference from the cancellations so I can make my house payment. And I need to start figuring out a way to drum up some more bookings, or I won't be living here very long."

At first he was thinking about her over-justifying saying no when he'd already more than let her off the hook, but then the very last part registered. He hadn't realized her budget was so tight. "Do you need help? Because I can—"

She jerked her head up, resentment blazing in her eyes.

Shit. Wrong thing to say.

"I don't want your money, Asher. I don't need a man to bail me out."

"I didn't mean it that way." Confusion and frustration swirled inside his chest, and he scrambled for a substitute solution that wouldn't piss her off and offend her independence. "I was going to say, I could put together a brochure for you, like the one for the climbing school. You could use them for promo."

Her expression relaxed, though a slight frown remained with her nod. "Sorry I jumped on you."

He shrugged as if it was no big deal, but in reality, he hated that he couldn't use his resources to take the pressure off of her shoulders. How ironic that he'd always wanted a woman who didn't want his money, and now that he had one, all he wanted to do was offer it to her. Ease her worries, make her happy.

Or are you simply trying to play hero so she has no choice but to fall in love with you? A knight in shining armor, riding to the rescue.

Well, that would be idiotic, wouldn't it?

After they finished eating and were putting the leftovers away in the kitchen, he asked, "You want to watch a movie, or catch up on a couple episodes of *That 70's Show?*"

She handed over the last container of fried rice. "I, um…I think I'm going to head back to my place."

There it was again. He gripped the handle of the refrigerator door as he closed it and faced her. The look on her face tightened the knots in his stomach once more. He clenched his jaw against his rising anxiety. "What's going on?"

"I just prefer to head home," she said defensively.

"Honor, at least be honest with me. If you're mad about the brochure, I don't have to—"

"I'm not mad about the brochure."

"Then what is it? Because after this past month, it seems to me we should be way past the point where me offering to help is offensive. Whether it's a brochure or even money."

"And I told you, I don't want your money. My business is exactly that—*my* business."

"Of course it is, and it always will be. But in general, I'm going to do things for you. And I'm going to buy things for you, and I don't think I should have to feel bad for that."

"Then don't and you won't have to feel bad," she retorted with a frown.

"That was so not my point." He blew out a sigh and raked a hand through his hair as he tried to figure out what the hell was going on. "This is going the wrong direction, and I don't even know that we're talking about the right thing. You've been pulling away since you got here."

Guilt flashed in her eyes before she averted her gaze. His stomach lurched as he waited for her to explain, but she turned her back, one hand braced on his island counter. He fisted his hands against rising fear.

"Honor. This is where we work on things together. Make sure we're both on the same page so it's not—"

"This isn't going to work," she interrupted.

"—so scary."

She swiped a hand over her cheeks as her shoulders rose with a deep inhale. "I need to go home because I can't do this."

As she took a step forward, he stuffed down a surge of panic and gently caught her shoulders. "Hey. Whoa. Let's talk this out first."

After a moment of resisting his hold, she relented and let him turn her around. The tears in her eyes squeezed his heart to the point it hurt to draw in a breath.

He pulled her into his arms, holding tight as he pressed her cheek against his chest. "It's okay. Everything is fine. We're fine."

And for a moment, he believed it. She was warm and pliant in his arms, her weight leaning against him in complete trust. He stroked her hair before pressing his lips to the top of her head, his racing heartbeat easing.

In the next breath, she stiffened and pushed away while

raising her anguished gaze to his. "I told you from the start this wouldn't work out."

"What's not working out?"

"This." She waved her hand back and forth in the space between them. "You and me."

Chest tight, he caught her hand and tugged her closer. He needed her back in his arms. When she was in his arms, what they had together overrode the doubt. She held back once again, but he kept hold of her hand.

"You and me are working great, Honor. I know you've felt it as much as I have. The past month has been amazing."

"It has been, but it's not going to last."

"Says who?"

"Everyone I know."

"I'm not saying that," he countered. "I'm saying the exact opposite of that."

She huffed out a sigh of exasperation. "You know what I meant."

"No, I really don't. Who says it's not going to last?"

"My family. My friends. *Your* parents."

"I don't give a shit what anyone else says—"

"It's not what they literally say, it's what's happened in their lives. It's right there for anyone to see, plain as day."

"*We aren't them.* This is about *you* and *me*, no one else. And I say we've got years and years ahead of us."

"Because you're a long-haul guy. That's not me."

She was back to avoiding his gaze, her voice sad and heartbroken. As if she wanted what she was convinced she couldn't have. It illuminated the distinction of her saying she *couldn't* do this, not that she *didn't want to* do this.

"You can be. It's all up to you and what you want."

"It's not a matter of what I want, it's what *is*."

The revelation in that sentence broke his heart. Hopeless.

"You want to know what *is?* Look at me." When her green

gaze rose to his, his heart damn near beat out of his chest. He squeezed her hand with a gentle smile. "I love you."

Panic filled her expression. She yanked her hand free with a shake of her head. Stepping back out of his reach, she said, "You can't love me."

"But I do," he said firmly. "With all my heart."

"You can't," she repeated, her voice trembling like a frightened, cornered animal. "You're supposed to be on guy-time."

"What the hell is guy-time?"

Tears filled her eyes. "It doesn't matter. You've known from the beginning where I stood on all this."

"You mean how you've felt about love?"

She nodded.

"Funny thing about that, you've never actually said it." She took a breath to speak, but he held up his hand. "There was the whole hypothetical conversation early on, but never once have you said out loud to me that you don't believe in love."

Her brows dipped, her expression uncertain.

"My theory is, it's not that you don't believe in love. You just haven't known what it was until now—what it *is*. You haven't seen it and experienced it for yourself. But now that you have, don't you see you don't have to be afraid?"

"I'm not afraid," she argued. "I'm realistic. Nothing lasts. Things get screwed up and then it's over."

"Not always."

"Almost always."

He tilted his head slightly to try a different angle. "Hasn't this felt different for you? At the beginning, I had to fight what I felt for you because I thought you were engaged. And once I found out you weren't, denying what's between us was as impossible as not breathing. I've never had that with anyone before you."

Her wide gaze met his, and he swore he saw a flicker of

the hope that had been missing before. But when he moved toward her, her expression closed off, and she backed up.

Sonofabitch.

"There are exceptions, Honor. You even said so yourself."

"Not in my family."

"In *my* family, there are. My grandparents, my aunts and uncles, and despite the mess right now, even my parents. We could be an exception, too. We *are* the exception for your family."

She shook her head. "No. I told you."

She was so adamant, his voice rose in frustration. "You're so damn scared you won't even *try* to see what's right in front of you."

"I'm not scared," she almost shouted. "Stop telling me what I am. I *know* what I am."

"You're realistic?"

"Exactly." His sarcasm went right over her head as she stated, "Hartman's don't do love. It's not in our DNA."

"Do you hear how stupid that sounds?"

Her eyebrows rose. "Wow. Nice."

"Hey, I'm just being honest. I've been nothing but honest with you the whole time."

"So have I. You knew where I stood."

"That's the second time you've said *stood*," he pointed out.

Her gaze narrowed. "Stand. You know where I *stand*."

She was like fucking Roxanna, unable to admit when she was wrong. And she was so damn wrong right now.

"What I know is you're lying to yourself. You do believe, or at the very least you *want* to believe, but you're too afraid to love someone because it's all about taking a God-awful risk."

Her gaze flicked away, and he softened his tone.

"It's worth it, Honor, I promise. I'm right here in front of you, and I'm not going anywhere. All you have to do is trust your heart. What we have can last as long as we want it to. I believe that with every fiber of my being." His breath hitched at the next part, but he forced the words out. "Which leaves it up to you. Do you want it to last or are you too afraid to even try?"

In the silence of her telling pause, the truth stabbed deep into his soul. This was what Rox had meant with her cryptic text. *Don't push her.* It hadn't been about the trip. It was about this, right here.

Unfortunately, he couldn't take back his words, and he was reminded of the first day he saw the beautiful, stubborn woman in front of him. Standing on the lawn as her client kneeled in front of her, he'd thought *a woman madly in love shouldn't look away from her lover's eyes—or the ring—when he was on one knee offering her the rest of his life.*

He didn't have a ring, and he wasn't on one knee, but the offer of the rest of his life was just as potent. And Honor was staring at the door as if she couldn't wait to get out of his house and his life forever.

"What people want isn't always what's best, Asher." Her raw, raspy voice dropped to a choked whisper. "This is the way it has to be."

Then she ripped out his heart and walked out the door.

CHAPTER 31

*H*onor shoved the bowl of yellow batter out of reach in frustrated dismay. No matter what she did, no matter how she adjusted the ingredients, it didn't taste right. Nothing she'd baked the past week had tasted right, so this time she'd pulled out the recipe she hadn't used in over four years to make sure she wasn't accidentally forgetting something.

There wasn't a damn thing missing from the recipe.

The only ingredient missing was…Asher.

Better now than later.

Her heart squeezed hard, intensifying the constant ache that had plagued her since she'd walked away from him. A moment later, she realized she was staring out the window at his house. Again.

A dozen times a day she found herself doing the same thing, longing for a glimpse of him. She'd check her phone to see if he'd sent a text before she remembered it was over. Then she got pissed off that he hadn't texted. Or called. Or walked across the street to take her in his arms and tell her he loved her.

But that proved her point, didn't it? If he really did love her, wouldn't he try harder? Or simply, um, try in the first place?

Instead he'd disappeared, and she'd found out from Roxanna he'd left early for the job in Wyoming.

She shouldn't care. She tried so hard not to, yet her emotions alternated between bursting into tears at the drop of a spatula and being angry when the littlest thing went wrong—like another batch of batter tasting like crap. Nights were the hardest, when she had nothing to distract her heart as she lay in bed alone, remembering the heat of him wrapped around her, whispered conversations in the dark, the sound of his voice, the touch of his lips.

Breaking things off had made total sense in her head. If she missed him this much now, imagine the devastation further down the road at the inevitable end. It was definitely better now than later—for both of them. She was saving him the heartache as much as she was saving herself.

Do you hear how stupid that sounds?

Yeah, that was her heart telling her head she was as stupid as Asher had said.

But the heart wasn't any smarter than the mind. He'd told her to trust her heart. Years of watching her mother do that very thing proved following one's heart led to foolish choices and unhappy consequences.

Better now than later.

She wondered how many more times she'd have to say those words before her foolish heart believed them. As she turned away from the window, she noticed a metallic silver Mercedes slowing down to pull into Asher's driveway. She recognized Janine Diamond exiting the luxury car, dressed in a fashionable white pants suit and heeled, red sandals. The woman walked to her son's front door and rang the doorbell, then removed her sunglasses to scan the neighborhood, her black leather bag clutched to her side.

Honor frowned a minute later when she moved to sit in one of Asher's front porch chairs as if to wait. Did she not know he was away for work?

"Not my business," she muttered, forcing herself to turn from the window.

Another taste of the batter on the counter prompted a frustrated growl, and she went to go get a load of laundry from the dryer. She forced herself to fold it and put everything away, but once back in her living room, she couldn't help another look out the window. Mrs. Diamond was still sitting on the porch, her cell phone in hand.

She hadn't seen or spoken to Asher's mother since the night of the anniversary party. With the upheaval in his family, they hadn't done anything with them while they were together. And he hadn't met her family at all, though she'd been forced to tell Glory about him when her sister and friends made their monthly trip to Lift Your Spirit and discovered her cupcakes in the shop. This morning, she'd had to tell Glory it was over already. She may have even cried, but pretended she'd stubbed her toe.

Another glimpse out the window twenty minutes later took her out the door and across the street before she thought about what she was doing. By then, it was too late because the woman had spotted her. Halfway up the driveway, it dawned on her maybe his mom was waiting because she knew Asher was on his way home.

Her heart thumped hard at the possibility of seeing him face to face. But it was a surge of hope that left her mouth dry, not dread.

"Honor?"

"Good morning, Mrs. Diamond. I noticed you sitting over here and wanted to make sure everything is all right?"

"It's Janine, please." The woman glanced across the street to her house. "I had forgotten Asher mentioned you two are neighbors. I came to talk to him, but he doesn't seem to be home, and he's not answering his phone or texts."

"As far as I know, Asher is in Wyoming for a photo shoot."

"Oh." Disappointment weighted the word, and her shoulders drooped. "That's right. I forgot about that, too."

Despite the flawless makeup and not a dark hair out of place, the strain of the past month was evident in the lines around the older woman's eyes and her subdued tone. "You've been dealing with a lot the last few weeks."

Janine averted her gaze, her lips pressed together as sadness and distress chased across her features. A lump of sympathy swelled in her throat, and Honor found she wanted to give the woman a huge, comforting hug. Like the night Asher had come home after seeing his half-brother for the first time.

That ache in her chest sharpened once more, and suddenly she heard herself say, "Would you like to come over for a cup of coffee?"

Now you're just torturing yourself with any connection to him.

The offer came out of nowhere. She hadn't expected to make it, but couldn't retract it. All she could hope is the woman would politely decline and be on her way.

"Oh, thank you. That would be nice," Janine said as she rose.

Cringe-worthy small talk about the weather made the walk back to Honor's house feel like a mile because she didn't know what else to talk about. She didn't want to ask about the governor's campaign because of the family scandal. She couldn't ask about Celia's wedding, because last she'd heard they'd decided to postpone it because of the divide between her parents. She *did* want to ask about Asher, but didn't know if the woman knew she and Asher had broken up, or even that they'd been dating in the first place.

So...the weather morphed to talk of where she did her baking as they approached her front door. The sound of a car turning into her driveway brought Honor around. She frowned in confusion when her own mother parked her red BMW from husband number three.

Had she forgotten to put a lunch date on the calendar? She didn't think so, but even if she had, it was only eleven a.m. and that certainly didn't explain why her mom was walking up the sidewalk with a bottle of tequila.

"Mom? I didn't know you were coming over." *With tequila.*

She stuck a heavily-jeweled hand on her jean capris clad hip, the bracelets around her wrist clinking. "What else am I going to do when I find out my girl's got a broken heart?"

"What?" She tried to scoff, but suddenly her pulse was racing and her eyes burning. "Where did you get that idea?"

"Glory called me."

Snitch.

"Come on, now. We're going to get drunk and cry it out." Before she could protest how much she hated this ritual, her mom moved around her. As she opened the door, she tossed her blond curls over her shoulder and gave Asher's mom a sweeping glance. "Hello. I'm Camilla Burns."

"Janine Diamond."

"The governor's wife," she confirmed with a nod. "I've seen you on TV. Would you like to join us?"

"Mom, I don't think—"

"I would love to."

Honor watched the two of them disappear into her house. Brash and flamboyant next to rich and regal. Talking and laughing, arm in arm as they headed straight for her kitchen.

What the hell is going on?

When Honor joined them, her mother was pouring

tequila into three glasses as she pulled her finger from her mouth. "Honey, this batter is awful."

"I know, Mom." She eyed the liquor her mother slid across the counter. "I'm not drinking at eleven o'clock in the morning."

From her stool at the island counter, Janine shook her sleek salon hair back from her face and lifted her drink in the air. "It's five o'clock somewhere." She downed the liquid in one swallow and banged the glass on the counter. Honor exchanged a wide-eyed look with her mom.

"Oh, I like you," her mother declared before doing the same with her drink and pouring them each another.

This time Janine took a more dignified sip. As she lowered her glass, she gave Honor a sympathetic look. "What did he do?"

She froze like a deer in the headlights. "Nothing." Then she grabbed her glass and took a huge swallow. The alcohol burned a hot trail down her throat and made her cough. Feeling both their gazes, she choked out, "What makes you think he did something?"

"Because he's a man," her mom answered.

Both older women nodded sagely, clinked their glasses, and this time all three of them drank. Honor slumped down onto the stool next to Janine. "He didn't do anything wrong."

"I see." Her mother nodded as she poured again. "So, he's like all the other men you've dated."

"No." *Not even close.*

Bottle in hand, she raised her eyebrows.

"He told me he loved me."

She gave a mock gasp. "The bastard."

"Hey, that's my son you're talking about."

"Right. Sorry."

Janine waved a hand and sipped. Her mother sipped.

Honor cradled her drink in her hands, swirling the clear liquid round and round the glass.

"You don't love him back?" Janine asked.

She glanced up to find them both watching her intently. She ducked her head and swirled the tequila some more. "Love doesn't last. You both know that better than anyone."

"The right love does."

Honor stilled her hands and shot her mother a look from beneath her lashes. "Really, Mom? You can say that with a straight face after four divorces?"

"My dear daughter, why do you think I got married four times?"

The guy was rich? You were lonely?

Both sounded hurtful, so she said, "I don't know."

"I was searching for *my* right love. I still am, and I will keep at it until I find it. I want a man who will love me and fight for me when the going gets tough. Not a single one of my husbands did that. Not even your father, I'm sorry to say."

Her mom had never said anything like that to her before.

You've never asked.

Guilt swelled a hard knot in her throat.

Janine sat up straighter, her hazel gaze shifting to her mom. "My husband fought for me. Twice. He's been fighting for me since the news of his love child broke."

"Oh, honey, you have to be in love to create a love child," her mom chided. "Sorry to say, but given what I've heard, you can hardly blame the boy or the woman in your case."

"I don't blame either of them."

Honor swiveled her seat toward Janine. "Asher said you both had signed divorce papers the night it happened?"

The woman nodded as she drained her glass and motioned for more. Honor's mom didn't lift the bottle.

"Mark came to the house the next day, begging me to

work things out. He said he'd never stopped loving me, and asked for us to start over. To give him a second chance."

"And you gave him one."

Her slim shoulders lifted in a helpless shrug. "I still loved him. He never told me he'd slept with another woman the night before."

"And if he had?" Honor asked. "Would you have worked things out?"

"I don't know." She looked down at her glass, left hand tapping the side, her ring clinking each time. Her hand paused as she stared down at the large solitaire and interwoven diamond encrusted wedding band. Her fingers shook, and she gripped the empty glass once more. "I honestly don't know that I would have forgiven him. It would've been too fresh."

"Given what you now know, do you wish he would've told you? Do you wish you'd have gone through with the divorce all those years ago?"

Janine stared hard at her ring for a long moment, then she lifted her head, her expression solemn, but no longer lined with stress. "No, I don't. How could I? We have a family together, five wonderful children, and thirty-five amazing years. Well, thirty-four. That year prior to our decision to divorce *was* awful. And though there were also some strained times through the years, we'd learned by then how to work hard at our marriage. Unless I take the time to really think about the crappy stuff, the things I remember first are the happy times. Lots of happy times with our kids." A soft, reminiscent smile took ten years off her face. "The answer is definitely no. I don't wish for anything to have changed any of that."

"Do you still love the man?" her mom asked.

"I do." Tears welled in her eyes as she splayed her left

hand against her chest and smiled at the both of them. "With all my heart."

Honor's pulse leapt at the same words Asher had said to her a week ago.

"Then forgive him and enjoy the rest of your years together."

Janine nodded and her mother turned to Honor. "And what about you? Do you love this guy of yours?"

Her heart stuttered before pounding high in her throat. What if she did—would it even matter? He hadn't tried to contact her all week. What if she was too late? What if he'd realized when she left that he didn't really love her? What if he didn't think she was worth fighting for?

All the *what if*'s were adding up to a mass of fear—the exact fear Asher had accused her of.

When she didn't answer, her mom leaned across the counter and took hold of both her hands. "Don't let fear keep you from something that could be amazing. It's time to jump, my dear. Have some faith and trust your heart. Trust his, too."

Eyes wide, she swallowed hard. "Geez, Mom, did you talk to him?"

"No, baby, but I know you. And, I tasted your batter, and I know exactly what's missing."

"What?"

"Love."

CHAPTER 32

*G*eared up and ready to go, Asher waited impatiently for the rest of his group to finish their pre-flight safety checks. There were two tandem jumpers, and he was one of three solo jumpers. He would be taking pictures both during free fall and once he pulled his chute, plus video via his helmet cam.

Another group was jumping before them, their plane right now taxiing down the runway. As he watched them take off and climb in altitude, the ever-present thoughts of Honor were right there clamoring for attention. This time he let them flow.

He'd been hurt when she'd walked out. Even knowing her fears, it hurt like hell that she'd tossed his love aside. Then he'd gotten pissed off that she hadn't even been willing to *try* and left for Wyoming early so he didn't have to see her across the street.

He'd spent the past week in the mountains, hiking, climbing, biking, pushing himself to the brink of his physical capabilities, exhausting himself physically and mentally so he wouldn't lie in bed at night thinking of her. Yet, hers was the last face in his mind when he closed his eyes, and she was the first person he thought of the moment he woke up.

After the first day, he'd wanted to call her and let her know he wasn't going to give up so easy. But fear was an insidious thing, creeping in to make him hesitate each time he opened his contacts. All his life he'd seen his parents and grandparents happy. Other than small disagreements, he'd never witnessed them fight, so the idea of them ever splitting up had never even crossed his mind—until the scandal broke. Even then, he'd been adamant with Loyal that they'd be okay. They'd work it out. But the last time he'd seen his mom and dad in the same room, he'd finally had to acknowledge the more likely possibility they wouldn't.

His fundamental beliefs were challenged once more. What if love wasn't enough? If he was the hopeless romantic sap Roxanna had called him at the wedding almost two months ago, and he gave Honor everything and she didn't want it—didn't want *him*—she would totally wreck him for life.

High in the sky, little dots tumbled out of the plane as all the doubts and fear of the past five days coalesced into one unavoidable truth—the two of them together did not depend on anyone else in the world but them. He'd said those words to her and then forgotten them himself.

Worth the risk, remember?

Yes, she was. He had to trust his heart, the same as he'd told her to do. The night of his parents' anniversary party, he'd felt deep down she was *The One.* Every day since had only reinforced that belief.

His pulse picked up speed as his thoughts gained excitement.

Now was not the time to give up. She was afraid to trust

in love, afraid to want what she didn't think was possible, so he needed to fight with everything he had to prove to her it was okay to want forever. Okay to *believe* in forever.

That's what he should've done five days ago. That's what he needed to do now.

"Asher."

Honor's voice behind him was like a miracle. He swung around fully expecting to have imagined it, but there she stood, right in front of him. With his heart pounding high up in his throat, he stared in shock.

She smiled hesitantly. "Hi."

"Hi." A second ago he'd been all fired-up to go get her, now all he had was *Hi?*

His brain absently noted the tandem harness over her sweatshirt and skinny jeans as he drank in the vision of her before him. Then the absent mental note registered, and he darted his gaze down, then back up. Now, he recognized the slight tremble in her smile, the stark contrast of the freckles splashed across her nose and unusually pale cheeks, and the trepidation in her luminous, green eyes.

"I'm going to jump," she said. The high breathlessness of her voice conveyed her anxiety.

"Why?" he asked.

Her gaze flicked past his shoulder, and her face paled even more. He glanced over his shoulder to see the skydivers floating into view, their colorful chutes deployed above their heads as they rode the air currents down to the ground.

"Because if I can do that, I can love you."

He nearly got whiplash when he jerked his head back around.

"I know it sounds stupid," she admitted with another shaky smile, "but it's what I need to do."

It was the stupidest most wonderful thing he'd ever heard.

He held her gaze and reached for her hands. She grabbed on and held tight, her grip surprisingly strong—almost painfully strong. He gave her a gentle smile. "You don't need to prove anything to me. You being here is enough. What you just said is enough."

"I'm doing this as much for me as for you."

"What's it going to prove to you?"

"Some guy once told me if I start here, everything else will be a piece of cake."

"I was talking about taking risks when it comes to extreme sports."

"Well, I figure if I can hurl myself out of a plane, living to tell the tale will be my cake, and the rest is just frosting."

He gave her a mock frown. "Now I'm *just* frosting?"

She gave him a cheeky grin. "It's my favorite, too."

He started to tug her forward for a kiss when the lead diver hollered out, "Final check! Let's go boys and girls!"

"Ready?"

"No." But she managed a sideways smile as they lined up for the gear check and her tandem partner went over everything with her again. He watched her nod and smile, and his heart melted at the courage she was summoning to do this.

As the owner checked Asher's harness, chute, and reserve chute, he gestured toward Honor with a slight nod of his head and asked in an undertone, "Did she book a video of this?" When Chet shook his head, Asher said, "If you let me video her on this jump, the whole shoot is on me. I'll stay for however many extra jumps we need to get it done."

Chet's brows rose, but he didn't hesitate. "Deal. You know her?"

"I'm going to marry her."

He grinned. "All right, then. Congrats, man." With a clap on the shoulder, he moved on to check the next solo jumper.

When it was time to go, Asher held Honor's hand on the

way to the idling plane. She squeezed his so hard the tips of his fingers tingled. They were trailing along at the back of the group when she suddenly pulled him to a stop.

"Asher."

He turned back, and his chest squeezed when her wide eyes locked with his. She looked absolutely terrified. "You okay? Because you really don't have to jump if you don't want to."

A tremulous smile curved her mouth. "I love you."

His heart jolted hard at the pure, unhindered emotion in her eyes. He moved closer, lifting his hand to her face, grinning with joy as he brushed his thumb over her cheek.

"I wanted you to know that before we jump."

He leaned in, his lips a hair's breadth from hers. "Tell me again when we're back on the ground."

She gave a jerky nod.

"You got this, Butter Cream."

The nickname made her laugh, and he pressed his lips to hers. Before he could deepen the kiss, Chet hollered, "Save it for later, Diamond! Those who don't jump will never fly."

Asher broke the kiss and led Honor to the plane as he hollered back, "Let's go make love to the world!"

She gave him a confused smile, but he'd explain the quote later.

When they were up in the air, climbing in altitude to the jump zone, the tandem pairs sat with their backs to the pilots, and Asher sat with the solo jumpers in the back, near the door. Honor and her partner were the first of the tandem pairs, and he'd jump seconds before them so he could film her freefall, then break away to take still photos after he pulled his chute.

He checked his equipment once more, turned on his helmet cam and caught her eye through their safety goggles.

When he gave her a thumbs up, she gave him two back. With the roar of the engine in his ears, he mouthed, "*I love you,*" and was rewarded with her huge smile just before Chet opened the door.

Her eyes went wide, and it was time to go.

CHAPTER 33

"*OH MY GOD! HOLY SHIT! HOLY SHIT! HOLY SHIT!*"

A half-dozen more *holy shits* were ripped from Honor's mouth by the 120 mph wind before Asher was right there falling with her and the guy strapped to her back. He gave her a thumbs up, and she managed to offer one back even as she remembered to keep her arms and legs extended as was drilled into her during orientation.

It was a pure adrenaline rush as they plummeted to the earth thousands of feet below. Before her brain could fully register the terrifying sensation, Asher gave her a smile and a wave and dove through the air away from them. His departure jammed her heart farther up into her throat, then there was a loud *whoosh,* and her whole body jerked as the parachute opened above their heads.

Suddenly she was floating—or at least it felt like it after the fall seconds earlier—and the ground below came into vivid focus. She could see the snow capped mountains, and green grass, brown fields, buildings, roads, and teeny, tiny little cars. The beauty of it all took her breath away.

"You doing okay?" her partner asked.

"Yep," she replied automatically. She couldn't remember his name because earlier she'd been too nervous about seeing Asher and then jumping. "That was insane."

He laughed. "Want to steer?"

She looked over to see him offering the handles attached to lines leading up to the parachute. "Really?" But she was already reaching to take control. He instructed her how to pull on one to turn right, and the other to turn left, and she spent a full minute turning back and forth, and even accidentally spun them around a few times before he took over again.

Her stomach was a little queasy after the spins, and suddenly it didn't feel like floating anymore as the earth seemed to rush up to greet them. Her heart raced, but her partner set them down like a pro, smack dab on their feet in the middle of an impossibly small target in the grassy field next to the runway. He unhooked their harnesses, then led her out of the way for the next pair coming in for landing.

She thanked her partner profusely, then turned on wobbly knees and searched for Asher. He was a dozen yards away, still attached to his chute, camera pointed at her. He lowered it a few inches to give her a grin, but when she smiled and started toward him, he brought it back up, snapping like crazy until she was only a few feet away.

She lifted her hands in front of her for emphasis as she laughingly exclaimed, "Oh. My. God."

"Right?" he agreed as he slung the camera back over his shoulder.

She launched herself at him and held on tight as his arms closed around her. "That was amazing. I can't believe I jumped out of an airplane."

"Want to do it again?"

She laughed against his neck. "No. I'm good. I love you, and I'm definitely good."

He set her on the ground and lifted both hands to her face. Looking deep into her eyes, he said, "I love you, too." Then he gave her the kiss that had been interrupted earlier.

This time, they were breathing hot and heavy and she was plastered against him when a round of cheers and applause broke them apart. Heat flooded her face when she saw the group they'd jumped with laughing and clapping.

Asher hugged her to his side as he waved them off. They followed the rest of the group across the runway toward the hangar, and he kept his arm around her while the owner chatted with him about finishing up the photo shoot the next day.

When the guy moved ahead of them, Asher leaned down to whisper in her ear, "No more work for me today. Let's get this stuff off and get out of here."

An hour later, they stumbled into his hotel room, lips locked together as he kicked the door shut. It was a freefall of clothes, and kisses, and bare skin as he followed her down onto the bed. When he joined them together with one deep thrust, every whirling emotion came into sharp focus in her body. It was like the parachute opening, and she suddenly understood *let's make love to the world.*

Knowing the whole future lay ahead of them elevated their lovemaking to a new level. Afterward, she lay tucked against his side, her hand on his chest, head just below his chin. The beat of his heart beneath her palm was strong and steady. Just like Asher. She relaxed in the certainty this is where she wanted to be for the rest of her life. With him.

Contented silence blanketed the room, but before sleep could take hold, she murmured, "I'm sorry for last week."

His arm tightened briefly. "It hurt like hell when you left, but I've come to realize we both needed to work a few things out."

"You were right about me being afraid," she admitted. "You were also right about it being worth the risk."

"I was reminding myself of exactly that before you showed up. As soon as I could wrap up the job, my plan was to go back home and fight like hell to get you back."

Unexpected tears sprang to her eyes, and she pushed up to lean over his chest so she could see his face. "You were going to fight for me?"

His solemn brown gaze held hers. "Whatever it took. I wasn't going to give up until you gave in. And I always will."

She blinked at the moisture in her eyes and reached up to brush the mussed hair off his forehead. "You have no idea how much that means to me."

"I should've done it right away."

"I think this is the way it had to be. And I'm okay with that if you are."

He smiled as he ran both hands down her back, cupped her ass, and slid her up until her lips met his. "As long as you're happy."

"As long as we're *both* happy." After a long, deep kiss, she rested her chin on her fist on his chest. "Speaking of happy, have you spoken to your parents?"

"This is an odd time to bring up my parents."

"Have you?"

"No. Not since before my trip."

"I did. Well, your mom, anyway."

He pressed his head back against the pillow, forehead furrowed. "When did you talk to my mom?"

"Yesterday. She stopped by your house, and ended up at my house doing shots of tequila with my mom."

His eyebrows rose in disbelief. "My mom was drinking tequila? How in the hell did that happen?"

"My sister knew about you, and she told *my* mom, whose remedy for a broken heart is to get drunk and cry it out."

"Okay…?"

"I had just invited your mom over for coffee when my mom showed up, and we all got to talking—"

"Between shots of tequila?"

"Yes, between shots of tequila, and it turns out my mom is shockingly wise when it comes to relationship advice."

"The woman who's been divorced four times."

"I know, right? But she really nailed it, and your mom finally realized that things happened the way they were supposed to happen so she would end up with you and your brothers and sisters. There was more than that, but the gist of it is, she loves your dad and the life they've had together, and I'm pretty sure if they haven't worked things out already, they are in the process."

"Wow. Really?"

"Yeah."

"That's…" He blew out a breath and gave her a tremulous smile. "That's so good to hear after the past month."

"I know." Seeing the emotion in his eyes had her blinking back tears again. "You should probably call them and see how it's going."

"Hmm." He cut his gaze to the alarm clock on the nightstand, then lifted both his hands to frame her face so he could plant a kiss on her lips. "How about later—when we're not naked in bed."

"Yeah," she agreed with a grin. "I'm good with that." She held his gaze, and her smile widened as she thought about something he'd said before. "So…whatever it took, hey? What would that have looked like?"

He tucked her hair behind one ear and traced her earlobe. "I was going to start with flowers and chocolate."

"It's a good start, but…" She lifted one bare shoulder. "It's a little generic."

"Begging would've been next. And when that didn't work —because God knows it didn't work the first time—I would've moved on to brow-beating and kidnapping so—"

She raised her eyebrows.

"—I could seduce you with cake." He grinned as if proud of having come up with that tactic. "Lots and *lots* of cake."

Honor laughed. "So we're back to calling it that?"

"It'll be our code word." He tapped a finger on her nose before sliding his hands down along her back. "Good plan, don't you think?"

"Browbeating and kidnapping? Sounds a little caveman-like to me."

"I meant the code word was a good plan." Then he shrugged. "But a man's got to do what a man's got to do."

"I probably would've beat you over the head with my rolling pin."

"You're totally over-looking the seduction part. I know how much you love my stick shift." He waggled his eyebrows.

She was sprawled on top of him completely naked and still her face heated. "This is getting to be too much."

He shifted his hips beneath her, and the flush in her cheeks spread through her whole body when she felt he was hard.

"Again?" But she wasn't complaining really. She wanted more, too. With him, she'd take more for the rest of their lives.

"If I've told you once, I've told you a dozen times. I can never—"

"—have too much cake," she finished with him.

Returning his grin, she rose up to straddle his hips and lost herself in the bliss of loving Asher. Of course life wouldn't always be easy; she fully expected they'd have some curveballs to deal with at some point, but something this good was worth whatever work and risk it took to keep it.

She now believed with all her heart and soul, with the two of them together, anything was possible.

Most especially love.

EPILOGUE

*H*onor put the finishing touches on Celia Diamond's square, four tier wedding cake, then stood back to make sure every flower and pearl accent was in place. The white drape cake was deceptively simple looking, yet timelessly elegant with its pearl accents and red and white edible roses. Mid-afternoon sunlight streamed through ballroom windows of the Diamond mansion, but the air conditioning kept the early August heat at bay, ensuring the frosting would be safe.

And the guests cool as well, she thought with a humorous tug at her lips.

A soft gasp came from her right, and then the bride stepped up beside her. "Oh, my God, Honor, it's amazing," she whispered. "Thank you so much for doing this for us."

"I was thrilled to be asked. Just remember, though, cakes are for eating. That's why you chose a different flavor for each tier."

"I'm going to have some of each one," she vowed with a grin. "And after watching everything I ate for the past two months, I'm going to enjoy every bite."

"Good."

Though Celia wore leggings and a button-up shirt, her make-up was done perfectly, her dark bob a combination of artful curls and loose braids, accented by red tea roses. She was always beautiful, but today the word stunning was appropriate. Honor couldn't wait to see her dress.

"Shouldn't you be getting dressed? What if Robert sees you?"

"He's down at the guest house with the guys, but yes, I'm going to put my dress on now. Elena said you'd arrived with the cake and I just had to come take a quick peek." Her smile radiated pure joy. "It's going to be a great day."

"Yes, it is," Honor agreed as she gave her a quick hug. "Enjoy every moment."

"I plan to. Are you coming upstairs to get changed?"

"As soon as I get my dress from the car."

"I'll see you when it's time," she said as she departed with a happy grin.

A few minutes later Honor carried her dress bag up to the second floor. Unlike three months ago, the hallway was busy with the wedding planner's employees, a couple bridesmaids, and Elena and her daughter, Solana. Honor had met the entire Torrez family at the rehearsal dinner the night before and liked each one of them.

She gave the two women a quick smile and wave before slipping into Asher's bedroom. With her gaze and mind focused on the bed, she shut the door behind her and flipped the lock.

"Took you long enough to get up here."

She gasped and whirled around, her heart in her throat as she saw Asher lounging against the wall next to the door.

"Don't *do* that," she exclaimed as she smacked him in the chest—his firm, muscled chest encased in a snowy white shirt to go with his tux. It felt like déjà vu from the last time she'd been up in this room.

As if reading her mind, he grinned and reached to catch her hand to tug her close. "Need help with your zipper?"

She rolled her eyes even as a grin tugged at her own mouth. "I have to get dressed, Asher. You're supposed to be at the guest house."

"Guys don't need an entourage to get dressed. You've been so busy this week, I haven't gotten near enough cake."

It had been a crazy week with Celia's large cake, plus two smaller ones on her calendar. She'd missed him, too, seeing as each night she'd worked past one a.m. just to get everything done. Three days ago, they'd managed to steal an hour together for themselves, but other than that, she'd been asleep almost before her head hit the pillow, while he spooned close from behind.

With one hand pressed to his chest, Honor rose up on her tiptoes and kissed his chin. "You can have all the cake you want at the reception."

"What if I want some now?"

Her pulse skipped and her breath hitched with anticipation. "We don't have time."

"The ceremony isn't for another forty-five minutes. Your job is done already, and I'm only an usher."

Celia had refused to let him be the official photographer because she wanted her brother to enjoy the wedding, not work the whole time.

"Ushers are supposed to seat people," Honor pointed out. "You know, *before* the ceremony."

"Merit's down there." He dipped his head to nuzzle her neck. "Well, either there or the wine cellar. I saw him chatting up the best man's sister on my way up."

She hummed with pleasure as his tongue stroked against her skin, and every breath she took teased her with Asher's sexy cologne. She shouldn't give in, but the man knew exactly how to wear down her resistance and make sure she loved every second of it.

"Celia's guests are probably wandering around aimlessly, wondering where to go."

"If they can't figure that out, then let them wander." His breath was warm against her ear, his large hands firm on her hips as he tugged her against his erection. "Gimmie me some frosting, Butter Cream."

Honor hadn't been able to get him to stop calling her that, but at least he only did it in private. And truth be told, she loved the nickname, because she loved him. Snaking her arm up and around his neck, she said, "As long as you help me with my zipper after."

"Deal."

Dinner was done, cake had been cut, and Asher had just finished his second serving of cake for the day. He was definitely going for thirds as soon as the bride and groom departed and it was okay for him to take Honor home.

But that wouldn't be for a couple of hours yet, so for now he stood behind her, his arms wrapped around her middle, his head resting against hers as they swayed to the music while they watched the wedding party and the parents out on the dance floor.

Her dress had been messing with his head from the moment she'd slipped it up her gorgeous, naked body. Turns out she didn't have a zipper, but she'd had him tie the halter top behind her neck. When he'd trailed his fingers down the exposed length of her spine, she'd shivered and he'd had to resist taking her again. They *had* had a wedding to get to.

The whole afternoon and evening, sexual awareness

simmered between them even as contentment permeated every pore of his body.

His body stirred yet again, and looking for a distraction, he focused on his parents swaying to the music, looking as much in love as the bride and groom. One would never guess the rocky path they'd navigated a few short months ago. After the tequila shots with Honor and her mother, his mom had gone home to work things out. Even after the second DNA test proved Grayson was his father's son, his parents' bond was stronger than ever as they worked the campaign side by side as a newly reunited team.

Asher swept his gaze around the ballroom, like he'd done every so often during the evening. Each time he located Loyal, he reconfirmed which brother he was looking at, then kept searching.

"No sign of Grayson all night," he commented.

"This would've been a huge deal for him to come to when he's only just started to talk to all of you."

Everyone but Loyal. "I know. I still hoped."

Honor rubbed her hand over his forearm. "He'll come around eventually. It's only been a few months. You have to give him time."

Yeah, he knew that, too.

He looked back at his older brother again, and noticed him frowning across the room. Following his gaze, he saw Roxanna sitting at a table, laughing with Shelby, Solana, Dev, and Reyes. The resentment between the two of them remained strong as they avoided each other at every turn.

Watching Rox as he continued to sway with Honor and drink in the addicting scent of her subtle perfume, he was reminded of the last wedding the three of them were all at. Roxanna had asked if he thought they'd ever have this—love, marriage—and look at him now. He hoped she'd find her right person now that he'd found his.

And speaking of love and marriage…

He suddenly found it hard to draw in a steady breath. Tightening his arms the tiniest bit, he pulled Honor back with him into one of the private little alcoves in each corner of the ballroom.

When she saw they were alone, she laughed softly and turned in his arms. "You read my mind."

Her husky voice sent a surge of desire through him, and he loved that she wanted him as much as he wanted her. But that's not what this was about. "I have a question to ask you…"

Her eyes went wide.

"It's actually a question *about* a question," he quickly clarified.

"Ok-ay," she said cautiously.

"There's going to come a time when I want to ask you a question, *the* question, but I don't want to freak you out, so… I thought if we talked about it ahead of time…we can be sure to be on the same page when the time comes."

She relaxed against him, smiling as she draped her arms around his neck. "And what page is that? 'Til death do us part, two point five kids, a dog, and a house in the suburbs?"

"I was thinking more like four kids and two dogs, because really, what would we do with half a kid?"

Her warm laugh filled his heart with so much love. "Dog hair and cake doesn't mix."

"We won't allow the dogs in your cake shop."

Her brows rose. "My shop?"

"The store next to Lift Your Spirit is moving to bigger space across the street in October. I thought I'd see if you would want the space. You did say it was a key location."

"Are you kidding right now?"

He grinned at the excitement that spread across her face.

"I mean, I am going to charge you rent and demand free cake for life, but the space is yours if you want it."

"I want it. I definitely want it," she assured him. Then she rose up on her tiptoes, her happy gaze shining bright. "And as for the other, I'll take that page any day you're willing to offer it."

He wanted to drop to his knees and offer it right now, but he hadn't brought the ring with him, damn it. That was okay, though, he'd plan something special just for her.

In the meantime...he dipped his head and covered her mouth with his. She leaned in and opened to him in that way that always made his pulse rev high. He lifted his hands to either side of her face and leaned his forehead against hers as he spoke the emotion in his heart that would last a lifetime. "I love you."

Her lips curved against his. "I love you, too."

Thank you for reading!

DID YOU KNOW?

Reviews from readers help authors to be able to continue to write the books you love, so I really hope you enjoyed Asher and Honor's journey to love in *Must Love Frosting* and would be thrilled if you'd leave a review where you purchased the book or at a favorite retailer.

How can you make sure you never miss a new book? JOIN my Newsletter and here's what you get:

*FREE bonus books
*New release announcements
*what's going on in my writer's life
*exclusive first-look bonus content
*cover reveals
*special sales

http://smarturl.it/WebSJNNewsletter

FREE reads!
Romantic suspense & Contemporary Romance
with heartwarming Happily Ever Afters
Sign up for my newsletter today!

Next up in the **Must Love Diamonds Series** is
Love Loyal and True.

A one-night stand? Sure.
A no-strings fling? No problem.
Love and Marriage? Hell no.

Loyal Diamond has proposed twice. He's had his heart
broken twice. He's not risking it ever again.

Psychic Roxanna Kent had a vision of a loyal and true soul
mate when she was a little girl. She didn't expect him to be
named Loyal, or that he would be bitter and jaded and
completely closed off to the love she has to offer.

Chapter 1

Roxanna Kent shivered as a passing firefighter swirled the air up past the hem of her thin, satin nightgown. An EMS worker had given her a blanket, and a two-sizes too large pair of slippers for her bare feet, but they were no match for the chilly Colorado October night—even with a blaze raging in her apartment building across the street.

Strangely, she didn't feel the cold, even though she was aware of her body shivering and the occasional chatter of her teeth. Numbness had set in once the last of her neighbors escaped the smoke filled halls. If she hadn't woken from her dream, heart pounding in terror, the smell of smoke choking her despite the crystal clear air, would she have still made it out alive? Who would've been there to make sure?

No one.

Surrounded by firefighters, police, EMS workers, fellow homeless apartment residents, and a multitude of onlookers, she'd never felt more alone in her life.

"Excuse me?" A hand on her blanket-wrapped shoulder drew her around to see a blond woman wearing a Red Cross jacket. "Do you have someone to call? Or can I call for you?"

"Um…" The one person—well, make that both persons—she would've called were out of town. Her best friend, Asher, and his fiancé, Honor, were in Alaska on a photo shoot-slash-engagement trip. She turned her head back toward the fire. "My phone is still in there. I don't know the numbers."

She hadn't even thought of it when she went into the hall to reassure herself the phantom smoke was a figment of her imagination and discovered it was all too real. She'd woken in time to pull the fire alarm before flames were visible, but as everyone worked together to make sure no one was left behind, the fire had spread frighteningly quickly. Her phone was likely melted by now.

The hand on her shoulder gave a gentle squeeze. "We're setting up a shelter at the community center for anyone who needs it. Volunteers are giving rides right over there."

Roxanna blinked and looked in the direction the woman pointed. She saw a few of the neighbors from her floor getting into cars. Unlike her, some of them had managed to grab some personal items. She'd have to go see what she could find from her shop before she—ooh, the second floor apartment. Asher owned her retail building, and he'd always told her she could use it if she needed to. She'd never needed to—until now.

She managed a weak smile of something close to relief. "Thank you, but I have a place to stay."

The blond pressed a card into her hand. "Call if you need anything."

At her nod, the woman moved on to a family huddled together in blankets. Roxanna roused herself out of her stupor to take stock of what she needed to do. Get over to Lift Your Spirit, pick out some clothes from her inventory, then head upstairs for a hot shower. The smoke smell infused into her hair was strong enough to tighten her throat and make her eyes sting.

She searched for a way to get through the chaos to the back of the building where her Jeep was parked until she realized she didn't have her keys, either. A couple of shaky inhales kept her from bawling right there on sidewalk and got her mind thinking. She kept a spare set at her shop, but she couldn't walk the two and a half miles in slippers and a satin nightgown, so she'd need to call a—

Nope. She had no money.

Damn. Now the sting in her eyes wasn't only from the smoke.

Swiping the tears from her face with one hand, she walked over to the volunteer staging area. A few minutes later, a black man named Leonard in his fifties, maybe early sixties, opened his passenger door for her.

"Thank you so much. I'm Roxanna." She slid in with a grateful smile, and once he was in his seat, she directed him to Lift Your Spirit.

About halfway into the ride, he said, "I think that's the psychic shop my granddaughter brings me cupcakes from every so often. Is that your place?"

She nodded as country music played softly on the radio. After barely two minutes of sitting, emotional and physical exhaustion were taking over. She'd never had such a strong premonition before, except for that one time she was nine.

"She brings me those chocolate covered cake balls, too," Leonard added. "They're very good."

"The cupcakes and the cake balls are Honor Hartman specialties." She'd started making the cake balls to use up her cake scraps, and customers had gone crazy for them. "She's opening a cake shop next door to me this fall."

"I'll make sure to watch for it." He turned off Aspen street to drive around to the back of the building. It was almost three a.m. when he braked outside the back door of her shop.

"Thank you so much for the ride, Leonard," she said as she opened the passenger door.

"Are you sure it's okay for me to leave you here?" he asked, head ducked to look at the alley as a slight frown drew his grey eyebrows together. Other than a black SUV and an older white four-door car parked a little ways away, the area was deserted at this time of night.

"There's an apartment upstairs. I promise, I'll be fine."

"I'll wait until you're safely inside," he advised.

Her heart warmed at his concern. "Thank you. You and

your granddaughter are welcome to come by anytime for a free treat. Or even a reading."

"I don't do this to get paid back," he protested.

Her senses were way out of whack with everything that had happened, but a moment of focus revealed the orange tones of his aura, confirming his generosity and kindness was genuine. "I know. And I'm offering simply because I want to. Get home safely yourself."

They shared a brief smile before she turned to punch in the key code to unlock the back door. Thankfully Asher had installed them on all the entrances when he first bought the building six years ago, so she didn't need a key. Energy saving motion lights came on in the hall as she stepped inside. With a final wave for Leonard, she shut the door and used the same code for the lockbox into the shop. From here in the back, she could see the soft, comforting illumination from the Himalayan salt lamps displayed in her front windows and throughout the shop.

From one heartbeat to the next, the orange glow flashed her back to the fire, and her heart leapt into her throat with her sharp inhale. As the smoke smell clinging to her hair and clothes filled her lungs, she tossed the blanket on a chair by the door of her reading room, and went the opposite direction into her office-slash-storage room.

Thinking of her car keys, she frowned at the unorganized chaos on her desk and surrounding surfaces, not quite sure where to start looking. Folders and papers were piled on the top of her desk, with one precarious stack reaching almost two feet high on the left side. After her accountant got married and moved out of state a few months ago, she kept meaning to clean and organize, but with so many other things to get done, it was hard to find the time.

You don't make *the time.*

No, she didn't. The bills were depressing, she couldn't

balance her profit and loss reports to save her life, and doing hours of paperwork here in the back room was lonely. She was so damn tired of being lonely.

More tears burned her eyes, but a few determined blinks held them at bay.

"Now's not the time to clean the desk *or* have a pity party," she muttered. Since she didn't need the keys right at this moment, she turned away from her disaster area, toward the storage part of the room.

Her part-time employees, Tessa and Darcy, kept everything ship-shape over here. Once Roxanna verified new orders and made sure the inventory was correct, they didn't let her near their organized shelves.

Thankfully, though, she didn't have to dig through any boxes since there was a clothes rack off to one side with older clearance items that hadn't sold. There were a few select items she might try to cycle through the shop one last time, but most she would donate to a local women's shelter and take the tax write off.

She found a brown T-shirt, and a brown, gold, and black gauzy skirt, then grabbed a second, extra-large, orange tye-dyed T-shirt to sleep in. It would be a toss up between lying awake the rest of the night or going comatose the moment her head hit the pillow.

Essential oils would help with the latter, so she made a quick trip out front for bottles of lavender and ylang-ylang, then grabbed socks and a pair of the new mid-calf, lace-up military boots she'd stocked for winter. With everything gathered in her arms, she made her way back out to the door in the hallway that led to the second floor.

Up in the apartment, she moved on auto-pilot, the light from the outside street lamps guiding her straight to the bathroom, where she shut the door and stripped down for a shower. A quick wash of her underwear in the sink ensured they'd be clean and dry when she woke up, then she stepped beneath the steamy spray.

After she scrubbed her hair and her body, she was in the middle of rinsing the suds away when the horror of the night replayed in her mind and the tears she'd been fighting resurfaced yet again. She didn't need her psychic intuition to tell her releasing the emotion was the best thing to do right now. She turned her face up and let them flow as the water washed them down the drain.

Fatigue weighted her limbs when she finally shut off the water and dried from head to toe. She probably wouldn't need it, but dabbed a couple drops of the ylang-ylang oil on her temples, wrists, and the back of her neck anyway, then pulled the orange T-shirt over her head. With her five foot nine height, the extra-large barely covered her bare butt cheeks, but right about now all she cared about was getting to the bed.

She wrapped a towel around her wet hair, wishing she'd thought to look for a comb or brush in the shop. Now it would have to wait until morning, when she went down to open up. She grimaced as she remembered she was working alone tomorrow. At least it was Sunday, the one day she opened at eleven a.m. instead of nine.

When she shut off the bathroom light, the dark quiet helped soothe her frayed nerves. There was only one bedroom, and the door swung open easily. Room darkening shades kept out the light from the street, but the faint outline of the bed was enough to guide her silent footsteps.

She stripped back the corner of the comforter and slid between the cool sheets with exhausted relief. A deep inhale to ease the tension in her shoulders sent a tingle of unease down her spine when the faintest hint of distinctly male cologne tickled her senses. When the mattress suddenly rocked beneath her, she froze and her heart surged up into her throat. Something warm and hairy brushed against her leg at the same time a muscled forearm snaked around her waist.

Roxanna screamed and swung wildly, kicking free of the sheets to scramble from the bed.

———✦———

Love Loyal and True releases July 23, 2019.

About the Author

New York Times and *USA Today* bestselling author Stacey Joy Netzel always promises Happily Ever After in her books, but the journey to get there is going to one heck of an adventure! She lives in N.E. Wisconsin with her family, a horse and some cats. She writes steamy romantic suspense and small town contemporary romance with sexy, rugged heroes, and strong, resilient heroines. Colorado, Wisconsin, and Italy are favorite settings for her books, and she is a three time winner of Wisconsin Romance Writers' Write Touch Readers' Award.

Hearing from readers is a very special thing for any writer, so pop in and say "Hi!" at any of the below locations. And once again, reviews are always appreciated.

Thank you, and happy reading!
~Stacey~

www.StaceyJoyNetzel.com
http://smarturl.it/WebSJNNewsletter

facebook.com/StaceyJoyNetzel

twitter.com/StaceyJoyNetzel

bookbub.com/authors/BookBub